BORDEN ISLAND
ROBERT E KREIG

WHITEKEEP BOOKS

Book Cover by Robert E Kreig

Edited by Sally Odgers

ISBN Print Version: 978-0-6457064-8-2

ISBN eBook Version: 978-0-6457064-9-9

Published by Whitekeep Books.

www.whitekeepbooks.com

www.robertekreig.com

First Printing, 2024

BORDEN ISLAND
ROBERT E KREIG

WHITEKEEP BOOKS

T he year is 2053.

A seismic shift reshaped the geopolitical landscape, ushering in an era where the reins of power transitioned from traditional nation-states to the commanding heights of international corporate conglomerates. This tectonic transformation, decades in the making, unfolded against a backdrop of mounting disillusionment with conventional governance, as promises made by elected officials dwindled into hollow echoes, drowned out by the cacophony of global crises.

The genesis of this epochal upheaval traces back to the tumultuous mid-2020s, a time when the digital sphere became a battleground for social justice warriors, their rallying cries reverberating across social media platforms. Their ire was directed not only at the failings of governments to address pressing issues like war, famine, and environmental degradation but also at the palpable disconnection between the rulers and the ruled.

Amid this maelstrom of discontent, astute corporate titans seized upon the rising tide of public disillusionment as an opportunity ripe for the taking. Beginning in the early 2030s, clandestine conclaves convened, where captains of industry from diverse sectors—mining, media, technology, and beyond—forged alliances under the banner of a corporate syndicate. Their aim? To supplant the faltering guardians of the status quo and assume the mantle of saviors, delivering on the unfulfilled promises of politicians past.

From the towering skyscrapers of megacities to the remote hamlets of the hinterlands, the corporate syndicate's influence knew no bounds. Their tentacles extended into every facet of daily life, from the provision of housing and transportation to the dissemination of information and the harnessing of renewable energy sources. With prices slashed and quality assured, the populace found themselves increasingly reliant on the benevolence of their corporate overlords.

Yet, as the old guard clung desperately to power, resorting to tax hikes and regulatory machinations in a futile bid to stem the tide of change, their efforts proved naught but a fleeting gust against the gathering storm. Across continents, governments crumbled like sandcastles before an incoming tide, their erstwhile leaders ousted in a whirlwind of upheaval.

In the ensuing vacuum, the United Nations emerged as a reluctant arbiter, tasked with shepherding humanity through this brave new world order. Gone were the days of singular rulers and centralized authority; in their place stood corporate boards, where elected representatives of the workforce wielded influence alongside seasoned executives. Here, decisions that once shaped the destinies of nations were deliberated upon, their echoes reverberating across the global stage.

Yet, even as the banners of multinational corporations fluttered alongside the flags of sovereign nations, a specter loomed on the horizon—a specter of accountability, embodied by the watchful gaze of the United Nations. For in this brave new world, where power resides not in the hands of the few but in the collective will of the many, the balance between prosperity and peril hangs ever precariously.

CHAPTER ONE

Colonel Eric Powers flung his backpack onto the floor of the front passenger seat of an open top SUV, modified with four rows of seats to transport personnel between the tarmac and the row of buildings by the fence line on North Boundary Road. He offered a polite nod to the driver, a young man wearing a fluorescent orange vest.

"Evening," the colonel muttered as he turned to see his unit following him, humping loaded packs over their backs, their white United Nations uniforms standing out like beacons in the darkness.

"Good evening," the driver replied, appearing disinterested in the newcomers.

The last pair approaching the vehicle, a young woman, and a muscular man, shared the responsibility of carting a heavy crate between them.

"You all right with that, Private Gonzalez?" Powers called in a thick, Scottish accent.

Private Gonzalez's face was flushed as she struggled to carry the heavy crate. She nodded and strained under its weight.

"Fine, sir," the woman called back.

Powers glared at the others as they threw their gear into the SUV, two men and one woman, all larger than the private, claiming their seats.

"Did it not occur to any of you to offer assistance instead of leaving it to Private Gonzalez to carry your shit?" Powers' voice held a hint of disappointment.

"Sorry Colonel," one of them offered, starting back to help.

"That's a good lad, Corporal," Powers said with a shake of his head. "Do your fucking job when it's too fucking late."

"Don't you fucking dare, Garrett," Gonzalez snapped, her anger evident. "Just get in the car and do your nails or some shit."

Garrett held his hands up in mock surrender as Gonzalez and the large man approached the back of the SUV.

"Tailgate's unlocked," the driver announced, his voice phlegmatic.

"Geez," the other male unit member remarked, pointing at the driver before turning his attention to the big man carrying the crate. "Another person with the limited personality skills of Lieutenant Harris. I thought you was the only one."

"Shut up, Roland," said the woman standing beside him. "Just get in the car."

"Fine," he said with a shake of his head, climbing into the third row of seats.

"Sorry," the woman offered, looking at the driver as she slid into the seat behind him. He simply shrugged in response.

Within seconds, Gonzalez and Harris loaded the crate and threw their backpacks on top before closing the tailgate.

"All aboard," Powers called as he flopped onto the seat beside the driver. The others clambered on, the large man and Gonzalez taking the rear seat. She leaned her head against his arm as the SUV lunged away, racing for the buildings to the north, passing signage displaying the logo for John F. Kennedy International Airport.

"I need a stiff cup of tea," he muttered to himself, noting that it was already 20:17.

"Is that tea with something extra?" asked the other female in the group, seated behind the driver.

"Ay." The colonel chuckled. "I'll make you one, if you like, Private Jackson."

"What's the added ingredient?" she probed. "No, let me guess. Whiskey?"

"Bang on the money." He nodded. "One cap or two?"

"Better make it two," Jackson replied.

As they neared the buildings, the driver veered toward a smaller structure situated about twenty meters away from the others. A solitary figure dressed in a sharp suit stood silhouetted in the doorway, the warm light spilling out from behind.

"This doesn't look good," Garrett remarked, seated behind Powers.

"If this puta tells us the chopper is delayed," Gonzalez said, sitting up, "I'm gonna get loca."

"Exercise control, Private Gonzalez," the colonel instructed. "It might be nothing."

Taking a deep breath, Gonzalez fixed her gaze on the figure as he drew closer.

"It'll be fine," Lieutenant Harris told her, his deep voice carrying an unmistakable Australian accent.

The figure waved enthusiastically as they slowed down in front of the structure, stepping out through the doorway to greet them as they came to a stop. The tension in the air was palpable as everyone waited for the figure to speak and reveal his news.

"Stay in the car." As Colonel Powers stepped out of the car, he motioned for his team to stay put. He returned the friendly greeting from the man in front of him before cutting to the chase. "Hello. Who are you?"

"Well, ah…" The figure shifted nervously, clearly taken aback by the direct question. "Straight to the point. They told me you were a no bullshit type of guy. I'm Daniel Rogers. You can call me Dan if you like. I'm a liaison officer for intra-communications section at the United Nations headquarters here, in New York City. They sent me out to inform you—"

"You're a technician?" interrupted the colonel.

"N-no," Rogers replied, fidgeting with his suit jacket.

"A sales rep?" Powers prodded.

"No," the other answered, growing more flustered by the minute.

"You're a clerk." The officer smiled knowingly.

"Not exactly." Rogers furrowed his brow.

"Sure, you are," Powers said, stepping closer to stand directly in front of the man. "Just a console operator who takes calls and passes messages between people in expensive suits, right? What were you told to do? Come down here and deliver an important message that couldn't wait until morning?"

"I-I-" Rogers' chin trembled uncertainly.

"Don't fret, laddie," the colonel reassured with a smile. "I'm just having some fun with you. Now, what's the message?"

Rogers glanced back at the SUV where Powers' team waited, their tired and serious expressions giving nothing away.

"You're to remain here for about an hour or so," he stated hesitantly. "There's food inside—coffee, tea, and soda."

"What happens in an hour or so, Dan?" Gonzalez called.

"That's when you'll be transported to Ottawa for delegation escort duties," Rogers replied, his nervousness evident in his voice.

"Maldito gilipollas," Gonzalez cursed. "I fucking knew it."

"Private," the lieutenant reprimanded her.

She threw her hands up in frustration, but quickly composed herself.

"I'm all right L-T," she returned.

Powers shook his head disapprovingly.

"Now, you've gone and upset Private Gonzalez," the colonel told him. "You need to understand, Mister Rogers, we just came from a three-day babysitting job in Sudan. Before that, five days in Puerto Escondido with no break between. Puerto Escondido wasn't too bad, but have you ever been to Sudan?"

"No," Rogers said.

"Lovely place," Powers told him. "We spend the bulk of our time in El Obeid. It's a developing city and has come a long way in the last twenty years, according to the suit and tie we escorted through the region. His job was to assess the housing development in the city. Nice, tall apartment blocks. Glass and steel. Stunning.

"Not one of them fitted with air-conditioning," the colonel continued. "Not even the ones claiming to be at *lock-up* stage. Miles of solar panels everywhere because they get lots of sun all year round. They even built solar receptors onto the windows of the towers. Very smart.

"But not smart enough to hook up the vented air-conditioning that was on the bloody blueprints. It would have been nice to have air-conditioning. You know why?"

"I'm assuming it was hot?" Rogers replied.

"Fucking oath, it was hot," the colonel agreed. "Now, we're tired. It's nice you have some food in there for us because we're all very hungry. We'd like some down-time after a job like that. You can understand that, can't you?"

"Of course." The other nodded.

"Good." Colonel Powers grinned. "Because here's what you're going to do when you go back to headquarters to pass your letters and make your calls. You're going to tell the suits there, that when we return from this job, my team and I are going to take a two-week break at full-pay and if they don't like it, they can suck my fucking big, fat, furry, ginger nuts. Got that? Make sure to write that down, I don't want you messing it up."

***

The sound of a whimsical and light tune, reminiscent of a classical string piece, filtered merrily through the small studio apartment. The occupant, a young woman, stood under the warm spray of the shower, her mind drifting away with the relaxing rhythm of the water. Suddenly, she tilted her head, unsure if the sound she heard was the ring tone or just resonating sounds in the bathroom playing tricks on her brain.

But then, she heard it again. A crescendo of violins, playing a cheerful allegro. And she knew. After turning off the faucet and grabbing a towel to wrap around herself, she hurried to the kitchen where the phone awaited her. It was mounted on the wall next to her fridge, a flat panel that seemed out of place in her modest living space.

Pressing the green speaker button, she answered with a tired but polite, "Hello." Annoyed by the pooling water at her feet, she glanced down at the floor as she waited for the other person to speak.

"Sorry to bother you at home, Hope," a woman's voice declared from the other end.

"Deputy Secretary," Hope replied, sounding slightly surprised. She checked the clock beside her bed and saw that it was 8:25 PM. "I thought I still had an hour before I needed to call you. Did I miss a message?"

"No, nothing like that," the deputy secretary responded. "I just wondered if you had your tablet device with you, or is it still here at the office?"

"You're still at the office?" Hope asked incredulously. "Are you going to go home and pack? Will you have time?"

"I keep a bag here for situations like this," the other person explained calmly. "Speaking of which, don't pack too much. They'll be supplying us with jumpsuits and jackets. You'll just need toiletries and a change of underclothes. Maybe some pajamas if you wear them."

"Already ahead of you there," responded Hope, crossing the room to her bed where a group of plush toys covered her pillows. In the center sat a large, old teddy bear propped against the headboard, its soft, fading brown to tan fur looking inviting. She unzipped a green canvas gym bag that lay on top of her bed and began examining its contents. A towel, bathroom bag, two pairs of underpants and sports bras, a t-shirt, two pairs of socks and one pair of jeans. Beneath all of that lay her unicorn and rainbow adorned onesie. She thought about removing the jeans but heard a familiar inner voice of common sense remind her, *you just never know.*

"Good," the woman on the phone remarked, her voice crisp and professional. "Are you excited? This is your first field trip on a United Nations delegation."

Hope smiled at the question. "Very much," she replied eagerly. "I've never been to Canada before."

"Really? Well, don't make any plans for sightseeing," the deputy secretary said, her tone serious. "It's a quick, overnight inspection. Nothing more."

Hope nodded silently, knowing that this was strictly business. "I understand."

"All work and no play, unfortunately," the voice on the other end added wryly. "Listen, before I forget. The tablet. Do you have it with you?"

"Yes." Hope's eyes flickered to the bedside table, where her tablet lay charging on a sleek wireless dock. Next to it, her trusty vibrator rested, also recharging for its next use. A sudden wave of embarrassment washed over Hope as she imagined the deputy secretary somehow peering through the phone panel and seeing her private belongings. She quickly snatched the sex toy and slid it underneath her underwear in the top drawer of the bedside table, hoping to hide it from view. In her haste, the toy accidentally turned on, emitting a loud and unmistakable buzzing sound against the bottom of the drawer. Frantically, Hope retrieved the object and fumbled with it before finally managing to turn it off and hastily slamming it shut inside the drawer. Her cheeks flushed hot with embarrassment as she prayed that the deputy secretary hadn't heard her awkward encounter with her intimate possession.

"What was that noise?" the voice asked curiously.

Shit!

"I... ah... just knocked something over on my bedside table when I reached for the tablet," Hope improvised, trying to sound nonchalant. "It's nothing, really."

"Good," the deputy secretary uttered. "So, can you bring the tablet with you?"

"Of course," replied Hope dutifully, placing it on top of her bag so she wouldn't forget it.

"Don't bother calling me in an hour," the deputy secretary instructed her. "I'll send a car to pick you up at ten. See you at the airport."

"Thank you, Deputy Secretary," Hope replied, returning to the phone.

"Sally," the other insisted. "Keep the formalities for when we're in public, please."

"Sorry," said Hope sheepishly. "I can't. Not yet. Deputy Secretary Tinsley is the best I can do for the moment."

"Okay then." The deputy secretary chuckled softly. "I'll see you later."

The phone went silent, leaving Hope to let out a breath and return to the bathroom. She grabbed another towel to mop up the puddle by the fridge and the trail of water leading to it around her apartment.

Her gaze gravitated to the open sliding door of her built-in closet, on the other side of her bed. Numerous pairs of high heeled shoes rested neatly on racks at the base while hangers bore several long dresses, pants suits and a couple of jackets suited to New York winters.

Stay in there, Hope.

Hope shook the thought away and moved her gaze to the old bear sitting on her bed. Her eyes welled up, smiling gratefully at the plush animal before she returned to the bathroom where she hopped back into the shower, determined to finish what she had started before the unexpected call from her boss.

CHAPTER TWO

As Hope scrolled through the endless document on her tablet, her eyes grew tired, and her mind started to wander. She couldn't help paraphrasing the monotonous political dribble in her head as she prepared to share the information from UNIDO with the UN representative, Deputy Secretary Sally Tinsley, who sat beside her and who was currently sleeping. The woman's middle-aged face was peaceful, and strands of dark hair fell across her cheek as she dozed.

Hope brushed a strand of her own dark hair out of her face and behind her ear, taking a moment to glance around the cabin at the other passengers. Some were talking quietly, while others were deep in slumber. In front of her sat two individuals, dressed in blue coveralls like her and the deputy secretary, their titles and names stenciled on their right breasts. She didn't know them very well, having briefly met them in Ottawa before they boarded the shuttle craft.

One was a doctor and the other a civil engineer. The engineer seemed patient enough, nodding and listening to the incessant chatter of the doctor. At first, Hope wasn't sure if the medical practitioner was attempting to gloat or show off his superior intellect with his rich Oxford accent, or if he was simply trying to pass the time with conversation. After enduring his one-sided gabfest for nearly two hours, Hope deduced that he was probably just a nervous flyer.

A woman's voice crackled over the intercom, thick with a French-Canadian accent. "We're about five minutes out from our destination," she announced. "Make sure you bundle up before going outside. The current temperature on the surface is minus twelve degrees Celsius. That's about ten point four Fahrenheit for our Yankee friends."

The sound of a deep, guttural groan echoed through the small cabin, causing Hope to turn and see six others seated behind her. Four men and two women were dressed in white coveralls with their abbreviated names and titles stenciled on their chests. Each one wore two patches on the right shoulder—the flag of the United Nations and that of their home country beneath it.

Hope scanned over them quickly before pausing on a young man with rugged, chiseled features wearing the Australian flag on his arm. His short, cropped hair matched the length of his scruff, giving him a rugged and handsome appearance. His head was tilted lazily to the side, indicating he was in a deep slumber. Lt. Harris.

A small tattoo on the left side of his neck peeked out from under his collar—the numbers "0003" etched into his skin. The shuttle suddenly dropped, causing Harris' head to loll and come to rest on the shoulder of a young woman beside him, obscuring the tattoo from sight.

"Wake up, pendejo," said the woman with the Mexican flag on her sleeve. Pt. Gonzalez.

Harris stirred and opened his dark, emotionless eyes. Hope felt a tightness in her throat as she looked at him. She couldn't understand why she felt so drawn to him, but also filled with fear. Her gaze lingered too long.

"Do you want to take a picture?" Gonzalez asked sarcastically.

Hope quickly turned back around in her seat, every muscle stiffening as she clenched her tablet tightly in her hands.

"Play nice, private," said a stern, Scottish voice.

"Yes sir," Gonzalez replied obediently.

Deputy Secretary Tinsley stirred in her seat, disturbed by the shuttle's turbulent fall.

"Where are we?" she asked groggily.

"We're about five minutes out," Hope replied, echoing the pilot's earlier announcement. She relaxed her grip on the tablet and held it out toward Tinsley. "A report just came through from the Venezuelan team investigating the McIntyre facility. They found no issues and need your signature to log the report."

Tinsley gingerly took the sleek tablet from Hope's outstretched hand and scribbled her mark on the screen with her finger, before handing it back. With a press of a tab, they both watched as the digital signature was submitted.

"You've been glued to that thing since we left Ottawa," the Deputy Secretary remarked, nodding toward the tablet in Hope's hands. "Did it tell you anything new? Do you have any insight on why we have such an extensive security detail with us?"

Hope's voice was hushed as she replied, "No, not really. I overheard the doctor mention something about an anomaly."

"An anomaly?" Tinsley's eyebrows rose in curiosity. "Do tell."

"That's all I know," Hope replied softly. "To be honest, he's been talking nonstop to the other one there. I tuned out after a few minutes."

Tinsley smiled knowingly, peering out of the tiny portal beside her to see rows upon rows of spinning wind turbines arranged like stoic soldiers along the frosty shore, stretching into the distance. The sight was both mesmerizing and slightly forbidding at the same time.

***

The shuttle, a sleek craft not much larger than a motor coach, banked to the left and descended rapidly toward the frost-covered ground below. Its powerful engines roared, churning up a deafening whir that echoed through the frozen landscape. As it leveled its wings, the shuttle continued to descend and veer to the left, its port side aiming toward a steep, rocky incline.

A flurry of white, powdery dust erupted around the craft as it skimmed over the barren surface, leaving a trail of swirling clouds in its wake. The shuttle cut through the air with precision, heading straight for giant iron doors set into the face of a mountain. As it drew closer, slowing its approach, the doors opened with a resounding metallic clunk to reveal a dark, deep cavity carved deep into the rock.

Hovering just inches above the ground, the shuttle gracefully pivoted to its right, aligning its tail with the open doors. With a series of electronic beeps and whirs, three panels on the undercarriage slid open—one under the nose and two beneath the small wings—allowing sturdy landing gear to extend from hidden compartments. Stubby struts with caterpillar treads lowered toward the ground as the craft prepared for touchdown. With expert precision, it landed gently on the frozen surface, reducing its engines from a thunderous roar to a soft purr. As the white cloud settled back onto the ground, the port side hatch opened with a quiet hiss.

A short ladder, four feet in length, dropped from beneath the opened hatch as two men dressed in bright orange, fluorescent coveralls approached from the open doorway in the mountainside. The sound of their heavy boots crunching against the snow and ice echoed through the chilly air. One of the men made a beeline for the ladder while the other moved to a large compartment door at the tail end of the craft. As the first man ascended the ladder, the other opened the compartment and quickly glanced inside at the cargo before turning to face the large doors and whistling loudly. In response, more orange-clad individuals emerged from within.

"Bring out the Cat," he called with a wave of his hand.

The first man clambered into the shuttle, stepping into the front of the cabin where several occupants were bustling about, donning thick parkas, and preparing for their journey. "Hello folks," he said with a warm smile breaking through his thick, graying beard. "I'm Ken Wade, Chief of Maintenance here at Borden Island Facility. My colleague, Evan Gross, is tending to your luggage as we speak. So, all we need to do is get you inside where it's a tad bit warmer than out here."

"We have cargo below containing items of utmost sensitivity," the Scottish man at the rear of the cabin announced. "I believe my team would be best suited to handle its unloading."

Wade glanced at this man's label: Col. Powers.

"I understand, Colonel," Wade replied calmly. "But trust me when I say that we deal with sensitive material on a daily basis. You will be better off heading directly inside where we have hot coffee, tea or even hot chocolate waiting for you. Actually," he added with a smirk, "you'll have to make it yourself, but it's there. My team will unload your equipment with care and have it safely inside before you can take your first sip."

Powers looked as if he were about to argue but was cut off by Doctor Isaac Palmer, a man in blue coveralls and a matching parka. "Well then, let's not keep the hot chocolate waiting," he said with a slight shiver. "It's freezing out here."

Wade smiled, seemingly relieved that he didn't have to argue with the Colonel any further. "Right this way, Doctor," he replied politely. "Mind your step."

"We'll go first," the colonel interjected, causing the four individuals in blue coveralls—including Tinsley—to look at him quizzically. "For your protection. It's protocol," he explained.

"Of course." Tinsley nodded politely.

The colonel turned to Harris. "You're up," he commanded.

"Yes sir," the lieutenant replied dutifully. His voice was deep and gravelly, with a strong Australian accent. He made his way down the narrow aisle toward the open hatch where Wade was already standing on the ground below. "Jackson, Gonzalez, with me," he called back to his team.

The two female members of the security detail fell into perfect formation behind Harris, their steps synchronized with his as he strode forward. He shot a quick glance at Hope as he passed her by, his face seemingly blank and emotionless. But his piercing gaze seemed to paralyze her, causing a knot to tighten in her stomach.

With casual ease, Harris stepped through the door of the shuttle and gracefully dropped to the ground. The two women following him mimicked his actions, each sitting on the ledge of the hatch before lowering herself to the surface.

"All good," Harris called back to the group behind him.

Doctor Palmer turned to Colonel Powers with a quizzical look. "I thought they were supposed to say, 'all clear' or something like that."

"Lieutenant Harris is a special breed," replied Powers with a small smile. "He has his own way of doing things."

"Special breed," whispered a young man in white coveralls beside the colonel. His badge proclaimed him as Cpl. Garret. A wry grin spread across his face.

"You're next," the colonel said, gesturing for those in blue to exit the shuttle.

It wasn't long before all passengers stood on solid ground, except for the two remaining flight crew members who stayed at their stations. A large vehicle on caterpillar treads approached the shuttle, pulling a trailer behind it on skis.

"This way," Wade shouted over the fading drone of the shuttle's engines and the approaching rumble of the land vehicle. He guided them toward a set of open doors that led into a large facility.

Hope pulled her parka hood over her head as a cold wind bit at her cheeks. Without hesitation, she followed Wade through the doors, joining in with the others as they trudged through a fine mix of tiny ice crystals and stone that crunched loudly beneath their heavy snow boots. The sound resembled that of a marching parade as they fell into line behind Wade.

The cold air bit at their skin, causing them to shiver and huddle closer in their blue uniforms. Cvl. Eng. Glenn Schwartz's teeth chattered as he muttered, "Fuck, it's cold."

"Welcome to the seventy-eighth parallel." Wade chuckled; his warm breath visible in the frigid air.

Hope, her face hidden under her hood, glanced to her right and saw Harris standing beside the Mexican woman, Gonzalez. To her left marched Jackson, the other female soldier, wearing the Canadian flag on her sleeve. She should have felt safe surrounded by soldiers, but instead she felt a sense of curiosity and confusion in their presence.

"Did you remember to take the tablet?" Tinsley's voice interrupted her thoughts as she walked a few paces behind.

"Yes, Deputy Secretary," Hope replied, patting her stomach to indicate that the device was safely tucked underneath her jacket.

"Thank goodness." Tinsley huffed in relief. "I thought I left it on the seat in the shuttle."

"That's why I'm here," Hope reassured her. "To make sure you have everything you need."

"And to cover my ass," Tinsley added with a wry smile.

"And to cover your ass," Hope acknowledged.

Wade led the group through a massive doorway and into an expansive cavern. As Hope took in the scene before her, she shook her head in disbelief. The space was a strange mix of natural rock formations and man-made structures, like some Frankenstein experiment gone wrong. Huge iron beams and concrete walls supported the cavern's roof, creating an odd contrast against the dark volcanic rock surrounding them.

"This," Wade announced with a sweeping gesture to their right, "is our garage." The group stood in awe as they took in the sight before them. The space was massive, filled with vehicles of all shapes and sizes. Some were sleek and modern, while others appeared to be cobbled together from spare parts.

"The small vehicles," Wade continued, "like the one retrieving your luggage, are generally used for field trips."

"Field trips?" Schwartz asked eagerly, his eyes lighting up with curiosity.

Wade nodded, a smirk playing across his lips. "Yeah, usually that means one of the lab nerds downstairs wants to do something science-y, or we need to perform maintenance on one of the wind turbines on the coast."

Tinsley couldn't resist pressing for more information. "Science-y? What does that entail exactly?"

"Who knows?" Wade shrugged nonchalantly. "One time, Professor Ford asked me to take him out to the beach so he could observe the wildlife. The guy studies quantum physics. Why he wanted to look at seals, I don't know. But who am I to question the chief of operations? Anyway, if you would follow me."

He led them toward a series of pod-like structures, neatly organized in rows along the walls of the cavern. They made their way toward a larger building beside a set of giant metal panels, monstrous elevator doors.

"These are our workshops and living quarters," Wade explained. "And this big one here serves as our conference facility, recreational room, and general quarters. Help yourself to some coffee, tea, hot chocolate—whatever you fancy. Professor Ford should be up soon to go through the induction process before taking you down to your designated quarters."

Palmer's eyebrows raised in question. "Quarters?" he asked, gesturing toward the large, looming buildings in front of them. "Didn't you just say these were the living quarters?"

Wade came to a stop and turned to face the doctor.

"I apologize," the chief of maintenance replied. "These are *our* living quarters—for the maintenance personnel, that is. The rest of the staff have their own quarters down in the facility."

Hope glanced between the two men; her curiosity piqued. "Why don't you all live down there as well?" she asked.

"Why don't we live down there?" Wade repeated, considering the question carefully. "I'm not sure how much you know about this project, Miss...." he trailed off, waiting for her to provide her name.

"Aguilar," she supplied. "Hope Aguilar. I'm assistant to the Deputy Secretary."

Wade nodded in acknowledgment before continuing. "Miss Aguilar, knowing what lies down there is enough for me to say that I prefer to be up here where it's colder, less comfortable, and easier to escape from if need be."

Tinsley looked at him with a mixture of surprise and concern, stepping closer to get a better look at the man dressed in bright orange jumpsuit.

"You don't believe it's safe?" she probed.

Wade's response was blunt and direct. "Isn't that why you're here, Deputy Secretary? To tell us if it's safe?"

A thick silence descended upon the group as they took in his words. The sound of tools and machinery echoed through the cavern but seemed distant and far away.

Their train of thought was interrupted by the return of a tractor-like vehicle from the shuttle, its trailer loaded with luggage and cargo. Its engine roared loudly as it passed through the large open doorway.

"We need to tow the shuttle inside," the driver called out.

"Okay," Wade responded with a wave before turning back to the group. "This way," he said, leading them toward the larger building. "We have a TV and a couple of nice sofas for you to relax on while you wait for the professor."

CHAPTER THREE

Deputy Secretary Sally Tinsley sat on the left side of a plush, cream-colored sofa by the door. With her elbow resting comfortably on the armrest, she swiped her finger across the sleek tablet screen, pausing momentarily to read something before continuing. Her sharp gaze darted to Lieutenant Harris, who stood at attention nearby, before scanning the rest of the occupants in the room.

The room was set up like an open plan living space. A cozy lounge area with a large flat-screen TV mounted on the wall served as the focal point. Above the television, a digital display shared the current time and outside temperature.

At precisely 16:49 EST, the temperature was a chilly -12.3 degrees Celsius or 9.86 degrees Fahrenheit. Hope returned from the compact kitchen, navigating her way around several sets of cheap cafe tables and chairs as she balanced two steaming mugs in her hands. The other travelers positioned themselves strategically around the room. Colonel Powers claimed a spot on the L-shaped sofa directly in front of the TV, while Corporal Garret and another soldier, Private Collier, opted for seats nearby.

Offering a warm smile to Privates Jackson and Gonzalez, who were enjoying their coffee at one of the small tables, Hope expertly maneuvered around them to reach another sofa lining the wall where Doctor Palmer had made himself comfortable. He lay stretched out with his head propped on one armrest and his sturdy boots resting atop the other.

"Deputy Secretary," said Hope politely, extending a mug toward Tinsley. "I apologize for not being able to find chamomile tea. This is English Breakfast instead."

Tinsley graciously accepted the cup from her assistant, who carefully situated herself beside her on the sofa. Hope cast a quick glance toward the kitchen where Schwartz could be seen preparing a cup of instant coffee. She then turned her gaze to one of the many windows that overlooked the vast cavern outside. There, Harris stood silently watching the bustling activity of the workers clad in bright orange jumpsuits. Hope brushed a stray strand of hair behind her ear with her finger, slowly tracing the outline of her earring and sending a pleasant tingle down her neck and spine.

Tinsley's voice was a mere whisper, but it carried an unspoken warning. "Be careful," she cautioned the assistant, turning to face her with a serious expression, reading the young woman's thoughts. "Your infatuation with him might be dangerous."

Hope knew better than to underestimate her boss, especially when it came to matters of the heart. Tinsley was a shrewd politician, and her position as deputy secretary was not given lightly.

"He is certainly handsome and appears to be in good health," Tinsley continued, her gaze fixed on the man in question. "But let's not forget that he is a soldier, my dear. And that is all he is."

Hope's brow furrowed at the dismissive tone in Tinsley's words. "You don't think he's capable of romantic feelings?" she asked.

"Look at him," Tinsley replied, gesturing toward the man who stood guard nearby. "While everyone else relaxes, he remains poised and ready for action. He hasn't even taken a sip of coffee or water since we arrived. He is solely focused on his duty."

Hope did look at him, unable to resist stealing a glance at the lieutenant. Her gaze hungrily roamed over his body, tracing the lines of his broad shoulders and the defined muscles of his arms. She couldn't help admiring his strong jawline and the way it clenched with determination. And when her gaze landed on his perfectly sculpted behind, she felt a flush creeping up her cheeks, betraying her inner desires.

Suddenly, a loud rumble filled the room, causing everyone to sit up straight.

"What's that?" Palmer asked as he looked around.

"The doors are closing," Harris answered, his eyes trained on the view outside the window. "They've moved the shuttle inside. Captains Moreau and Gauthier are on their way."

Powers thanked the lieutenant before returning his attention to the screen. "Any sign of Professor Ford yet?"

"Not yet, sir," Harris responded.

As they waited for further updates, Tinsley turned to Hope with a raised eyebrow.

"That is all he is," she said in a hushed tone, emphasizing her previous warning.

A short time later, two more figures in white coveralls burst through the door. The first was a young woman with a determined look, identified as Capt. Moreau by the Canadian flag patch on her arm. Following her closely was a man with a slight limp, Capt. Gauthier, sporting the stars and stripes on his uniform.

"Fuck, it's freezing out there," he huffed, shaking off the snow that clung to his boots.

"Why aren't you wearing your jackets?" Powers asked, noticing their lack of appropriate attire.

"They're still on the shuttle, sir," Gauthier replied, making his way to the kitchen.

"We didn't think we'd need them," Moreau chimed in, her French-Canadian accent strong as she followed him into the room. "They towed us in while we were in the cockpit. We thought it would be warmer once they closed those doors."

"What can I get you?" Gauthier asked, grabbing two mugs from a shelf above the sink.

"Coffee," Moreau answered without hesitation.

"Looks like they have only instant," Gauthier noted, putting down the cups and reaching for a tin.

"I'll take a double scoop," Moreau said, opening the fridge and retrieving a carton of full-cream milk from the door.

"Do they have skim?" Gauthier asked.

"Don't be such a pussy," Moreau teased, grabbing another carton.

With her mug cradled between her hands, she turned and leaned against the kitchen counter, taking a long-awaited sip. Her eyes closed as she relished the warmth spreading through her body. When she opened them again, her attention landed on the Deputy Secretary sitting on the couch by the door.

As soon as she saw the Deputy Secretary, her body tensed with excitement and respect. She stood up straight, still gripping her warm mug of coffee.

"Deputy Secretary," she exclaimed, making her way across the room toward the esteemed visitor. "It is an honor to be in your presence. I have been an admirer since you were assigned as one of the administrators of the UNIDO division."

Tinsley rose from her seat to shake the captain's hand.

"That was quite some time ago," she replied. "You don't look old enough to have been around during that time."

"I was eleven," Moreau responded. "You were twenty-three at the time, very young to hold such a position. And you were still studying political science at the University of Toronto. They must have seen great potential in you."

"Look at Dona, already smitten," Gauthier teased.

"Oh, shut up, chatte," Moreau snapped at her co-pilot before turning back to the Deputy Secretary. "You see what I have to deal with?"

"We all have our struggles," Tinsley offered with a smile. "Where are you from, Captain?"

"Montreal," Moreau answered.

"I am originally from Didsbury," Tinsley revealed.

"I know this," Moreau said, glancing over to grab a chair from a nearby table and joining Tinsley at her table. "I know everything about you. Not a very big town, correct?"

"It's big enough," Tinsley replied, passing her tablet off to her assistant Hope who began checking for any new emails or messages. "Which part of Montreal?"

"Lakeside Heights," Moreau replied.

"Sounds like a fancy neighborhood," Schwartz chimed in.

"If you enjoy having passenger jets flying over your house every ten minutes," Moreau retorted. "Then yes."

Tinsley smiled.

"But you did enjoy it, didn't you?" she asked.

A wide grin spread across Moreau's face.

"Yes," she replied. "It fascinated me. I always wanted to be up there in control of one of them."

"Have you ever flown one? On the controls... stick... whatever they call it?" Tinsley inquired.

"No, not yet," Moreau admitted. "But I am hoping this job will give me the experience and skills to apply for a pilot position once my service time is over."

"She flew us here today," Gauthier interjected. "And let me tell you, it was a smooth flight. All I do is answer calls and do crossword puzzles when I'm paired up with her."

"Is that true?" Tinsley turned to Moreau.

"I like being in control," Moreau responded honestly.

Tinsley took a sip of her tea, studying the young woman before her.

"Why the UN?" she asked.

Moreau pursed her lips, considering the question carefully.

"I originally joined the army to fly troop transports," she explained. "But eventually, I requested a transfer to med-evac missions. Then, a sergeant at the academy suggested I apply for a position with the UN. So, I did."

"I see," Tinsley nodded thoughtfully. "But why?"

Looking down at her coffee, Moreau watched the steam swirl around the rim of her mug before answering.

"I saw footage of the combined force's assault on Bosaso about seven years ago," she said somberly. "Have you seen it?"

"I have," Tinsley replied quietly.

Hope's fingers scrolled through her messages, but she remained attentive to the conversation unfolding beside her. She gave the captain a quizzical look.

"Bosaso?" the assistant asked, her eyes flitting between the two women beside her.

"Twelve attack vessels swooped in, unleashing a barrage of missiles and rockets on the town," Moreau explained, her voice heavy with emotion. "The flames engulfed everything. It's hard to imagine anything surviving such destruction. But just to be sure, the crafts landed and deployed one hundred soldiers. They killed every living thing in sight because they believed a terrorist threat originated from that region."

A deep sigh escaped Hope as she witnessed Moreau fighting back tears.

"Even if there was a threat," the captain continued, frustration evident in her voice. "Why massacre innocent men, women, and children? It makes no sense." She took a sip of her coffee before concluding, "After witnessing that horror, I knew I couldn't continue transporting troops to carry out such atrocities. That's why I joined the med-vac unit and eventually applied to work for the UN. I want to make a positive impact."

Some time passed as they waited for news updates on the TV screen and engaged in casual chatter. Hope returned her attention to scrolling through messages on her tablet while Harris kept watch out the window.

"Someone is approaching," Harris suddenly announced, turning briefly to glance at Colonel Garrett.

"It better be this Professor Ford guy," Corporal Garrett grumbled, rising from the sofa to join Lieutenant Harris.

As if on cue, the door swung open, and a tall man entered the room. He wore glasses and his attire consisted of jeans and an untucked plaid shirt. Hope craned her neck, tilting her chin upward to take in his full height. His short back and sides hair, peppered with strands of gray, and his long beard were unkempt, and somehow gave him an air of ruggedness.

With a pleasant smile, he greeted the group. His name tag, neatly displayed on his shirt pocket, identified him as Allen Ford—Chief of Operations. As he looked around the room at all the faces, Tinsley stood and reached out to shake his hand.

"Sally Tinsley," she introduced herself. "Deputy Secretary of the United Nations Industrial Development Organization. It's a pleasure to meet you."

"The pleasure is mine," replied Ford, warmly shaking her hand before turning to greet the others. "I see you found the coffee stash all right. I hope you have an appetite fit for a king. Our cafeteria staff downstairs have been working hard preparing roast veal, an assortment of vegetables, along with pumpkin soup and apple pie for dessert. We don't have any dietary requirements or allergies to consider, I assume? No one informed us if that's the case."

An uncomfortable silence filled the room.

"Excellent." Ford grinned, clapping his hands before rubbing them excitedly as he made his way toward the television. With a press of a button on the side panel, the screen switched from the news to a dark background with bold white lettering reading "Innovative Energy Corporation." The words then transformed into the acronym "IEC."

"Well then, let's get started on the essentials," Ford announced. "Welcome to Borden Island."

All eyes turned to give Ford their full attention as he began his tour of the facility. The room buzzed with eager anticipation, each person leaning forward in their seats to catch every detail.

"The construction of this state-of-the-art facility began in July of two-thousand and thirty-five," Ford began, his voice commanding and confident. "After years of hard work and dedication, it was finally completed in September of twenty forty-nine. Our research equipment was set up in the labs the following year, and we have continued to upgrade and improve our facilities since then. In fact, the entire facility was brought up to its current state only six months ago with the assembly of the miniature hadron collider."

He gestured toward a screen behind him, which lit up with a three-dimensional animation of the facility. The image zoomed in on a cross-section of the building, giving a clear view of its impressive size and complexity.

"As you can see, there are three levels beneath us," Ford continued. "The first level consists of living quarters, recreational facilities, and the cafeteria I mentioned before. We currently have three hundred and twenty-seven members of staff, not including the maintenance crew. Each staff member has their own quarters on Level A, where we will be descending to shortly."

Garrett let out a low whistle. "It must be massive down there."

Ford nodded with a small smile. "Oh yes, it is quite impressive. Allow me to show you." He touched the screen again, and the animation zoomed into the elevator shaft before opening onto Level A. The cafeteria and a large open space were located at the center, surrounded by corridors branching off in different directions leading to smaller rooms.

"Those rooms," Hope said, pointing at some of the smaller spaces on the screen. "Those are the living quarters?"

Ford nodded again. "That's correct. They may not be luxurious, but each room is equipped with a bed, small built-in desk, closet, and basic bathroom facilities including a shower, sink, and toilet."

Private Jackson raised an eyebrow. "And where does all the water come from for these facilities?"

"We have an automated desalination facility near our wind turbines on the coast," Ford explained. "The water you used for your hot beverages earlier came directly from the sea." The animation returned to the elevator shaft and continued its descent before opening to a detailed floor plan of Level A, showcasing the layout in even more detail.

The animated image returned to the elevator shaft and descended further before opening to a floor plan.

"This is Level B," he continued, his voice echoing through the sterile hallway. "Our various tech and research labs are located here as well as our medical facilities." The walls were lined with glass walls and sleek metal doors, each one bearing a number and designation. "We have two operating theaters, fully equipped and ready for use in case of casualties."

Schwartz's brow furrowed in concern. "And have you needed to use those facilities?"

Ford's expression darkened. He nodded slowly and took in a deep breath. "Unfortunately, yes."

"The anomaly," Tinsley interjected, her voice filled with curiosity.

The chief of operations looked at her, perplexed. "Wh-Where did you hear that?"

"I'm here to assess the functionality of this facility, Professor Ford," she replied coolly. "The fact that I heard that word associated with this facility on my way here has me somewhat concerned."

"I apologize, Deputy Secretary," Ford said, looking down at his shoes. "You were already scheduled to visit us when the incident occurred."

"Incident?" Tinsley repeated, her tone now sharp with urgency.

"I have every intention of explaining." Ford raised a hand, almost as if surrendering to her. "I just don't know where to start."

She glanced around the room at the others who had arrived with her. "How about you start here?" She gestured toward Schwartz. "I know why Glenn is here. He and I have crossed paths before. But I really don't understand why such a large peacekeeping team is here." She turned to face Ford again. "Are we in a war zone? They're definitely not here as my protection detail."

"Deputy Secretary," Colonel Powers interjected, his voice crisp and authoritative. "According to our orders, we're here solely as your protection detail. However, I did notice that our equipment seems to be a bit excessive for such a seemingly mundane job." He gestured to a large crate nestled among the other cargo in the cavernous room outside the conference room.

Tinsley nodded, her mind racing with possibilities. She moved her gaze to Palmer.

"I must admit, I'm perplexed as well. Why would we need a pediatrician on a mission like this?"

Ford waved his hands by his side, his shoulders half shrugging as he searched for an answer.

"My understanding is that all of the personnel were declared fit and ready for service here, including no pregnancies," Tinsley pressed.

"Yes," Ford said. "You're correct. There were no pregnancies detected during the physicals."

"But we have a pediatrician in our midst," she stated, her tone now sharp with suspicion. "Professor Ford, is there an infant in this facility?"

A thick silence hung in the air, tension building among those gathered in the room. Even Harris, usually stoic and calm, had shifted his attention fully to the man standing by the television, waiting for an answer to Tinsley's question.

Ford swallowed hard and frowned. "Yes."

CHAPTER FOUR

Intrigued and questioning glances darted among the various occupants of the room. All eyes seemed to converge on Allen Ford, the director of the facility, and Doctor Palmer, who were already aware of the situation with the infant.

"Where is the child?" Tinsley inquired, her voice cutting through the tense atmosphere.

"He's in the medical section," Ford responded, his tone weary and strained. "Under constant observation."

Tinsley nodded, her expression grave. "Is he healthy? Is he being properly cared for?"

"As best as we can with what we have," Ford replied, his eyes flickering with a mixture of exhaustion and guilt.

"And his mother?" Tinsley pressed on.

Ford's features twisted into a pained expression as he struggled to find the right words. "She...passed away," he said, his voice cracking slightly.

The news was met with stunned silence from all those present. Harris, maintaining a stoic facade, tilted his head ever so slightly in question.

"What happened?" he asked, his gaze fixed on Ford.

The colonel turned to look at Harris, while the lieutenant gazed intently at the professor, waiting for an answer. Ford appeared disoriented, opening and closing his mouth as if grappling with some internal struggle.

"What happened?" Harris repeated coldly.

"I— it's not a simple explanation," Ford stammered. "Where do I even begin?"

"The beginning is usually a good place," Harris retorted.

Hope scanned the room and noticed that all eyes were now focused on Harris. It was the closest she had seen him come to expressing any human emotions.

"There's footage." The professor's voice quivered, his hands shaking as he spoke.

"Of the incident?" Colonel Powers leaned forward; his brow furrowed in concern.

"Yes," the other replied, his eyes downcast. "It shows Amy... Doctor Caldwell at her monitor in the Shrine... ah... in the Energy Generation Chamber, during a test performance of the equipment. The incident..." He paused and swallowed hard. "It's probably best if you just saw it for yourselves."

Private Collier gestured to the large screen television in the corner of the room.

"You have our full attention," he said solemnly.

"We don't have it here," Ford told them, his voice strained. "It's stored on a secure server in my office. My intentions are to hand a copy over to the authorities when we release Doctor Caldwell's remains. But we've been stranded here without transportation for another week."

"You have some now," Captain Gauthier pointed out, gesturing to the shuttle visible through the window.

"Yes," the professor said, "But according to company protocol—"

"We're with the United Nations," Tinsley interrupted. "Protocol is our business."

"I understand," Ford replied, his shoulders slumping in defeat. "I had hoped you might be able to take her back to her family. That's why I sent a notice of possible biological risk."

"Biological risk for a dead body?" Schwartz raised an eyebrow skeptically. "Surely you have adequate storage and facilities for that?"

"We do have a morgue," admitted the professor, his voice cracking with emotion. "But we were not prepared for this..."

"Why didn't you contact the authorities immediately after the incident?" Hope questioned.

"We can't," he answered. "Our communications are limited solely to the company. We cannot reach out directly to anyone else. Even family and friends have to go through the company's servers when contacting us and vice versa."

He stopped and locked eyes with Tinsley, his gaze pleading for understanding. The room fell into an uncomfortable silence as they watched the professor struggle to hold back tears. "It's been two weeks since it happened. I started writing a resignation letter and fully intend to submit it to you to hand over on my behalf. I was hoping we could continue this conversation down in the facility but, here we are.

"The purpose of this facility is grand," he declared, his tone imparting a sense of awe. "To create an alternate power source for our planet—something renewable, safe, and sustainable." He went on to explain how their research had led to the use of a modified miniature hadron collider, which could potentially produce a small singularity capable of supplying cities with power indefinitely.

As he crossed the room slowly, his footsteps echoing against the walls, his expression shifted from confident to troubled. He made his way toward the deputy secretary, his eyes searching for some glimmer of understanding. "I was wrong," he admitted. "I came in here toeing the company line, but what happened to Amy wasn't an accident. It was unforeseen, unexpected..." His voice trailed off as if unable to find the right words. "But it was no accident."

Tinsley cleared her throat and straightened her posture, her voice carrying a serious tone as she addressed the professor. "Mister Schwartz, my assistant and I have been tasked with assessing the safety and structural integrity of this facility, as well as its impact on the surrounding environment." She punctuated each point with a wave of her hand. "Our protocol demands careful examination and the submission of thorough reports. It is our responsibility to make recommendations based on our findings, which will then be published for public review." Tinsley's gaze bored into Professor Ford, who seemed slightly taken aback by her professional demeanor. "We understand that Innovative Energy Corporation has plans to have this power plant operational within the next six months. However, we urge you to also submit your own recommendations to them."

He appeared beaten down, his shoulders slumped and his eyes downcast. "You're someone who's familiar with the cutthroat world of politics," he said, his voice heavy with resignation. "You understand how ruthless corporations can be. We all bow down to them. I'm just a scientist, fascinated by this field, working for one powerful company. I do what I'm told so my family can have food on the table and a roof over their heads. Any recommendations to shut down this facility should come from an external organization. Someone not involved in this project, completely removed from Innovative Energy Corporation."

"And you think that's us?" Schwartz asked skeptically. "My report will primarily focus on the structure of this place. I am just an engineer."

"And I'm here to assess the safety of the protocols in place in this facility," Tinsley added, pushing her glasses back along her nose with a finger. "While I have some sway in the execution of UN policies, I have no authority when overriding the agreements between the UN and corporate entities, including current operational procedures and policies the company has in place. I can report on them and ask for legal actions to take place, if I believe they are in breach of the United Nations accord of international corporation conduct. But I cannot break any aspect of those agreements without reasonable cause, including transporting the deceased body of an employee. I'm sorry."

Ford, appearing beaten, started for the door.

"Come," he said, motioning for them to follow him. "I'll show you."

With Ford leading the way, they approached a towering set of iron doors, seemingly carved into the dark rock of the cavern. The professor confidently pressed a button beside the entrance and waited for the heavy doors to slide open with a rumble, revealing a large elevator beyond. Its size was impressive, easily large enough to accommodate a small vehicle or several people and their equipment.

"Wow," Hope murmured in awe.

"It needs to be big to transport bulky equipment and supplies down into the depths," Ford explained. "This elevator services all levels for that purpose. There are two other shafts that connect Levels A, B, and C for personnel, but this one is the only one that goes directly to the surface."

Harris spoke up, his curiosity piqued. "Is this the only way to get to the surface?"

Ford shook his head. "No, there are other exits as well." He pointed to a smaller door tucked into the far corner of the vehicle bay. "Emergency escape stairs lead up from below and connect to that door, as well as another behind those pods over there." He gestured toward rows of structures on the opposite side of the cavern. "And there are two more escape hatches that lead directly outside."

With that, the group shuffled into the elevator, their footsteps echoing off the steel walls. Colonel Powers stood at the front, his posture rigid and commanding. But as he raised a hand to stop Moreau and Gauthier from entering, the tension in the air became palpable.

"Not you two," he announced with a stern voice, pointing directly at them.

Moreau furrowed her brow in confusion but held her tongue.

"I need you two with the shuttle," Powers clarified. "Make sure it's ready to go at a moment's notice. If we need to evacuate, I want you to be prepared. This is an active operation from this moment onward. Understood?"

Moreau glanced at Tinsley with an apologetic expression, hoping to continue their conversation. Tinsley nodded and pressed her lips together. Hope felt a twinge of disappointment in her heart. She thought the two women had hit it off, both from the same nation and sharing similar values. Maybe this was the start of a new friendship for the deputy secretary—something that Hope believed Sally Tinsley lacked in her personal life.

"Yes sir," the two captains answered, their voices echoing off the gleaming walls of the elevator as they stepped back to allow the others to board. As Hope glanced at Gonzalez, a fellow Mexican, her heart ached for a sense of familiarity in this foreign place. Her eyes met those of a beautiful woman who seemed to have a perpetual scowl etched onto her features, as if bitterness and resentment were her constant companions.

Attitude with a side order of shit, Hope considered.

She pushed down the desire to connect with someone from her homeland, filing it away for future consideration. Perhaps later when she wasn't surrounded by strangers and on edge in this new environment.

As the doors closed with a soft hiss, she turned to face Harris, hoping for any sign of emotion in his expression. All she saw was the stoic facade of a soldier.

Just a soldier and nothing more.

"Are you all right?" he asked, the concern evident in his voice. "You appear troubled."

"I'm fine, thank you," she forced out, trying to sound confident despite the nervousness quivering in her voice.

The elevator descended smoothly and silently, its metal walls encasing them like a metal coffin.

Stay in there, Hope, a voice called inside her head, echoing the constant memory that haunted her.

Hope took a deep breath and tried to calm her racing heart. Every second spent in the enclosed space took her further from the surface and increased her desire to be up there with the pilots.

"You're not fine," Tinsley whispered, leaning closer to Hope's ear. "What is it?"

"I'm claustrophobic," she admitted, feeling a wave of shame wash over her.

Tinsley's eyebrows shot up in surprise. "Why didn't you say so before?"

"I don't know," Hope replied honestly, listening to the low whirring of the elevator motors humming softly through the walls. "I thought I'd be okay. I haven't experienced it since..."

Down.

Down.

The air seemed to thicken around her, suffocating her as the elevator continued its descent deeper into the earth. The memories flooded back, overwhelming her mind with their intensity. Darkness closing in from all sides, pressing against her like a tangible presence. Cold hardness against her back as she pressed herself against the wall for balance, security. In her mind, she huddled in a dark corner, curled up in fear, holding her pooky bear tightly. A distant voice, echoing from far away.

Stay in there, Hope.

"Close your eyes and take deep breaths," Tinsley offered, her voice filled with concern. "I really don't know what else to do."

Down.

Down.

Down.

The cocoon of fear crept over her neck and scalp, tightening its grip as the elevator descended further and further into the depths. All she could think about was how anything could go wrong... a malfunction, leaving them stranded in the shaft... a cave-in, burying them alive.

Stay in there, Hope.

Down.

Down.

Down.

"It's fine." Hope forced a smile, trying to push away her fears. "Perhaps it will pass when we get to Level A."

Into the depths of the earth they went, like a descent into the belly of a beast. And for Hope, it felt like being swallowed whole.

Chapter Five

As the elevator doors slid open, a cool rush of air greeted Hope's face. She quickly stepped out, trying not to draw attention to herself. As she took a deep breath, the sense of relief instantly replaced the feeling of confinement from the metal box. Tinsley followed her into a vast space that reminded Hope of a food court in a shopping mall. Tables were neatly positioned in rows and columns, surrounded by plants and trash bins with tray disposal shelves on top.

Hope scanned the area, expecting to see familiar signs for fast-food outlets. Instead, she saw a large cafeteria situated across the expanse of tables and seats. Glass-fronted cases lined the length of its facade, illuminated by bright heat lights that shone down on steaming food. A few hot and cold drink dispensers stood to the far right, while a tray dispensary filled with various plates, bowls, cups, cutlery, and napkins sat to the left. A long bench stretched in front of the glass cases, where people could slide their trays as they collected their food.

Behind the facade, about twenty people dressed in white outfits with hairnets and aprons worked diligently at stainless steel benches and appliances. One woman caught Hope's eye as she looked up from her task.

"Not ready yet, boss," she called out across the vast space. "Probably another half-an-hour?"

"It's all right, Tracey," Ford replied. "We're a little early. I'll take our visitors to my office to go over a few things before we trouble you."

Tracey waved her hand before returning to her work.

"That's Tracey Zelski," Ford said to the group as they walked toward a corridor to their right. "Our head chef. She runs a tight ship. They make some pretty good grub in there. Not great. But good enough. My office is this way."

They followed him, passing three smaller sets of elevator doors on their way to a corridor. Hope turned and noticed another set of three elevators on the other side of the large one they had just emerged from.

"I thought you said the labs were further down," Schwartz said.

"That's correct," Ford replied, leading them down the corridor.

"But your office is on this level?" Tinsley asked.

"Yes," Ford confirmed. "Most of my research is done downstairs in the Energy Generation Chamber. It's not a suitable place for meetings with staff members, so an office was included on this level for convenience."

With that, Ford opened the first door on the right side of the corridor, just past the elevators, and led them inside.

As they entered the room, a soft light flickered on automatically, revealing a square space lined with mostly empty bookshelves. In the center of one wall stood a dark panel, while a corner desk with a computer and high-backed chair could be seen tucked against the far wall. Two light-colored sofas faced each other in the middle of the floor, separated by a small coffee table. The room exuded an inviting aura, adorned with maple wood furnishings and plush rugs covering the hardwood floor. Hope felt comfortable in this space, especially compared with how she'd felt in the pod room in the cavern and the elevator she had just escaped.

"I'm surprised," she remarked as she stepped aside to allow the others to enter behind her.

"With what, may I ask?" Professor Ford responded as he sat at his desk and turned on his computer with a tap of the screen.

"I was expecting something more industrial," Hope explained.

"The intent is for staff to stay in these rooms for three months at a time, with one month off before returning for another three," Ford informed them as he navigated through folders on his computer using a mouse. "The company wants its employees to feel at home while they're away from home."

Hope furrowed her brow in confusion. "Then why isn't the maintenance crew located down here? Surely there are enough rooms."

"There are more than enough rooms," Ford confirmed, opening a folder, and scrolling through files. "And all of them are quite comfortable. The pods were originally brought in to house the workers who constructed this facility. They were meant to be removed before the official opening, pending approval from UNIDO. But after the incident, the entire maintenance crew staff decided to occupy them instead of staying down here. And I can't blame them."

"How many people know about the incident?" Colonel Powers asked, standing to the side of one of the sofas as Deputy Secretary Gonzalez took a seat.

"Most of our staff," Professor Ford replied. "Some have heard rumors, but only a few know the full extent. A couple of the maintenance crew were in an adjacent area during the test when the incident occurred. They shared what they know with the others, and since then, everyone has opted to stay above ground."

"What did they know?" Gonzalez questioned.

Ford pressed a button on his keyboard and swiveled in his chair, gesturing to the screen mounted on the wall.

"Watch," he instructed as an image appeared.

The security camera footage showed a high-angled shot of a circular platform in a dark room. Numerous rod-like objects, attached to iron beams resembling scaffolding, extended from the edges of the room toward the center, stopping just short of reaching the edges of the platform. These rods seemed to surround the platform on all sides, at least from what could be seen in the footage.

The CCTV footage captured a small figure hunched over a computer console, completely dwarfed by the massive structure surrounding her. Her fingers flew across the keyboard with precision and purpose, though her movements were barely visible on the screen.

"What is that?" Tinsley asked, squinting at the pixelated figure.

Ford's eyes widened in awe as he replied, "That, my friends, is the heart of the project. A singularity fabricator."

Schwartz chimed in, "I don't see anything resembling a hadron collider. Didn't you say it was part of this project?"

The professor nodded. "Ah, yes. The miniature hadron collider is actually built into the surrounding sectors outside the chamber," he explained. "There's a tunnel that forms a giant ring inside the mountain. The hadron collider was constructed inside that tunnel and part of it passes close by the Energy Generation Chamber. There's an access passage just outside the chamber with a terminal room at the other end. As I mentioned before, the maintenance crew was monitoring power consumption and controlling the hadron collider in that room while Doctor Amy Caldwell prepared to transfer energy to the singularity fabricator from the terminal you can see on screen."

The group watched intently as Caldwell reached for a microphone on her desk and announced, "The hadron collider is now at full capacity. Any discrepancies on your end?"

"No, Doctor Caldwell," a man's voice responded.

"The person speaking is Ken Wade," the professor informed them. "You met him earlier."

"Transferring energy to the fabricator," Caldwell stated confidently as she typed away on her keyboard.

Bolts of electricity burst forth from the tips of rods surrounding a circular platform in the center of the room, creating an intricate web of crackling energy. In the midst of this chaos, a spherical form slowly expanded until it reached the rods, reminding Hope of a crystal ball.

"Do you see this, Allen?" Caldwell asked into the microphone.

Ford's voice came through the speakers, awestruck as he replied, "Yes, it's incredible. Are we getting any readings yet?"

Caldwell turned back to her computer and clicked a few buttons.

Ford shook his head. "I was supposed to be down there for this. Stupid stomach bug."

Hope felt sorry for him.

"Energy output stable!" Caldwell exclaimed with excitement. "The readings are off the charts. If they're accurate, we're receiving one hundred thousand gigawatts of energy every second. We should try to increase it even more."

"Agreed," Ford's voice responded through the speakers.

Caldwell jumped out of her seat and pumped her fist in triumph before returning to the microphone.

"I forgot you can't hear me if I step away." She laughed breathlessly. "We did it, Allen. We actually did it. This could solve the world's energy crisis."

"Not could!" Ford's voice was filled with exhilaration. "We have solved it."

Caldwell let out a joyous whoop and pumped her fist in the air again before breaking into a round of applause.

Suddenly, the sphere flickered and something palpable and monstrous appeared within its shrouded depths. The group watching the footage held their breath as the energy shrouded sphere returned to its original state.

"What was that?" Private Jackson's voice trembled with fear.

"What was that?" Ford's voice echoed through the monitor, tension evident in his tone.

Caldwell hurried back to her computer, confusion etched on her face. "What are you talking about?"

"Something just appeared in the singularity," Ford explained urgently. "Check the readings."

She frantically typed commands into her keyboard. "Everything seems fine."

"Let's shut it down," Ford instructed. "I think we need to run some tests."

Nodding quickly, Caldwell pressed a few keys, willing the machine to power down. The rods stopped flaring at their ends, but the sphere remained ominously active.

"Did you shut it down?" Ford asked.

"Yes," Caldwell replied, her hands shaking. "I've exited the program. It shouldn't be functioning."

"Ken?" Ford called out.

"The collider is off, Professor," Wade's voice replied over the speakers. "There's no power supply to the fabricator from this end. I can realign the rods if you want."

Before Ford could respond, a deafening growl filled the lab, followed by a piercing shriek that sent chills down their spines.

And then, without warning, a surge of tangled light shot out from the sphere and struck Caldwell in the stomach.

She screamed in pain as she was flung across the room, her body skidding to a halt a few feet away from the terminal.

The sphere flashed again, with ribbons of electricity crackling across its surface before disappearing.

The silence that followed was deafening, broken only by Ford's panicked voice. "Amy? Can you hear me? Ken, something has gone wrong. We need to get in there."

"On my way," Wade's voice responded urgently.

The screen flickered and turned black, removing the only source of light in the darkened room. Professor Ford's voice quivered as he addressed the gathering, tears threatening to spill from his eyes. "Ken managed to realign the rods, but not before..." His voice trailed off, overcome with emotion. "Doctor Caldwell survived another six hours," he continued, his gaze drifting to a corner of the room. "Long enough for our medical doctor to safely remove the baby."

"Excuse me, Professor," Doctor Palmer interjected, her brow furrowed. "That woman didn't look like someone in the third trimester, or even second. It would have been extremely unwise to attempt removal at such an early stage. The chances of survival are slim to none."

Ford nodded sadly. "I know," he admitted. "Amy only discovered she was pregnant a week or so before that footage was recorded. I can't explain it, but somehow the baby is alive and relatively healthy."

"Relatively healthy?" Palmer pressed.

"Yes," Ford replied with a hint of uncertainty in his voice. "I've requested a pediatrician to come and assess the situation. This is uncharted territory."

"I would like to see the infant," Doctor Palmer stated firmly as Professor Ford rose from his desk.

"Soon," Ford replied, gesturing toward the door of his office. "But first, we should get everyone settled in."

As they began to exit the room, Hope glanced back at the large elevator they had descended in just moments ago. Its doors were still wide open, revealing twelve men in orange coveralls carrying luggage and cargo from the shuttle.

"This way," Ford instructed, leading the maintenance crew to follow him.

"We can take those," Colonel Powers offered, pointing to a large black crate being carried by two men.

"It's no problem," the professor replied, determined to lead the way. They made their way across the dining area toward another passageway that led away at an odd angle to the right. Powers pursed his lips in frustration, clearly displeased with something.

Curiosity got the better of Hope and she asked what was inside the crate.

"Nothing special," Powers said. "Just some hazmat suits for the delegation and my team, and weapons."

Hope felt a twinge of discomfort at the mention of weapons.

"Weapons?" Deputy Secretary Tinsley questioned with concern.

"Standard protocol," Powers assured her with a wry smile. "We're required to take them everywhere we go. Just precautionary. Don't worry, we won't be needing them during this inspection."

As they walked, Hope still felt drawn to the towering figure of Lieutenant Harris. She blushed as she noticed his proximity and felt a sudden surge of heat.

"Colonel, may I request to see that footage again?" Harris asked, his tone urgent.

"I'll speak to Professor Ford about it," Powers replied. "Anything specific you saw?"

"I want to study the object in the orb and something in the last moments before it vanished," Harris explained.

"Care to share what's gripped your curiosity, Lieutenant?" the colonel pressed.

Harris's gaze darted to Hope, seemingly unsure if he should answer the colonel's question in front of the young woman.

"I'm not sure, sir," he finally responded.

Colonel Powers nodded, his sharp gaze lingering on the crate before them.

"I'll make the request," he said.

"Thank you, sir," Harris replied with a grateful nod.

The group suddenly came to a halt in front of two identical doors.

Deputy Secretary and Miss Aguilar," Ford announced, turning to one of the maintenance crew members who produced a handful of lanyards with plastic key cards attached from his pocket. The man in orange swiftly sorted through the mess and selected two cards, offering them to the professor. "Your rooms."

Hope and Tinsley stepped forward eagerly, each taking a key card from the man's outstretched hand.

"Does it matter which room we take?" the deputy secretary inquired.

"If you mean, have we assigned specific rooms for you," Ford replied with a small smile. "No. The rooms are all identical, so you may choose whichever you prefer."

Tinsley pressed her card against the panel by the door on the left, but nothing happened.

"Perhaps this one will work instead," Ford suggested, gesturing toward the neighboring hatch.

Following his suggestion, the deputy secretary placed her card against the panel and with a soft hiss, the hatch slid open.

"I'm sorry but I cannot correctly identify which luggage belongs to whom," Professor Ford apologized politely.

Without hesitation, Hope pointed to a worn and battered green canvas carry bag in one of the maintenance crew member's hands.

"That one is mine," she declared before stepping aside to allow him to enter their chosen room.

"And that suitcase is mine," Tinsley claimed as she pointed to a large black hard-covered bag on wheels.

As the maintenance man wheeled the bag into her room, Ford turned to the deputy secretary. "We will meet in the dining area in approximately fifteen minutes for dinner."

"I would still like to see the infant," Doctor Palmer interjected.

"I understand," Professor Ford replied kindly. "While you are settling in, I will check with the medical team to see if a visit can be arranged for this evening. This way, Doctor. Mister Schwartz. Your rooms are just a little further this way."

The professor gestured for the group to follow as he led them further along the corridor, their footsteps echoing through the sterile passageway. Tinsley leaned in closer to Hope and spoke in a hushed tone.

"What do you think Lieutenant Harris saw in that footage?" she asked.

Hope shook her head in confusion.

"I don't know," she replied quietly.

"There is something peculiar about him," Tinsley continued, turning to steal a glance at the lieutenant. "I can't quite put my finger on it."

"Maybe he's just very dedicated to his job," Hope offered. "As you said. Just a soldier."

"Perhaps," Tinsley conceded, but her gaze remained fixed on Harris.

Hope followed her line of sight, studying the lieutenant's features. She watched as he lowered his head to whisper something to Gonzalez, feeling an unexpected pang of jealousy. Her attention then drifted to Powers, who turned and caught her looking.

"You and Colonel Powers seem to be getting along well," Hope commented slyly to Tinsley.

"You sound like a giddy schoolgirl," Tinsley retorted with a laugh before disappearing into her room. "It's just professional courtesy. But if you'd like to join me, I'm heading to the dining area in ten minutes. I could really use a coffee."

CHAPTER SIX

Hope returned to the bustling dining area, filled with the chatter of hungry workers and the clanging of dishes. She spotted the deputy secretary conversing with one of the kitchen staff, a young woman with strawberry blonde hair that caught the light in an ethereal glow. With her tablet tucked under her arm and pressed against her chest, Hope made her way over to them.

"I'd love to say it's all fresh produce," said the woman. Her voice was warm and friendly as she gestured toward the drink dispensers. "Unfortunately, supplies don't come frequently enough. The vegetables are snap frozen and shipped up from Ontario. Same with the meat. All the dry goods come through Vancouver, but they arrive on the same transport. We have enough storage back there to keep a year's worth of stock." She motioned to the kitchen area behind the counter before turning her gaze to Hope, offering a genuine smile. "You want a cup of coffee?"

"Ah," Hope said, considering the various dispensers lined up on the counter. "Tea, preferably."

"Cups are there," the other woman said, pointing to a bench beside the drink dispenser. "The machine to the right offers Earl Grey, English Breakfast, Black Tea, Green Tea, Herbal Tea, Chamomile, Peppermint, Chai and Hibiscus. It's all real, not synthetic. Snap frozen like everything else here." She spoke with pride and confidence in her work.

"Including the staff," Tinsley chimed in playfully, lifting a cup of steaming black coffee to her lips.

"Including the staff," the other woman echoed with a grin.

"This is Tracey Zelski," the deputy secretary said to Hope. "Head chef."

"Nice to meet you," Hope said, reaching for Tracey's hand in a firm handshake. "Hope Aguilar."

"You too," Zelski replied, her grip soft but firm. Hope noticed the young woman subtly biting her lip and wondered why. "I like your hair."

"Thanks," said Hope, taking her hand back and smiling politely. Her hair was pulled back in a simple ponytail, nothing exceptional. She wanted to say something that acknowledged the compliment without appearing too interested, as Zelski seemed to be in her. "I hear you run a tight ship here."

"Yes," the head chef confirmed with a hint of disappointment flashing in her eyes. "We have to be extremely organized all the time. The goal is to keep the facility running around the clock, matching shift changes throughout the day."

"Wouldn't that just mean keeping food stocked up in those display cabinets there?" Hope gestured toward the glass cases on top of the counter as she pressed a button on the dispenser for chamomile tea.

"Technically, yes," Zelski answered. "But we're currently trying to choose between two options. The first is whether we should have sections for continuous breakfast, lunch, and dinner so those on different shifts can eat when it's most convenient for them. The second is that we should stick to a regular schedule where everyone eats breakfast at breakfast time, lunch at lunch time, and dinner at dinner time."

"What do you think is the best option?" Tinsley interjected.

"I don't know." The chef shook her head. "I think it's easier for my crew to focus on one thing at a time, but it's not fair for the rest of the staff if their shift is at odd hours. What would you do?"

"I don't think that decision is up to me," Tinsley replied, glancing over at Hope for input.

"How long have you been a head chef?" Hope asked Tracey, genuinely curious about her experience and expertise in the kitchen. The scent of freshly baked bread and sizzling meats filled the air, making Hope's stomach grumble with hunger.

"This is my first job with that title," Zelski admitted, her tone humble yet proud. "I worked at the usual fast-food joints when I was still in school. I graduated from Ontario with a Masters of Food Science and was recruited by IEC Immediately afterwards, I became a head chef."

"Well," Tinsley said with admiration. "Congratulations."

"I can only speak from my perspective," Hope chimed in. "If I were in your shoes, I'd consider the needs of the people here before the convenience of the kitchen. In my opinion... and it's just my opinion..."

"Of course," Zelski nodded attentively. "Please, go on."

"I'd organize your team into specialized sectors," Hope continued, feeling a surge of excitement at her own idea before a sense of self-criticism descended upon her. A nervous talker, with limited social skills, she knew she had committed to something by opening her mouth, and now she had to let it play out. "You could assign the breakfast menu to one sector, the lunch menu to another and so on. And within the kitchen itself, specific appliances could be assigned to each sector based on how many of each appliance you have available."

"We have six stove tops and ovens, and loads of bench space," Zelski said thoughtfully, glancing over her shoulder to where her crew bustled around like a well-oiled machine—carving meat, stirring gravy, prepping roast vegetables for serving—all in perfect synchrony. "It could definitely work."

"Perhaps you could also ask your staff for their input," Tinsley suggested. As she spoke, a loud metallic crash echoed through the room from the kitchen.

"I'll do that," the head chef replied, already heading back to the kitchen through a swinging saloon door at the end of the counter. "Thanks for the suggestions. And now I should go and see what that kerfuffle was." Zelski disappeared into the kitchen, her voice lost among the clanging of pots and pans.

Hope turned to follow Tinsley toward a cluster of tables in a corner of the dining area.

"She's an interesting one," the deputy secretary remarked with a sly smile. "Wouldn't you say?"

"I agree, she seems very nice," Hope replied, scanning the dining area. She estimated roughly fifty people scattered throughout, all dressed in civilian clothing and enjoying their meals and hot beverages. The smell of freshly brewed coffee wafted through the air.

"Just nice?" Tinsley teased as they settled into a cozy booth near the drink dispensers. "I think she's interested in you."

Hope felt a flutter in her chest, uncertain of how to respond.

"I got that feeling too," she admitted with a shy smile, playing with the edge of her cup.

Tinsley locked eyes with her over her mug of steaming coffee, silently conveying her message without saying a word.

Hope's heart raced as she waited for Tinsley to continue, unsure of where this conversation was heading.

"So?" Tinsley prodded after a moment, setting her cup down on the table and leaning forward.

Hope's mind raced, trying to decipher Tinsley's cryptic words. What did she mean? Was she asking about her feelings toward someone else? Or about herself?

"I probably shouldn't ask this," Tinsley said hesitantly, her professional facade faltering for a moment. "It's unprofessional. But have you ever considered...you know?" Her gaze flickered to Hope's lips for a brief moment before returning to meet her gaze once again.

Hope's heart skipped as she registered the meaning behind Tinsley's words. How could she not have considered it before? But now, with the question hanging in the air between them, Hope wasn't sure how to respond.

The assistant's composure changed to defensive mode, feeling slightly uncomfortable discussing such personal matters with her superior. But at the same time, there were few people in their lives they could confide in, so she found herself letting her guard down and opening to Tinsley.

"No," she replied, trying to keep her voice steady. "Not for a long time."

"Not for a long time?" Tinsley repeated, a playful grin tugging at her lips.

"I like men," Hope said matter-of-factly, though it wasn't entirely true. "I've only been with a couple of them. But I know I like them."

"Not for a long time?" the deputy secretary probed further. "You *have* been with a woman?"

"I was still in school," the other replied, dropping her voice to a whisper. She glanced around the restaurant, making sure there were no eavesdroppers nearby. The closest person was more than halfway across the dining area. "And it was one time. If you use that against me..." She trailed off, unsure of what she would do if this information became public.

"I wouldn't do that," Tinsley reassured her, reaching her hand across the table to offer a comforting touch. She nodded toward the tablet resting on the table between them. "Anything new?"

"Nothing really," the assistant answered as she checked her emails on the tablet. "Some messages and inquiries that I've already responded to. Nothing that requires your immediate attention. Just notifying people that you're currently out of the office."

"Okay." Tinsley sipped her coffee again before glancing around the room. Her gaze landed on Harris, who sat on the other side of the dining area, partially obscured by a large fern. He appeared engrossed in his work on a tablet device, typing away at top speed and occasionally pausing to read or watch something on the screen before continuing again.

Hope's eyes followed the deputy secretary's gaze toward Lieutenant Harris. She had to crane her neck to catch a glimpse of him.

"What do you think he's up to?" the deputy secretary asked, her voice low and filled with suspicion.

Hope took a sip of her tea before responding, "Perhaps he gained access to the footage."

Tinsley's expression revealed her deep contemplation of Hope's words as she watched Lieutenant Harris intently.

"What do you think he saw?" she probed further.

Hope made a soft sound as she swallowed her tea, gathering her thoughts before answering, "He told the colonel he wasn't sure. But we all saw something in the light. What did he see that we didn't?"

As they observed Harris from afar, the kitchen crew bustled around them, loading trays of steaming food into glass cases. The aroma of roast meat drifted toward them, tempting Hope to grab a plate and indulge.

"Don't ever be alone with him while we're here." Tinsley's tone was serious and forbidding.

Confusion crossed Hope's face as she replied, "Sorry?"

"I don't trust him," declared Tinsley. "Something about him isn't right."

Hope considered this for a moment before offering an alternative perspective. "Maybe he's just a focused military type person? I'm sure you've seen plenty of those before."

Tinsley shook her head vehemently. "No, it's more than that. There's something off about him. Just promise me you won't be alone with him."

The thought of being alone with Lieutenant Harris sent shivers down Hope's spine.

"Do you think he might hurt me?" she asked, leaning forward to get a better look at him.

"I don't know." Tinsley's response was cautious. "Maybe you're right and he's just focused on his job. But I still don't want you to take any chances."

Hope nodded, sitting back in her chair, knowing deep she would do whatever it took to get close to Lieutenant Harris, including telling a lie to the deputy secretary. "I promise."

Hope diverted her attention from her idle chat when she caught a glimpse of movement out of the corner of her eye. She turned to see Colonel Powers making his way across the room, his heavy boots thudding against the floorboards. He leaned against the table where Lieutenant Harris sat, hunched over a tablet device, intently studying its contents. The two officers engaged in a discussion, with Powers peering over Harris' shoulder and gesturing toward the screen. As they conversed, Powers caught sight of Hope and Tinsley and met their gaze, flashing them a grin before turning his full attention back to Harris.

"He's an interesting one," Hope remarked, echoing Tinsley's earlier words. "Wouldn't you say?"

"Don't even start," Tinsley warned.

"Why not?" Hope smiled mischievously. "He is rather handsome."

"He's also married," Tinsley told her.

"What?" Hope turned to look at the colonel, focusing on his left hand, where she noticed a glint of gold. "I hadn't noticed."

"That's because you're young and tend to notice other things first." Tinsley chuckled, taking a sip of her coffee. "These are the things us single thirty-eight-year-old women tend to pay attention to before making fools of ourselves."

Powers approached their table now, stopping beside them and addressing them politely. "All settled in?"

"As much as we can be," Tinsley replied. "And yourself?"

"I live out of my bags," the colonel confessed with a slight chuckle. "I never fully unpack until I get home."

"Would you care to join us, Colonel?" Hope offered kindly, gesturing to an empty chair by her side.

"Oh, thank you, no," he declined graciously, gesturing over his shoulder toward Harris. "My team and I will be sitting over there. We soldiers don't always have the same table etiquette as diplomats."

"Has Lieutenant Harris found anything of interest?" Tinsley inquired, nodding toward the soldier.

Powers quickly followed her gaze and turned back to them with a thoughtful expression. "I'm not entirely sure. He claims to see something emerging from the orb just as that bolt of light struck Doctor... Doctor Callie..." He struggled for a moment before Hope supplied the name.

"Doctor Caldwell," Hope interjected.

"Yes, that's it," Powers confirmed, pointing to the young assistant. "Harris believes it's an arm, but to me it just looks like a mess of lightning bolts. Whatever it is, I have no doubt Harris will be able to decipher it. He's quite remarkable."

"I'm sure he is," Tinsley observed shrewdly, her gaze narrowing slightly at the mention of Harris.

Powers picked up on her tone and furrowed his brow in slight confusion.

"I should head back over," Colonel Powers said with a warm smile. "The rest of my team will be making their way out here soon. Enjoy your meal, ladies."

Hope returned the smile and Tinsley offered a polite one as Powers turned to cross the floor back to Harris.

Hope's gaze lingered on the deputy secretary for what felt like an eternity.

Tinsley calmly sipped her coffee, keeping a watchful eye on the lieutenant.

"Sally," Hope hissed, using her boss' first name for the very first time, drawing Tinsley's attention. "That was quite out of character for you."

Placing her cup down on the table, Tinsley took a deep breath.

"I apologize," she said, shaking her head slowly. "I don't know why, but I just can't seem to trust that man. There's something about him that doesn't sit right with me."

"You're a diplomat," Hope gently chided.

Tinsley nodded in agreement, reaching her hand across the table to take Hope's.

"You're right," she admitted softly. "I just let my guard down for a moment. Maybe..." She glanced over at Harris who was still focused on studying the screen.

"What?" Hope tilted her head curiously.

"Maybe I should request for him to accompany us while we inspect this facility," Tinsley suggested. "Perhaps I should try to break down this barrier I've put up... Get to know the man instead of being so quick to judge."

A flutter of excitement filled Hope's stomach at the thought of being in proximity to Harris.

"Maybe," she agreed, calmly taking a sip of her tea.

***

The soft glow of the overhead lights reflected off polished silver trays as they were effortlessly carried by the familiar figure of Schwartz. He moved past Hope's table, the loaded tray balanced perfectly in his hands, before placing it gently on the empty table beside hers. As he sat down, Tinsley smiled politely. The smell of roasted veal wafted through the air, accompanied by the savory aroma of blanched broccoli and baked potatoes smothered in rich gravy.

"Good evening, ladies," Schwartz greeted them with a charming smile. Hope felt a little self-conscious as she quickly swallowed. "I hope this is good," he added, picking up his knife and fork from the tray. "I'm famished."

"It's really good," replied Hope, smiling warmly. She couldn't resist cutting another piece of meat and relishing its tenderness coated in the delicious gravy.

Schwartz dug into his meal with gusto, taking a moment to glance around the room. "The soldiers don't like sitting with us civvies, I guess," he remarked, gesturing toward the nearby group of troops.

"Colonel Powers indicated they're messy eaters," Tinsley quipped with a smirk.

Schwartz chuckled and continued to scan the room before finally settling his gaze back on the two women. "What's your take on this place so far, Mister Schwartz?" asked Hope, hoping to spark some conversation.

"Well," he began, gazing up at the ceiling lights that hung from iron rafters like long tubes. "It's Glenn. Mister Schwartz is what my neighbor's kids call me." He paused for a moment before continuing with a thoughtful expression. "But this place is well-constructed. Sturdy. It needs to be considering the seismic activity records."

Hope couldn't hide the hint of concern that crept onto her face. "Should we be worried?" she asked hesitantly.

Schwartz's expression softened as he quickly reassured them. "Nothing to worry about. The seismic activity is barely readable. But earthquakes can happen anywhere, and here they occur more frequently due to subterranean volcanic activity in the region." He paused for a moment before adding, "Which makes me wonder why the architect didn't consider geothermal power instead of wind turbines... or a combination of both."

"So, we're safe?" Hope prodded, seeking further reassurance.

"Absolutely," Schwartz replied confidently. "According to the reports, this facility was designed with those factors in mind. I still need to check the rec room and walk the corridors on this level, but so far, I'm impressed with what I've seen."

Just then, Doctor Palmer joined them at the table with his own tray. "May I?" he asked politely, gesturing toward the empty seat next to Tinsley. "I don't wish to intrude."

"Of course you can join us, Doctor," Tinsley replied graciously, gesturing for him to sit down.

"Thank you," the doctor responded gratefully before placing his tray on the table and taking his seat. "I thought maybe I should sit on my own somewhere else, this being a delegation only table, and that being the security force only table over there. Me, the outsider, and all."

"You're more than welcome, Doctor." Tinsley smiled. "Besides, that UN insignia on your coveralls makes you an unofficial member of our little team."

Palmer nodded, lifting his knife and fork with the intent to dig into his meal. His plate was filled with an array of steamed vegetables and nothing else.

"On a diet?" Schwartz teased lightly.

Doctor Palmer looked up from his plate, confusion evident on his face. Schwartz motioned toward his meal with a slight smirk. "Oh no," he clarified. "Not at all. I'm fifty-six years old and on diuretics, alpha-blockers, and calcium channel blockers. I limit my meat intake and try to exercise as much as I can. No junk food, fizzy drinks, or sugar in my tea." He let out a small sigh before continuing with a touch of humor, "You'd think I'd feel great with all these healthy habits, but the food I need to eat is so bland and unexciting."

Hope stifled a giggle at the doctor's candid confession.

"You may well laugh, young woman," the doctor told her with a wry smile, stabbing his fork into a cluster of green beans. Each one was plump and perfectly cooked. "I would if it weren't happening to me. I guess there is some good news, though. Professor Ford just informed me that I can see the child at six o'clock."

Schwartz checked his watch, the digits slowly moving toward the designated time.

"That's only twenty minutes," he said, glancing up at Tinsley who was delicately swallowing the final portion of her meal. She placed her fork and knife carefully on the plate.

"Tell me, Doctor," she said in her calm, professional voice. "What do you know of this infant? Obviously, a premature birth, if not induced. Do we know anything?"

"Unfortunately, no," Palmer responded with a heavy sigh. "The baby is not even three weeks old yet. It's surprising that he hasn't been transferred to a neonatal medical facility more equipped to handle preterm infants instead of being kept here in this makeshift power station. They are doing their best, but without specialists or proper equipment, it's a miracle that the baby is still alive. And from what I've gathered, the birth was not induced. They had to perform an emergency cesarean, which is a risky and complex procedure requiring expert skill and knowledge. I haven't been allowed to see the baby yet, which is quite concerning considering IEC initially requested me to come here for that reason."

He speared another mouthful of vegetables with his fork before shoveling them into his mouth with gusto.

"I'd like to join you when you go to see him, if you don't mind," Tinsley put in, her face lined with determination. She was not one to back down from a challenge.

"Absolutely," he replied with a nod. "The more, the merrier."

"I'm glad you said that," Tinsley said, turning to look at the soldiers surrounding them. "I'd like to ask Lieutenant Harris and Private Gonzalez to accompany us."

"Bring the whole party," the doctor remarked with a chuckle, preparing to shovel another load of beans into his mouth. "The more the merrier."

CHAPTER SEVEN

Hope felt the presence of Gonzalez and Harris standing behind her as she stared down at the floor of the elevator, clutching the tablet to her chest. The metal walls seemed to be closing in on her, suffocating her with their sterile, cold embrace. Schwartz and Doctor Palmer stood in front of her, facing the door with no regard for her tense posture.

Desperate to calm her racing heart, Hope closed her eyes and took a deep breath in through her nose, exhaling slowly from her mouth. But the whirring sound of the elevator motors only grew louder in her ears, drowning out any sense of peace or control she tried to grasp.

"Are you all right?" Harris asked quietly, his voice low and monotone. It seemed more like an obligatory question than a sincere one. Hope thought she was doing a good job hiding her anxiety from others, but it seemed that the lieutenant had picked up on it.

"I'm fine," she replied, still gazing at the floor.

Stay in there, Hope, taunted the mocking inner voice.

But before she could dwell on those thoughts any longer, Tinsley stepped closer and hooked her arm around Hope's, linking their elbows together.

The journey was mercifully brief. The doors finally slid open, offering relief and what equated to fresh air for Hope. She knew it was just recycled air pumped throughout the entire facility, but it felt like a welcome respite after being trapped in the small interior of the elevator.

As they stepped into a wide corridor, Hope scanned the signage on the opposite wall. Among markers for various research laboratories and technological sections, one sign caught her attention: Medical Laboratory.

"It looks like we go this way," Palmer announced confidently, starting down the long hallway. The walls were stark white and broken only by evenly spaced doorways, floor to ceiling windows, blank walls, and noticeboards, giving off an almost antiseptic feel. It was almost like being in a hospital.

"I hope so," Schwartz chimed in, looking at Hope with a small grin. "Otherwise, I'll have to add that to my list of substandard properties. Incorrect signage is just so drab."

Despite her nerves, Hope chuckled at his dry humor.

They continued down the corridor, greeting several people in lab coats and civilian clothing along the way. Another sign loomed above them, indicating offices and labs located in an intersecting corridor branching off to the left and right. But their destination, the medical laboratory, lay further ahead, and they pressed onward.

It wasn't long until the passageway ended abruptly with a large set of double doors directly in front of them. In bold lettering on the doors, the words MED LAB stood out prominently.

"This must be it," Palmer said, reaching out to push one of the doors open.

"You think?" Gonzalez joked.

"Private," chided Harris in a low voice.

"Sorry, sir," Gonzalez replied sheepishly as they all entered through the doorway.

The hospital room was vast, the walls stretching out to accommodate a long row of beds. Each bed had its head-end pushed against the wall, creating a sense of orderly precision. The air within the room was sharp and sterile, making it difficult to breathe. The stark white sheets on the beds looked almost ghostly, their emptiness only adding to the eerie atmosphere.

To the right side of the room stood two imposing doors, standing tall like watchful sentinels. The first door bore a sign that read "Operating Theaters," while the second door was labeled "Consultation Room." In front of these doors sat a gleaming reception desk, where a young man and woman were busily typing away at their computers. Their attention remained glued to the screens, filled with endless streams of medical information. Behind them stood a towering bookcase, overflowing with thick volumes of patient records, medical journals, and neatly organized ring binders. Filing cabinets for data storage lined one side of the bookcase, completing the picture of order and organization.

The pervasive feeling of sterility seemed to fill every corner of this vast space. Doctor Isaac Palmer stepped into the room and made his way toward the reception desk, greeted by the young man's voice tinged with a hint of French accent.

"Hello," the man said politely. "Are you here to see the doctor?"

"Yes," Palmer replied in a calm tone. "My name is—"

"Doctor Isaac Palmer!" a woman's voice announced from their left. All eyes turned to see a dark-haired woman in a crisp white lab coat approaching. From her appearance, Hope deduced that she must be in her mid-thirties—older than herself, but perhaps around the same age as Deputy Secretary Sally Tinsley. The woman extended her hand toward Palmer with a warm smile.

"I'm Doctor Hazel Wilkins," she introduced herself. "But everyone just calls me Hazel."

"Doctor Wilkins," Palmer acknowledged with a nod, establishing the level of professionalism he preferred. "The pleasure is mine."

"I wasn't expecting such a large delegation," Wilkins remarked, turning to address the other individuals in attendance.

"I apologize," Tinsley stepped forward, adjusting her glasses before offering her hand to the doctor. "I insisted we come along. The news of the infant has raised some concerns. I'm Deputy Secretary Sally Tinsley. This is my assistant, Hope Aguilar, and Glenn Schwartz, our civil engineer."

"Among many other titles," Schwartz added with a small smile as he shook hands with the doctor.

"Lieutenant Harris and this is Private Gonzalez," Tinsley continued, gesturing toward the two soldiers. "Apologies for not knowing your first names."

Gonzalez opened her mouth to introduce herself before Harris cut in coldly.

"Our names don't matter," he stated flatly.

Wilkins smiled politely, glancing at each of their faces before speaking again.

"Well then," she said breathlessly. "Shall we go see the boy?"

"If I may?" Palmer stepped forward eagerly, scanning the room for any signs of the child's location. "I'd like to examine him."

"He's currently in the observation room at the far end of the room," Wilkins replied, pointing to a window on the left side, past rows of neatly lined beds. "But I must warn you all to prepare yourselves. I'm not sure what you've been told, but when I made the initial request for a pediatrician, the child displayed some remarkable similarities to acromegaly. However, upon further examination, I believe my original diagnosis was incorrect. This is something else entirely."

"Gigantism?" Palmer questioned with interest.

"No," Wilkins shook her head firmly. "I don't believe so."

Palmer's eyes flicked toward the window, a deep furrow forming on his brow. "Do you know if there is a history of related symptoms in the family?" he pressed, his voice laced with concern. "Perhaps a growth on the pituitary gland?"

"I don't know," the other doctor responded hesitantly. "But I don't believe that's the issue. In any case, the boy won't let us run any scans on him."

Hope's stomach twisted into knots at this news.

"Won't let you?" Palmer gave her a quizzical glare. "He's an infant."

"You should take a look," Wilkins gestured toward the window. Hope felt an uneasy sense of foreboding.

Together, the group made their way to the observation room, passing by rows of empty hospital beds on their way. The room beyond the window was sterile and brightly lit, everything painted white with matching furniture.

In the center of the room sat a lone hospital bed, occupied by a young child dressed in all white. He couldn't have been more than three or four years old, with sandy hair that fell lazily over his forehead, partially obscuring his striking blue eyes. He sat cross-legged near the edge of the bed, completely engrossed as a young woman sat beside him on a plastic chair, reading aloud from a picture book.

"Is this some kind of joke?" Palmer exclaimed, turning to the other doctor. "Where is the actual infant?"

"And who is this boy?" Tinsley added with confusion.

"This is the infant," Doctor Wilkins replied. "I assure you; this is no joke."

As she spoke, the boy turned his attention toward them and stared at each person in turn with an intense and almost predatory gaze.

Hope felt another knot tighten in her stomach as she struggled to maintain composure.

"He sees us," Schwartz noted, waving to the boy. In response, the boy's sinister grin widened, sending a shiver down Hope's spine.

"Yes," Doctor Wilkins nodded gravely. "And he shouldn't be able to."

The engineer furrowed his brow in confusion.

"What do you mean?"

"That's a two-way mirror, Mister Schwartz," she answered.

The boy's leering gaze slowly traveled along the line of people, and when his attention landed on Hope, she felt her heart jolt. It was as if he could see right through her, recognizing her as an outsider and an intruder. With each passing second, the air in the room seemed to grow thicker and heavier, making Hope wish she had stayed in the elevator. Just when she thought she couldn't take it anymore, the boy's piercing gaze shifted toward Gonzalez standing beside her. He never broke eye contact until he had completed his inspection.

"Mother," he hissed with venom. "Mother will come."

A chill ran down Hope's spine at his words. The young woman in the plastic chair lowered her book and watched the boy closely, patiently. Her appearance gave the impression of someone who had heard the boy's words many times before.

"Mother will devour," he continued, his voice full of malice. "Mother is hungry."

Suddenly, the boy's eyes locked onto Harris at the end of the line of observers, wide and unblinking. His gaze was filled with terror, as if he were trapped in an invisible prison. The boy began to tremble uncontrollably, his body shaking with fear. A silent scream hung open on his lips before finally erupting into a muffled shriek that sounded as if it came from deep within him. As his attendant leaned closer to offer comfort, he whipped around and glared at her with feral rage before turning back to face Harris.

Without warning, the boy launched himself off the bed with surprising speed, darting beneath it as if his life depended on it. He disappeared from view like a scared animal fleeing into hiding.

"Soulless one," the boy hissed. "Soulless one."

Hope struggled to contain the waves of fear crashing within her. She glanced sideways at each person gathered around her, seeing in their eyes a reflection of her own emotion.

Confusion and terror filled every face except Harris', who stood motionless, transfixed by the shape huddled beneath the bed.

"What the fuck was that?" Gonzalez blurted out.

"Private," Harris scolded, his voice calm but firm. "Language."

"Forget that, Lieutenant," Gonzalez said excitedly. "Did you see that? What was that thing?"

She looked to Doctor Wilkins for an answer. "What was that?"

Wilkins shook her head in bewilderment.

"I've never seen this kind of behavior from him before," she replied.

Hope turned back to Harris, whose attention remained fixed on the boy. But when she looked at the kneeling woman by the bed, her voice gently calling, desperately trying to coax the boy out of his dark refuge, he seemed to shrink further into the shadows. His squinted eyes held a wild, feral look as if he were a trapped beast.

"Soulless," the boy whispered, his breaths coming in short pants. "Soulless." He repeated the word over and over, his gaze never leaving the hulking figure of Harris.

As Hope watched the boy sink deeper into the shadows, Gonzalez's words echoed in her mind, *What the fuck was that?*

***

The group huddled together; their heads bent close over a pristine white table near the humming coffee dispenser. Their voices were low and hushed, carrying an air of secrecy. Doctor Palmer remained in the medical lab, while Lieutenant Harris sat at a separate table nearby, his focus solely on the tablet device in front of him as he examined footage from the Energy Generation Chamber.

"How on earth is that possible?" Disbelief filled Schwartz's voice as he stared aimlessly at the steam swirling around his coffee cup. "That's not a baby, it's a boy."

"Wha—" Gonzalez started before quickly retracting her question and taking a different approach. "How old is he supposed to be?"

"Not even three weeks old." Hope's reply was accompanied by a heavy sigh as she too stared down at her mug, her hands resting flat on the table.

Gonzalez shook her head in disbelief.

"How many people here know about this kid?" the soldier asked.

"You're suggesting that some of the staff may not know about him?" Tinsley questioned.

"Do you think the kitchen staff know about him?" Gonzalez pushed further. "If I knew about him, I would want to be on the next transport out. The look on his face when he saw us..."

"I think the maintenance crew knows about him," Schwartz offered. "There's a good chance if they know, everyone here knows."

"He saw us," Hope interjected softly.

"I nearly pissed myself," Gonzalez admitted with a shudder. "Jodidamente espeluznante." She glanced at Hope. "*Fucking creepy.*"

Hope nodded in agreement.

"He saw us," she repeated, her voice barely above a whisper.

"Through the two-way mirror," Schwartz added, still trying to make sense of it all. "But how?"

"Vio mi alma," Gonzalez muttered under her breath, her eyes wide with terror.

Hope met her gaze and understood how she felt.

Tinsley and Schwartz exchanged confused glances, not understanding the exchange between the two women.

"Vio—" Tinsley began before Harris cut in with a strained voice, his finger frantically rewinding the footage on his tablet.

"He saw my soul," he translated for them, his eyes fixed on the screen.

"He saw us," Hope repeated, her own eyes wide with fear as the memory of the boy's intense gaze flooded her mind once again.

Tinsley turned to Harris with a furrowed brow. "He saw us. What did he see when he looked at you?"

The sheer terror that had washed over the boy the moment his eyes locked onto Lieutenant Harris remained etched into Hope's memory. He had scrutinized each of them with a hunger that felt almost primal, like a predator assessing its prey. But when his gaze landed on Harris, his demeanor shifted from hunter to hunted.

Harris slowly turned to face the deputy secretary, his dark eyes meeting hers in an intense stare that sent shivers down her spine.

"Nothing," he replied quietly but firmly before returning his focus to the tablet once again. "He saw nothing at all."

***

Doctor Palmer strode across the well-lit dining area, his attention locked on the coffee dispenser machine. With practiced precision, he placed a mug under the outlet and pressed the Espresso button, eager for his much-needed caffeine fix. The rich aroma of freshly brewed coffee filled the air as the black liquid poured into the vessel, filling less than a quarter of the cup. Not satisfied with this meager amount, Palmer pressed the button again and again, repeating the process three times, filling his cup to the brim before turning to face his colleagues.

The four individuals seated at the table watched with anticipation as Palmer approached, their eyes trained on him like hawks. He shrugged as he pulled up a chair next to Tinsley.

"So?" Schwartz asked, breaking the silence.

"Seems like a normal little boy of maybe three years old," Doctor Palmer remarked, taking a sip of his extra strong coffee, and relishing in its bitter taste. "Except, he's only three weeks old."

"How is that even possible?" Gonzalez blurted out, unable to contain her confusion. "Why does he—"

Palmer shook his head before taking another sip of his potent brew.

"There's nothing that I can see that indicates any abnormalities except for the rate of growth," he explained calmly. "But my examination was limited to basic instruments: a stethoscope, medical torch, otoscope, blood pressure monitor, a set of scales, and a tongue depressor."

"Otoscope?" Gonzalez questioned, furrowing her brows in confusion.

"Those funny torches doctors use to look in your ears," Schwartz chimed in helpfully.

"Yes," Palmer nodded in agreement. "And I found nothing peculiar during my examination."

Hope noticed Harris tearing his gaze away from the computer screen and focusing his full attention on Palmer.

"You saw the way he looked at us," Gonzalez interjected anxiously. "That was pretty fucking peculiar."

Harris seemed ready to reprimand her, but after a moment of contemplation, he relaxed his posture.

"I agree," Palmer confirmed. "He kept staring at me like that the whole time I was examining him. As if I was a meal. He was compliant and cooperative, but I couldn't shake off the feeling that he could lash out at any moment and tear me apart. Let me tell you, I'm very relieved to be out of there."

"Did he say anything?" Tinsley inquired curiously.

"Oh yes," Palmer replied with certainty. "Very articulate. His vocabulary is well beyond that of a three-year-old child."

"And definitely beyond that of a three-week-old infant, then," Hope added wryly.

Palmer nodded, lost in his own thoughts as he reflected on his encounter with the mysterious young boy.

"Physically," the doctor began, his voice firm and analytical, "he appears to be a normal three-year-old, but the way he speaks about the staff is unlike any child I've encountered before. His vocabulary and manner of speaking are more in line with that of a professional. It's as if he's absorbing information at an alarming rate." The doctor paused, taking a sip of water before continuing.

"He spoke highly of the level of care he's received here, specifically mentioning Doctor Wilkins and her team of nurses. And it wasn't just flattery; he discussed the capabilities and functions of various medical equipment in great detail. Even devices like the multi-scanner, which performs MRI, CT, and PET scans. He may not want to go near them physically, but his understanding of their technical features is impressive."

The doctor looked around the room cautiously, ensuring no one was within earshot before continuing. "I even asked him about some other items in the med lab—things that most medically trained individuals wouldn't understand—and his explanations were accurate and beyond my own comprehension. He has knowledge beyond his years, delving into concepts of engineering and software programming."

"And then there's the Energy Generation Chamber," Harris interjected, turning toward the doctor with intense interest.

"Yes," Palmer said gravely, his voice heavy with concern. "He claims to know how it functions, but what frightened me the most was when I mentioned his mother."

"Doctor Caldwell?" Schwartz chimed in, a crease forming between his brows.

"Yes," Palmer replied, shaking his head slightly. "He made it clear that she is not his mother." He glanced toward the bustling kitchen area where staff were cleaning, lowering his voice to avoid being overheard. "He seemed quite detached from her, only able to recall basic facts like her job as a doctor of quantum physics from Ontario. But then he began talking about his real mother. And that's what scared me. He told me that his true mother would come for him. He said she's searching for him now and won't stop until they are reunited. All that needs to happen is for the door to open or the seed to germinate."

"The door?" asked Schwartz, leaning forward in interest.

"The singularity," Palmer clarified. "According to the boy, the chamber creates a doorway to other realms."

Tinsley pondered aloud. "Like an entrance to the afterlife?"

"I don't believe so," the doctor mused. "I think he means another dimension, perhaps. You see, at first, I thought he was talking about Doctor Caldwell going to Heaven, or something of the likes. And when I mentioned her name, he told me that his real mother is ancient and nameless. She will come for him, he said. And when she does, she will devour him and this world."

"And the seed he mentioned?" Schwartz prodded.

Palmer shook his head in confusion. "I'm not sure. When I asked, he just grinned maniacally. The look he gave was so uncomfortable, I had to get out of there."

A heavy silence fell over the group as they processed the unsettling information.

"I think it's best if I show you this," Harris announced, rising from his seat, and bringing a tablet to the edge of the table where the others sat. He lifted it up so that everyone could see and pressed a button on the attached keyboard.

The footage showed Caldwell standing before the illuminated sphere in the center of the Energy Generation Chamber. For a moment, electricity crackled wildly around the orb before suddenly changing direction and focusing on one spot near Caldwell's face.

Hope felt her heart race as she watched a powerful bolt of light and intricate webs of electricity reach out toward the lab technician. She had seen this before and couldn't bring herself to watch it again.

"What is this, Lieutenant?" Tinsley asked, his voice tense with worry.

"Possibly a transference," Harris replied coolly.

He pressed another button, pausing the footage at a crucial moment.

"Look," he said, pointing to a specific area on the screen. "Do you see it?"

Squinting, Schwartz shook his head. Tinsley leaned forward, mirroring the engineer's confusion.

"It's just light," Gonzalez commented with a shrug.

Harris pressed the edge of the screen, advancing the footage frame by frame. They all watched closely as the image slowly progressed.

"Watch for when the beam of light comes into contact with Doctor Caldwell," Harris instructed, his eyes intent on the screen as he tapped the screen again and again. The light touched Caldwell's stomach, causing tangled webs of electricity to wrap around her body.

And then, within the bright light, something dark and elongated began to emerge.

Hope gasped in shock.

A long tentacle, resembling that of a cephalopod, reached out from the orb and touched Caldwell's abdomen.

Harris suggested, "Maybe the boy is the seed."

Chapter Eight

Harris carefully closed the tablet's case, his fingers moving with precision and deftness. He tucked the keyboard and trackpad neatly away before scooping it under his arm. With purposeful strides, he headed toward the corridor that led to the bedrooms.

"Where are you going, Lieutenant?" Gonzalez asked, rising from her seat to follow the officer.

"To see the colonel," Harris replied calmly.

Tinsley furrowed her brow, curious about his sudden departure. "Why now, Lieutenant?" she called after him.

He stopped in his tracks, turning to face Tinsley with a calm expression.

"I apologize, Deputy Secretary," he replied. "But I believe it is necessary for our security team to investigate the Energy Generation Chamber for any substantial evidence of what occurred. The footage is compelling, but physical samples would undoubtedly strengthen our findings."

Hope raised an eyebrow as she listened to Harris speak. He was like a well-oiled machine, immediately ready to take action while the rest of them sat dumbfounded by what they had just witnessed.

"You can stay if you wish, Private," Harris offered to Gonzalez. "I understand if you want to process what you saw with the others here."

Gonzalez hesitated, torn between following her superior's orders or staying behind with her colleagues.

"What about you, Lieutenant?" Tinsley asked. "Don't you want to discuss what you just saw?"

"No, Deputy Secretary," Harris replied firmly. "I think it's best if I focus on finding answers. There's a possibility that this life form—or whatever it was—may have left something residual in that room. It could potentially be contagious, and we need to know more." Harris paused, waiting for Tinsley's response. "If there's nothing else, Deputy Secretary, I'll take my leave."

"Of course." Tinsley nodded in agreement.

"Private?" Harris turned to Gonzalez.

"I—I think I'll stay for a little while, if you don't mind, sir," she replied, sinking back into her seat.

"Not at all." He turned and disappeared down the corridor.

Hope studied the young soldier, taking note of her tense posture and the way she held her cup but didn't take a sip. Her eyes were filled with fear and uncertainty.

"Are you okay?" Hope asked gently.

"No," Gonzalez answered honestly, her voice trembling. "Are you...after seeing that fucking thing?"

Hope swallowed hard and shook her head.

"Now he's going to see the colonel," the private continued, despair creeping into her tone. "And I'll have to go down there, where that thing was. Mierda de mierda."

"Stay here with us," Schwartz suggested, trying to offer support. He was met with a scathing look from Gonzalez. *Really?*

He turned to Tinsley for help. "I mean, we could request a security detail given the circumstances. Right? Why not ask Colonel Powers to assign Private Gonzalez to our team for the remainder of our time here?"

"It doesn't quite work like that," Tinsley explained patiently. "I've already made a request to the colonel for Lieutenant Harris and Private Gonzalez to be our personal escorts during this inspection. But the colonel reminded me that the privilege of an assigned security escort is limited to delegations sent into war zones or special situations predetermined by the UN."

"Down with the establishment," Palmer interjected, raising his fist in rebellion.

Despite the seriousness of the situation, Hope had to suppress a smile at his antics.

Gonzalez shook her head, her expression resigned.

"It's all right," she told the engineer. "My job is to follow orders. If the colonel tells me to go, I'll go."

"That's right," the assistant put in, attempting to sound optimistic. "The lieutenant is merely proposing an investigation. It doesn't necessarily mean the colonel will agree." Her words offered a glimmer of hope amidst their dire predicaments.

***

The six soldiers stepped off the elevator into the Energy Generation Chamber, accompanied by Ken Wade and another maintenance crew member, both wearing backpacks over their hazmat suits. Wade moved to a panel to the right of the elevator doors and began flicking switches, illuminating the room with bright lights that reflected off the metallic surfaces.

"Welcome to the Shrine," Wade announced proudly, gesturing toward the expansive chamber before them.

Gonzalez gasped as she tilted her head back to take in the full scope of the cavernous space. It was even more impressive than she had imagined from the footage. The room, roughly the size of a large cinema, expanded below the grated floor and maintained an ellipsoid shape throughout. The walls were coated in a dark, synthetic polyisoprene material, with multiple long beams protruding toward the center of the room. And there, where the beams almost converged, sat the platform where the orb in the footage had appeared.

Wade made his way to a workstation several meters from the platform, flanked by a maze of wires and equipment resembling something out of a sci-fi movie. "I haven't been down here since..." he started, trailing off as he picked up a half-full mug from the desk and inspected it briefly before setting it down. "Nobody bothered to clean this up. I should probably dispose of it."

"No," Harris interjected sternly. "We may need it for analysis. Don't touch anything."

Powers shook his head in disbelief as he pivoted slowly in place, taking in every detail of his surroundings. He pointed to a man-sized panel that blended seamlessly into the wall's surface. "What's that?" he asked.

"That's the entrance to the hadron collider access tunnel and the terminal room for monitoring power output," he explained. He motioned toward Billy, the other maintenance worker who stood nearby. "We were both in there, monitoring the generator's power levels when...well, you know what happened."

Powers nodded grimly, moving closer to Wade's side to inspect the contents of the desk.

"Generator?" Corporal Garrett asked, breaking the silence. "I thought this thing here was supposed to generate electricity."

"To get the Energy Generation Chamber up and running, we need to use power from the collider," Billy explained patiently. "Once the singularity forms, it will produce its own power independently."

"In theory," Wade interjected, glancing at Billy before locking his gaze with Corporal Garrett. "It's only ever happened once. And you saw what happened with that. I hope this thing never gets turned on again."

"Wouldn't that be nice," Professor Ford's voice crackled through their earpieces. "Do you copy?"

"Loud and clear, Professor," Wade responded.

"We can see you on the monitor. Do you see anything unusual?"

"Not yet," Wade replied, gesturing toward a device on the workstation. "I was just about to bring out the Geiger counter."

The soldiers scattered throughout the room, scanning every inch of the floor with their eyes and instruments. Private Teresa Jackson crouched by the elevator doors, running her gloved fingers over the grated surface. It felt strange, not quite like any metallic surface she had encountered before.

"What's the floor made of?" she asked, her voice echoing off the walls.

"Stainless steel coated with synthetic polyisoprene... the same material covering the walls," Billy explained as he strode toward the platform in the center of the room. The dark, metal floor gleamed under his feet, refracting the bright fluorescent lights above.

Wade clicked on his Geiger counter, a compact device that emitted a soft hiss and occasional crackle. He aimed it at the floor, scanning for any abnormal radiation levels.

"I'll check that. I want you to run a diagnostic on this console and send the data up to the tech analysis team," Wade instructed.

"All right," replied Billy, retrieving a tablet from his backpack.

As Wade made his way toward the platform, Gonzalez nervously watched him through her visor. Corporal Garrett jogged to catch up with them and joined in their inspection.

"I'll get you to check the skirting. Look for anything out of place—burn marks, cracks, things like that. I saw a lot of electric strikes on the edges. Could be some damage that needs our attention," said Wade, assigning tasks to the team.

Meanwhile, Billy switched on the terminal and plugged a thin cable into his tablet. He waited patiently for the computer to boot up, while Colonel Powers watched over his shoulder.

A log-in screen appeared, and Billy entered his details before moving his finger across a touchpad and tapping a few more keys. A small window opened on the screen, allowing him to enter a basic code.

RUN DIAGNOSTIC.

As lines of letters and numbers scrolled through the window in a language only understood by computer experts, Billy connected the other end of the cable to the computer terminal.

"What's that do?" Powers asked curiously.

"With luck it's recording the diagnostics test," Billy replied, placing his tablet on the desk next to the computer. "Then, if all goes according to plan, it will transfer the data to the tech team upstairs."

While they waited for the test to finish, Harris was down on his hands and knees, shining a penlight through a grate on the floor.

"Lose something, Lieutenant?" Powers asked with a hint of amusement.

"No, sir," Harris replied. "I think these are burn marks."

Powers crouched down beside him, and Gonzalez joined them to examine the marks more closely.

"Isn't this where she stood when it happened?" the private asked.

"Yes, I believe so." Harris glanced at the terminal and then to Wade and Garrett who were still working at the platform, measuring the room with his eyes, aligning objects viewed in the footage with his position. "Yes, it is." The gravity of their investigation hung heavily in the air as they observed the possible evidence of the catastrophic event.

Colonel Powers pointed to the floor, his finger coming to rest on tiny marks etched into the material coating. Surrounding these minuscule burns were patches where the metallic glint of exposed metal could be seen peeking through. These marks were so small, they could have easily been overlooked.

"What do you see?" Ford asked from his spot nearby. "We can't see anything from here."

"We can see bare metal," the colonel relayed to him.

In Professor Schwartz's cluttered office, the three UNIDO delegates and Doctor Palmer crowded around a large monitor fixed on the wall. The screen displayed footage of the chamber in question and all eyes were glued to it. Schwartz turned to Ford, who sat at his desk with his own computer open, watching intently.

"What does that mean?" Schwartz asked, gesturing toward the screen. "I'm guessing the polyisoprene coating prevents electricity from arcing. But what does it mean if metal is exposed?"

"I'm not entirely sure," Ford replied, tapping his chin thoughtfully. "The chamber was specifically designed to support the immense power needed to generate a singularity. All energy is directed toward the center of the room, just above the platform where the singularity is meant to form. The bolts of electricity you saw were not part of its intended function. The whole purpose of this chamber was to create a point in space and time of infinite density, harnessing an infinite amount of power infinitely—essentially creating the purest form of renewable energy; enough to sustain and power the entire world's population."

"There appears to be more over here," Wade announced from his position near the platform.

"Looks like some scrapes and minor damage," Garrett added as he joined Wade.

"Damage?" Ford questioned, furrowing his brow.

"Dents on the skirting," Garrett clarified, running his hand over one particularly deep dent in the solid steel platform. "Almost like someone kicked it in multiple places all the way around."

"According to the plans, the skirting is solid steel beneath that coating," Schwartz interjected, his voice laced with disbelief. "There's no way anyone could make a dent by kicking it."

"You did see that fucking thing on the footage, right?" Gonzalez chimed in, breaking the tense silence.

Schwartz took a deep breath, feeling slightly embarrassed. Of course, no one had kicked it.

As Wade and Garrett ran their hands over the surface of the platform, they came across a section where the Geiger counter suddenly crackled and buzzed loudly, startling them both.

"What's going on?" Ford asked, trying to make sense of the unexpected noise.

"Did you press something?" Garrett questioned his colleague.

Wade shook his head. "I didn't touch anything."

Suddenly, both men quickly pulled their hands away from the platform as if they had been shocked or bitten.

"What the fuck was that?" Garrett exclaimed, looking at his fingertips in confusion.

The Geiger counter fell silent once again.

"Wade?" called out Professor Ford, concern evident in his voice.

"Shit," Wade cursed, examining his gloved hand where tiny, charred circles were now visible on his middle finger and forefinger. He showed them to Garrett. "Look at this."

Garrett instinctively checked his own glove, running his fingers over the soft material and feeling for any abnormalities. To his surprise, he also found tiny black circles on his thumb and three of his fingers.

"Wade, talk to me," Ford pressed, a look of concern etched across his face.

"Sorry," the chief of maintenance answered, rubbing his hand against his pants. "I just got zapped."

"Zapped?" Powers asked, suddenly attentive and moving toward them with a sense of urgency.

"Probably just built-up static energy," the maintenance man reassured them, although his voice betrayed a hint of uncertainty. He glanced at Garrett for confirmation. "We're fine. Right?"

"Yeah," the corporal nodded, trying to brush off the strange occurrence. "It's nothing. Just a shock. That's all."

"Just a shock?" Powers repeated incredulously. The rest of the security detail gathered around them, their faces mirroring concern and confusion.

"Yeah, it was nothing," Garrett repeated, hoping they would drop the subject.

"Harris?" Powers turned to the lieutenant. "Are you satisfied, or do you believe we need to investigate this further? I'd like to get out of here."

"I haven't found anything conclusive," Harris answered with a furrowed brow. "But I don't think we will find anything else. The markings here and on the platform are the only physical indication of anything occurring in this room."

"Billy." Powers glanced at one of the young maintenance crew members. "Can we lift anything from that computer that might help us here?"

"The diagnostic is almost complete," Billy replied confidently. "We've already saved the readings from the terminals on this level into the facility's database. We can access that from upstairs."

"Professor?" Powers turned to the camera mounted on the wall. "I suggest we shut this area down."

"We can't shut it down permanently," Ford said. "The company has already indicated that we're behind schedule and there's an urgent need to repair the damaged sections for future tests."

"Future tests?" Tinsley interjected; her voice laced with disbelief. "You're considering future tests after what happened to Doctor Caldwell?"

"The company expects us to continue," Ford responded. "I'd like to shut the entire facility down, but they want more data."

"Lieutenant," the colonel said in a commanding tone, his voice echoing off the steel walls of the underground facility. "Tell the professor and our friends upstairs what you told me."

Harris eagerly nodded, turning to face the camera mounted on the wall. His expression was serious, his eyes focused and determined. "There's every chance that the entity captured in the footage left something residual behind," he stated with conviction.

"Residual?" Professor Ford asked with curiosity.

"Something superfluous," Harris clarified. "Something that is still a part of itself but separated. I believe it did so with the boy."

"Which is why he is exhibiting such unusual abilities?" Tinsley chimed in.

"I'm not entirely sure," Harris admitted. "But I think we can all agree that his development doesn't fit within the natural order of our physical world." He paused, glancing around at his colleagues before continuing. "I thought there might be a slim chance that the entity left more physical evidence behind. Something tangible apart from secondary confirmations, like burn marks."

"And did you find anything of the sort?" Ford, another member of the team, asked with a note of disappointment in his voice.

"No," Harris replied solemnly. "But I can't rule out the possibility that something may have fallen through the grate and ended up beneath us."

"Or if the entity is capable of leaving any physical traces of itself for us to find," Hope interjected.

"Precisely," Harris agreed.

As they pondered their next steps, Ford laced his fingers together and pressed them against his lips, deep in thought.

"Billy?" he called out after a moment. "Are you finished down there?"

"All done," came the reply from Billy. "Just shutting down the terminal now."

The professor nodded slowly in acknowledgment before speaking up. "All right then, come back upstairs. We'll program the elevators' access to all levels except Level C."

"On our way," Wade replied, moving toward the panel to access the elevator controls. With a press of a button, the doors slid open with a hiss.

As the team on the monitor turned away from the camera and began making their way toward the elevator, Hope watched as two maintenance crew members and the six military personnel stepped into the lift. She noticed Garrett, one of the soldiers, flexing his hand absently as the doors closed behind them with a final thud.

***

The group huddled in the dining area, gathering near the humming dispenser machines. Hope cradled another cup of coffee, regretting her choice of beverage as she felt the caffeine coursing through her veins, keeping her awake and alert. She checked her watch again; 23:37. The room was illuminated by a soft glow from the artificial lights above, casting shadows on the faces of those gathered.

"I can't shut down the chamber," Ford said defensively, his words directed at Tinsley. They were engaged in a heated discussion over whether to close down the lowest level of the facility until a full investigation could be completed. "The company wants more data, and they want it by the end of next week. It's out of my control."

"Can't you add something to your report to delay another test?" Tinsley asked, turning to Schwartz for support.

"Unfortunately not," he replied, bringing obvious disappointment to the deputy secretary's face. "There is nothing in my expertise that suggests issues with the construction of this site. If I add anything else to my report, I'll face severe consequences. Our concerns lie outside of my knowledge and abilities. My hands are tied."

Tinsley nodded in understanding.

Hope scanned each of their faces, finally resting on Corporal Garrett who winced and rubbed his fingertips together nervously. Her gaze then shifted to Wade, who fidgeted with something in his pocket.

"I understand," Tinsley said resignedly to the professor.

"The best we can do," Billy interjected, "is shut down the area until we can replace the coating on the floor and platform. That could take us what..."

"Two weeks," Wade suggested. "Maybe even longer if our supply of synthetic polyisoprene coating is low."

"A good effort," the professor chimed in, "but they have access to our stock records. Our mainframe is linked to their system. They know everything. They may give us two weeks, but they'll be checking in daily for progress reports. We can only pull the wool over their eyes for so long."

"What about you guys?" Billy asked, turning to Tinsley and Hope. "Can't the UN shut it down?"

Tinsley shook her head.

"We can submit a recommendation for closure to the UN on behalf of UNIDO," she explained. "But unfortunately, progress moves slowly in the political arena. It could take weeks..."

"Or even months," Hope said.

"Months," repeated the deputy secretary, "before any action is taken. And even then, all they may do is pass our request onto the next level of processing."

Private Collier shook his head in disbelief. "I can't believe this company wants you to run another test. Didn't they see the video?"

"They did," Ford confirmed. "And they read the reports submitted by Ken and me." He gestured toward Wade.

"So, what's their reasoning?" Collier pressed further. "Don't they care that someone died down there?"

Ford let out a heavy sigh and shrugged helplessly.

"In their defense, Private," Colonel Powers said, his voice carrying a weight of authority. "They have given the people here three weeks to grieve and process the incident."

"Why can't they wait a little longer, then?" Hope asked.

"From a corporation's perspective," Powers continued, his tone matter of fact, "this facility must be costing them a fortune, and all it's doing right now is a whole bunch of nothing. I'd say the needed data the professor mentioned was needed weeks ago in preparation for the deputy secretary's visit." He looked at Ford for support.

"Absolutely," the professor chimed in, his lips trembling slightly as he lifted his mug to hide his emotions. "The UN delegation was placed on the calendar months ago. So, yes, we required the data for that, and we just don't have it. What happened to Doctor Caldwell blindsided us."

Hope felt a sudden wave of pity for the man as she watched him check his watch. Lieutenant Harris also seemed to take notice of the professor, studying him intently.

"So, the company isn't being evil," Powers clarified to the soldier. "They've got a business to run."

Collier nodded slowly, clearly understanding but not entirely convinced.

Garrett flexed his hand unconsciously, drawing Hope's attention to it.

"How's your hand, Corporal?" she asked.

He glanced over at her before looking down at his fingers with a slight frown.

"It feels tingly," he admitted, worry creeping into his voice. He turned to face the colonel. "I think I should get it looked at, sir."

"Yeah," Wade agreed, pulling his hand out of his pocket to examine it closely. "Me too. That static build-up might have had more of a kick in it than I thought."

"Go to the Med Lab," Ford instructed, also noticing Wade's pink-tinted fingers. "You might need a salve or something."

Wade nodded, starting to make his way out of the room.

"Go with him," Powers told the corporal.

"Sir," Garrett replied, turning to follow the chief of maintenance.

As the two men left for the elevator, Ford checked his watch again and sighed.

"It's late, ladies and gentlemen," he said, looking tired but determined. "I've got maybe four hours to sleep before I'm required to attend a tele-meeting with some members of the board. I hope you don't mind, but I need to hit the sack."

"As do we," Colonel Powers said, standing up from his seat to signal for the other soldiers to do the same.

"Good night, Colonel," Harris said politely, still seated at the table.

"Not sleeping, Lieutenant?" Powers asked, raising an eyebrow inquisitively.

"I have a question I wish to ask Professor Ford before I retire, if you don't mind," Harris explained calmly.

"Knock yourself out." Powers chuckled, starting away with the rest of the group. "But don't keep the man up all night. You just heard what he said about needing sleep."

"I did." Harris nodded. "It won't take long."

Schwartz and Doctor Palmer followed the others as they made their way down the passageway toward their respective quarters for some much-needed rest.

"Night," Schwartz said, rising to his feet to follow the colonel away from the table. The doctor offered a quick wave before turning to the four remaining individuals.

Harris glanced at Tinsley and Hope, then spoke up in a formal tone. "Do you wish for us to leave, Lieutenant?"

His gaze then shifted to Ford, who sat stoically at the table. "What I need to ask the professor is of a personal nature."

"I don't mind," Ford replied, his voice calm.

Harris nodded and lowered his gaze to the table, gathering his thoughts before continuing. "The child—is he yours?"

Ford's expression remained unchanged as he peered at the soldier for what seemed like an eternity before finally asking, "Why do you ask?"

"I noticed your mannerisms whenever you speak about Doctor Caldwell," Harris explained. "I didn't want to presume, but I got the impression that your relationship with her was more than just professional."

The professor let out a long sigh before turning his gaze to the two women sitting across from him. "I am a married man," he stated matter-of-factly. "Or rather, separated. My wife and I haven't been living together for about six months now, but our separation began long before that. Amy and I had an instant connection when we first met."

He paused for a moment before answering Harris' question. "So yes, the boy is my biological son. The blood test results confirm it, but I asked Doctor Wilkins and the Med Lab staff to keep it discreet. The company knows, or at least those who need to know, know. I didn't think it was that obvious."

Hope felt a pang of sympathy for the man as she watched him struggle with his emotions. His words brought a knot to her stomach.

"As I said, Professor," Harris continued, "your mannerisms gave it away. But I don't think anyone else noticed."

"No," Tinsley agreed.

"Except Miss Aguilar," Harris finished, gesturing toward the young assistant sitting next to him. "I believe she may have noticed as well."

Ford turned to face her as she nodded in acknowledgment. Tears welled up in her eyes as she spoke. "I'm so sorry," she said softly.

The professor wiped his eyes, "Thank you."

With that, Harris stood up and made his way toward the corridor. "Goodnight," he said impassively before walking away.

Tinsley watched him go, looking confused. "Wait," she called out. Harris stopped and turned back to her. "Why did you need to know about that? Why did you ask?"

"I didn't need to know," the lieutenant responded with a small smile. "But I think the professor needed someone to talk to about it. And now he knows he has people he can talk to." He gestured toward both Tinsley and Hope before turning away once more. "Goodnight."

***

Corporal Eduardo Garrett anxiously waited in the sterile medical lab, sitting on a hard metal chair next to the front desk. His hand was throbbing with pain, and he felt a sharp, shooting sensation traveling up his arm and into his armpit. Wade had just been seen by the night doctor and emerged from the lab with bandages wrapped tightly around his fingers.

A young woman, her hair pulled back in a tight bun and glasses perched on her nose, glanced up from her computer screen and flashed a flirtatious smile at Garrett. He attempted to return it, but instead winced as another jolt of pain shot through his hand.

The receptionist stood up from her desk. "Are you all right?"

Garrett shook his head. "No, this is getting worse." He held up his injured hand for her to see.

The receptionist immediately called for the doctor, who appeared from a doorway at the other end of the room. He wore crisp trousers and a button-up shirt, giving off an air of professionalism.

"I'm ready for you now, Private Garrett," the doctor said, striding toward Garrett and examining his hand. "How is it feeling?"

"It's my arm," Garrett replied. "I think I got zapped by static electricity. But now the pain is spreading."

The doctor nodded, lifting Garrett's hand to inspect it closely. "Looks like something definitely got you here."

As another wave of pain pulsed through Garrett's arm, he winced and grimaced.

"Let's get you onto one of the beds," the doctor said urgently, gesturing toward a row of empty beds lining the wall. "We'll run an ECG test."

"Wait, am I having a heart attack?" Garrett asked in surprise.

"We can't be sure until we check," the doctor replied. "But it's better to be safe than sorry."

He led Garrett to the last bed in the row, closest to the observation window that looked into the room where the boy lay on a bed. The doctor motioned for Garrett to remove his shirt and rolled over a machine with a small display screen on a stand.

As he plugged in long cables with electrodes attached, the boy in the next room sat up slowly, observing with curiosity. His head tilted to the side as the electrodes were placed on Garrett's chest and back.

"Just try to relax," the doctor instructed, switching on the display unit.

"Relax?" Garrett scoffed.

A green line appeared on the screen, rising into a peak before flattening out and then rising again. It repeated this pattern rapidly, resembling a heart rate during intense exercise.

"It looks normal," the doctor said with a slight frown. "Slightly elevated. But within range."

The boy watched intently from his bed, lifting his chin to get a better view of Garrett's arm through the window.

"I'll keep you here for observation," the doctor continued. "Let me know if you experience another episode."

Garrett grimaced in pain once again, causing the ECG line to jump up and down erratically, like a seismograph during an earthquake.

"Fucking Hell!" Garrett exclaimed between clenched teeth.

As suddenly as it had started, the pain subsided, and the ECG returned to its normal pattern.

The doctor stood there in shock, not sure what to make of the sudden change. Slowly, Garrett turned toward the window where he met the intense gaze of the boy. It felt as though he was being studied by a predator eyeing its prey. The boy's eyes held a glimmer of excitement and malice as a wide grin spread across his face, sending shivers down Garrett's spine.

"Mother is coming," the boy whispered in a hauntingly low voice, sending shivers down Garrett's spine.

The pain erupted through his fingers, along his arm, bursting into his chest. As the line on the monitor jumped rapidly, unpredictably, Garrett fell back onto the bed and convulsed wildly, foam forming in the corners of his mouth.

The boy watched menacingly, hungrily, as his smile grew wider and wider.

"Help me," the doctor called to the receptionist. "Hold him down."

Blood spurted from the corporal's mouth as his teeth clenched tightly down on his tongue.

The boy snickered excitedly.

"Mother is coming," he hissed again. "Mother is coming."

CHAPTER NINE

Hope stood in front of the bathroom mirror, studying her tired reflection. Dark circles had formed under her eyes, evidence of the stress and lack of sleep she had endured since their arrival. She lowered her gaze to the pink onesie she was wearing, adorned with whimsical unicorns and colorful rainbows. At twenty-four years old, she'd never thought she would still be wearing kids' pajamas. But, here she was, deep underground in a onesie.

Shrugging off the nagging feeling of embarrassment, Hope went through her nightly routine of brushing her teeth and taking two melatonin tablets. As she turned off the light and made her way to the small bedroom, her thoughts turned to Lieutenant Dean Harris. Despite his stiff demeanor, she thought he might be more human than she initially thought.

Lying in bed, as sleep eluded her, Hope's mind continued to focus on Lieutenant Harris and on how he had managed to get Ford to open up about his relationship with Doctor Caldwell. Maybe there was more to him than just a strict military man. Her thoughts were interrupted by Sally's warning to stay away from Harris. But despite that warning, Hope couldn't shake off the desire to be with him.

Just as her eyelids grew heavy, memories of their arrival and everything that followed flooded her mind. But amidst the chaos emerged an image of Lieutenant Harris, appearing like a god through mist. She imagined his touch sending shivers down her spine and longed for his strength and closeness, even as another part of her fought against it.

Unable to resist any longer, Hope unzipped her onesie, sneaking her hand beneath rainbows and unicorns to her panties as she indulged in her forbidden thoughts. The tingling sensation spread throughout her body, but reality quickly set in.

You're just touching yourself, idiot. It's not him.

Frustration replaced desire and she let out a sigh of disappointment, unable to shake off the lingering thoughts of the lieutenant.

Stepping out of the large elevator onto the cavern's floor, Wade winced as his injured fingers throbbed beneath their bandages. The bright pink skin peeking through reminded him of the salve the doctor had applied earlier. A soft pulse in his fingertips mimicked his heartbeat, a constant reminder of his injury.

"Hello Kenneth," called a man in orange coveralls as he crossed the floor toward the vehicle bay. "Up late?"

"Hey Terry." Wade smiled through the pain, waving his hand with caution. "Yeah. Took longer than I thought."

"What did you do there?" Terry asked, nodding at Wade's fingers.

"Oh, nothing really," Wade replied nonchalantly. "Just some static from the platform in the Shrine."

"Static?" Terry raised an eyebrow in question as he started away. "Must have been quite a build-up."

"Yeah, I guess." Wade shrugged. "Listen though, Terry." Terry paused and turned back to face him. "Don't go down there without letting me know first, okay?"

"Sure thing," Terry agreed with a nod. "But honestly, I never go down there, anyway. That place gives me bad vibes, you know? The other guys can handle it if someone needs a light bulb changed or something. I'll just stick to repairing that snow mobile over there with the busted suspension."

"It's a lost cause," Wade remarked with a shake of his head before heading toward the pod structures. "Where's the rest of the night crew?"

"In the conference room drinking coffee," Terry replied.

"And what about the pilots for that monstrosity over there?" Wade gestured to the shuttle.

"Probably sleeping," Terry answered with a shrug. "They took one of the pods over the back, near the emergency door."

"Together in one pod?" Wade smiled, almost wincing from the throbbing ache in his arm.

"Yeah," Terry nodded. "More than just colleagues, I suppose."

"Guess so," Wade said with a tired sigh. "I'm off to bed. Goodnight."

"Goodnight," Terry echoed before continuing on his way.

Wade made his way past the conference room and toward his pod. Once inside, he stripped out of his coveralls, leaving only a t-shirt and his boxers on before climbing into bed. The red glow of his bedside clock displayed 00:49, a reminder of how late it was. He quickly set the alarm for 04:30 before the numbers flashed back to the time. With a final sigh, Wade closed his eyes and hoped to drift off to sleep quickly, wishing for the slight pain in his arm and the throbbing in his fingers to leave.

Hope's inner voice was a constant nag, urging her to go to Harris. But she adamantly refused, scoffing at the absurdity of the idea. She shook her head in disbelief, desperately trying to push away any lingering desires and resist the pull she felt toward him. As she lay in bed, staring at the dimly lit tablet on her nightstand, she couldn't help entertaining the possibility of giving in to her desires.

But what's the point? Her thoughts raced as she struggled to rationalize her decision. *Tomorrow, you will just be another lost soul wandering around the facility with Deputy Secretary Tinsley, before hopping back on the shuttle and returning home, never to see Harris again.*

Turning onto her side, facing away from the tablet and into the darkness of the room where the mattress touched the wall beside her, Hope considered picking up the tablet and reading something to help ease her mind. But a persistent voice in her head kept repeating one simple phrase.

Go to him.

Her mind was a chaotic whirlwind of conflicting thoughts and emotions—he could reject her; she felt ashamed and regretful of her actions. But then again, what did she have to lose? With a sudden surge of bravery, Hope threw off her covers and got out of bed. Taking her key card attached to its lanyard, she left her room, determined to end this internal battle once and for all.

The hallway was eerily quiet as she made her way toward Harris' room. The only sound was the faint hum of the air-conditioning droning softly through the corridors. Several times, she turned back to look at her own bedroom door.

This is ridiculous, she scolded herself silently. *He's probably fast asleep and doesn't need anyone disturbing him at this hour. Especially not an infatuated girl with foolish feelings.*

But the other voice inside of her persisted.

Go to him.

Finally, she stood nervously outside his door, heart pounding like a trapped bird in her chest. Her hand hovered over the door, uncertain if she should even knock.

Come on, she urged herself. *Knock.*

As Wade lay awake in bed, his mind raced with a tumultuous whirlwind of thoughts about the impending chaos the next day posed if he couldn't get to sleep. His fingers filled with pins and needles and a thrumming pulse ran along his forearm. He reached over to the light switch on the wall, his bandaged fingers trembling with anticipation. With a sharp intake of breath, he pressed the button, expecting a sudden burst of light to alleviate his anxiety.

But instead, a searing bolt of pain shot through his arm like a lightning strike. Wade's body jolted off the bed as he let out a guttural cry, his vision blurring from the sheer intensity.

"Fuck!" he cursed through gritted teeth, clenching his hand into a tight fist in an attempt to contain the pain.

But it was no use. The throbbing only intensified, feeling as if his hand were being crushed by a vice grip. His entire arm felt like it was on fire, and each pulsating wave felt like hot needles piercing through his skin.

"Fucking shit," he hissed through clenched teeth, desperately trying to find relief but only succeeding in burying his hand under his pillow.

Seconds felt like hours as Wade lay there, writhing in agony and squeezing his eyes shut against the unrelenting torture. He felt every nerve ending in his hand screaming for mercy, as if they were being stretched beyond their limits. The pain radiated up his arm and seemed to engulf his entire body, making him feel like he was being consumed from within.

Hope's heart raced as she stood in front of the door, her hand hovering tentatively before finally knocking. The sound of her fist against the icy surface reverberated through the quiet hallway, causing a flutter in her chest.

As she waited for a response, doubts crept into her mind. Was this really what she wanted? How could she give in to these feelings when there were so many reasons not to?

But before she could turn and walk away, the latch released with a click and the door swung open. Lieutenant Harris stood on the other side, his toned form glistening with sweat in nothing but skin-tight boxers. Hope let her eyes linger on his impressive physique before following the line down to his rock-hard abdominals, unable to ignore the semi-erect bulge visible through his underwear.

"Miss Aguilar? Is everything all right?" Harris asked, his voice breaking through her thoughts.

Hope tore her gaze away from him and noticed movement behind him. Private Gloria Gonzalez stood there, clutching a sheet tightly around her naked form. A pang of embarrassment and jealousy shot through Hope as she took in Gonzalez's beauty. It made sense that they would be together.

"Miss Aguilar?" Harris called again; confusion evident in his expression now.

Shaking her head, Hope felt her cheeks flush with embarrassment. "I'm sorry," she stammered, trying to push down the mix of emotions swirling inside her. "I didn't think you were...busy." She nodded to Gonzalez.

"I'm human, Miss Aguilar," Harris replied softly, a tiny smirk playing on his lips as he tried to ease the tension between them.

"And you're also very stupid," Gonzalez interjected, stepping forward to stand by Harris' side. "She's here because she wants you to fuck her."

Hope's eyes widened at the private's bold words, feeling exposed as she looked away.

But then Gonzalez's hand reached out and took hers, causing butterflies to flutter wildly in Hope's stomach. As their eyes met, a hunger burned in Gonzalez's gaze that sent shivers down Hope's spine.

Harris stepped aside, gesturing for Hope to enter the room. Her body acted before her mind could catch up as she walked through the door and allowed Gonzalez to lead her toward the bed by Gonzalez. Harris closed and locked the door behind them before joining them on the bed, removing his trunks without hesitation.

As Gonzalez undressed her with gentle care, Hope's heart pounded. It was clear that they were about to do something she had never done before, and she was both excited and scared. Her mind raced with thoughts of what they might be about to do, but her body craved it more than anything.

Gonzalez positioned Hope's body in a way that left her feeling vulnerable, but also incredibly aroused. Harris joined them, his muscular frame towering over them both as he pressed her against Gonzalez.

The sensations were overwhelming as their bodies intertwined, fueled by passion and desire. And as the night progressed, Hope let go of all inhibitions and felt alive like never before, lost in a sea of pleasure and exploration with Harris and Gonzalez by her side.

A sharp curse erupted from Wade's lips as he groped for the light switch, his injured hand throbbing painfully. The dim glow of the lamp illuminated the bandaged fingers that had been wrapped so carefully by the night doctor.

His breath caught in his throat as he saw streaks of red seeping through the white fabric. Blood was soaking through.

Grunting in frustration, he pushed himself up and swung his legs over the edge of the bed. With each step, he felt the pounding in his fingers growing more intense, the ache in his arm spreading into his shoulder.

Reaching the small washroom, he hesitated before grabbing a towel and wiping away the blood splatters on his face. Should he remove the bindings? A quick debate ensued in his mind before a sudden spurt of blood shot from his middle finger, landing on the sink with a sickening plop.

With no time to waste, Wade peeled off the dressing, revealing a pulsating mess of blood and tissue. His fingers throbbed with an intensity that made him dizzy.

Cursing under his breath, he dropped the bloody bandage into the sink and examined his finger, noticing a long-recessed line etched beneath the layers of glistening red.

Before he could even process what was happening, the line twitched and slowly parted like an opening mouth. A sense of horror crept over him as a thin tendril, milky in color, snaked its way out from within the wound.

Their lips collided in a fervent kiss, sparks of raw electricity igniting a wildfire within Hope's body. She let out a low gasp as Gonzalez's skilled fingers blazed trails of pleasure across her skin, sending her senses into overdrive. Each touch was like a lightning strike, electrifying her and making her primal instincts take over.

As Harris joined in, his gentle hands blended with Gonzalez's more urgent touches, creating an intense symphony of sensation on Hope's trembling skin. Their bodies melded together as they explored every inch of one another, unleashing a passion that consumed them. Hope was lost in a whirlwind of ecstasy, unable to think about anything else but the intense pleasure that consumed her.

With each touch from Gonzalez, Hope felt she was tapping into a hidden part of herself, one that had been suppressed for far too long. It was unlike anything she had ever experienced before, and yet it was something she wanted with every fiber of her being. The heat between them radiated like a furnace, engulfing her in waves of desire and euphoria.

The tendril slithered and twirled around Wade's finger, its slimy texture leaving a trail of cold slime against his skin. With each passing moment, it grew longer and thicker, pulsating with a cruel hunger for flesh.

Suddenly, thick veins bulged under Wade's skin, throbbing and pushing upwards as if trying to escape from within. A strangled cry escaped Wade's lips as he felt his heart beating so hard in his chest that it might burst.

The veins continued to spread like a network of spiderwebs, crawling up his arm and causing searing pain to shoot through him. Wade fell to his knees, unable to bear the excruciating agony any longer.

Now covering his entire biceps and triceps muscles, the twisted veins seemed to have a life of their own as they strained against his skin. And then they reached his shoulder, sending waves of unbearable pain coursing through him.

As he lay on the ground writhing in agony, Wade tried to scream but only managed a weak gasp as something scraped and clawed at the inside of his throat, suffocating him. He felt something dark and malevolent taking control of him, consuming him from within.

Hope's eyes smoldered with desire as Harris plunged deep inside her, sending waves of ecstasy coursing through her veins. Their eyes locked in a fiery gaze, sparking a passionate inferno that consumed them both. The scorching heat radiating from their union set every nerve ablaze, sending waves of intense pleasure coursing through Hope's body. With Gonzalez's hand exploring every inch of her inner thigh, Hope surrendered herself fully to the moment, giving in to the electric currents that pulsed between them. She was lost in a sea of ecstasy, floating on waves of pure desire and power.

As their bodies moved in perfect harmony, every touch, every kiss, sent shockwaves through her body, intensifying the wetness and heat between her legs with each passing second.

In this intense haze of passion and emotion, Hope shed all inhibitions and allowed herself to be consumed by the raw intensity of the moment. She was alive in a way she had never experienced before, completely immersed in the fire of their insatiable desire for each other.

With a sickening pop, the skin on his hand exploded in a shower of blood and flesh, revealing a writhing mass of wriggling tentacles that seemed to have a mind of their own. Wade's body convulsed as he watched in horror, tears streaming down his face, unable to comprehend the grotesque sight before him. The slimy appendages oozed out of his open palm, dripping with gore and leaving a trail of sticky residue as they slithered over his face. A searing pain shot through his head, causing him to let out a guttural scream as he felt his skull being crushed by an unseen force. The tentacles tightened their grip on him, cutting off his air supply and suffocating him. Frantically, Wade tried to call for help, but no sound escaped his lips. He closed his eyes, bracing himself for the worst as the tentacles continued to move and writhe in a frenzy, shredding bone, and muscle in their wake.

CHAPTER TEN

A sharp jolt of adrenaline surged through Captain Dona Moreau, snapping her out of a deep slumber. As she stirred awake, her hand rested gently on Curt Gauthier's bare chest, the warmth of his skin offering solace in the dimly lit room. With a slight groan, she lifted her head; her disheveled hair cascading over her face and shoulders, obscuring most of her view. With a tired sigh, she brushed it aside to gaze at the bedside clock, its glowing numbers gradually coming into focus as her eyes adjusted. The red digits read 03:48.

As the realization set in that she had only a few minutes left before her alarm would sound at 04:00, she felt torn between the temptation to sink back into peaceful sleep for the rest of their impending mission, or at least for the next ten minutes.

In the distance, a faint cry carried on the wind reached her ears, rousing her from any thought of going back to sleep. She strained to hear more but could only make out muffled voices outside. Probably just the maintenance crew, she thought wearily. But then another voice joined in, words indistinguishable but sounding urgent.

Moreau sat up against the wall and begrudgingly accepted that she would have to maneuver around Gauthier to use the washroom. Carefully straddling him, she tried not to disturb his slumber, but he stirred beneath her touch.

"Stay right there," he murmured with a lazy smile, reaching up to caress her breasts before letting his hands trail down to cup her buttocks.

"I need to pee," she stated matter-of-factly as she continued on her way. "You've got ten minutes until the alarm goes off."

He grunted in protest, but Moreau ignored him as she made her way to the bathroom. Another cry from outside caught her attention.

"What's that?" Gauthier asked, looking toward the door.

"I don't know," she replied dismissively, focused on her own needs.

He rolled over onto his side, his gaze lingering on her figure as if trying to memorize every detail.

"I'm going to take a quick shower," Moreau informed him with a mischievous grin. "And then I want some coffee. We need to run through pre-flight checks in twenty minutes."

"We have plenty of time," Gauthier argued, stretching out with a contented groan. "We're not leaving until after lunch anyways. Come back to bed."

"Twenty minutes," she repeated firmly, closing the bathroom door behind her.

Ten minutes later, dressed in her white coveralls, Moreau sat on the edge of the bed and began lacing up her boots while Gauthier took a shower. Through the open door, she heard an uproar coming from outside, a voice shouting frantically from across the cavern. She tugged tightly on her boot laces and stood up, straining her ears to make out the muffled words over the sound of water splashing in the washroom.

Driven by a nagging curiosity, she edged toward the door and gently cracked it open, unleashing a gust of chilling wind into the stuffy room. The distant voices grew louder and more frantic, escalating into a violent cacophony that sent shivers down her spine. A gut-wrenching cry pierced through the chaos, followed by a woman's terrified response.

"What the hell is going on?" Moreau muttered, pushing the door open wider to peer outside. Her view partially obstructed by a row of massive pod structures, but she saw people dressed in orange scurrying around near the conference room. Their frantic shouts bounced off the walls, creating a chaotic symphony of panic.

"What happened?"

"Don't go in there!"

"Shit!"

A surge of alarm coursed through Moreau's body, twisting her stomach into knots as she slammed the metal door shut and raced over to bang on the washroom door. Her heart drummed against her chest as she urgently ordered Gauthier to "get out" before frantically rummaging through her backpack for her equipment.

The cool metal of her gun brought some semblance of reassurance as she strapped on a belt with holstered weapon and loaded magazine pouches, moving with swift precision. The sound of running water abruptly stopped and Gauthier emerged with a towel wrapped around his waist.

"What's happening?" he asked, rubbing at his damp hair.

"I don't know," Moreau answered, grabbing five loaded magazines from her backpack, and swiftly sliding them into her belt pouches. "But something is seriously wrong out there."

Gauthier tried to brush off the situation. "It could just be a minor incident."

"It could be," Moreau agreed with a tinge of doubt, slinging her backpack over her shoulders. "But we can't take any chances. Let's gear up."

Sensing the urgency in Moreau's voice, Gauthier quickly dressed and they cautiously made their way along a narrow walkway between towering structures. Moreau gripped her gun with white-knuckled intensity, ready for any potential danger ahead. Gauthier stayed alert, scanning their surroundings for signs of peril.

The panicked cry of a voice echoed through the dark cavern walls, bouncing off the rocky surfaces and making it nearly impossible to pinpoint its source. Moreau's hand tightened around her weapon as she stealthily made her way forward. The narrow walkway felt claustrophobic, surrounded by looming structures that seemed to close in with each step.

"Shit," someone shouted in terror. "There's three of them!"

Gauthier stayed close behind Moreau, his weapon drawn and ready for any threat. With their pod door slightly ajar just in case they needed to make a quick retreat back inside, they moved cautiously toward the commotion.

"It's coming from the conference room," Gauthier whispered.

A bloodcurdling scream pierced the air, causing Moreau's heart to race faster as they approached the chaotic scene ahead.

"Fuck!" another voice bellowed, the sound reverberating through the cave. "Fuck!"

Without hesitation, Moreau quickened her pace and raised her pistol in preparation for whatever danger lay ahead. As they rounded a corner between two pod structures, the full scene came into view—people in orange coveralls scattered in small groups throughout the area. Some cowered near vehicles and tool shelves while others huddled behind pods or sought refuge inside them. But a larger group stood frozen, their gaze fixed on something on the ground.

But nothing could have prepared Moreau for the horror that awaited her.

In front of her, a man was bent over on all fours, his face buried deep within another person's torso. As he pulled away from his grisly feast, his face and hands smeared with blood and coiled strands of what appeared to be intestines writhing and squirming like living creatures.

"Holy shit," Gauthier gasped, his gun trained on the man.

He fired a single shot, hitting him square in the shoulder.

The figure collapsed to the ground like a marionette with its strings cut. The sudden sound of gunfire snapped the others out of their stunned trance, causing them to flee in terror from the gruesome sight.

Moreau's stomach churned as she stared in horror at the victim's mutilated body. Blood and tissue spilled out from a gaping hole where his abdomen once was, almost appearing black against the stark white of exposed bones. The stench of bile filled her nostrils as she fought back waves of nausea.

"I... I can't...I think I'm going to be sick," she stuttered, unable to tear her eyes away from the grotesque scene.

But before she could move, the fallen creature stirred, coiled tentacles unfurling from around its head, thrashing wildly as it hoisted itself off the ground.

"Shit," Gauthier cursed, unloading his entire clip into its chest until it stumbled and fell to its knees.

"We have to get to the shuttle," Moreau urged, gripping Gauthier's arm tightly.

He nodded, tossing his empty magazine, and swiftly reloading his weapon.

But as their attention fell upon the conference room window, terror gripped them in its icy grasp. The sight before them was nightmare-inducing—two humanoid figures covered in writhing tentacles stood motionless inside, their cold, calculating gazes fixed on the pair.

Before they could even process what they were seeing, the victim lying on the ground suddenly convulsed and sat up, his body twisting and contorting as thin, serpentine forms burst forth from every pore and orifice.

The sickening sound of blood-smeared tentacles drowned Gauthier's horrified gasp out as they violently erupted from the man's wounds. Without a moment to spare, Moreau bolted toward the shuttle with Gauthier close behind.

But just as they thought they had escaped, a deafening crash made them whirl around. One of the figures had shattered through the window of the conference pod and was now bearing down on them with terrifying speed, its tentacles lashing out like deadly whips.

Amidst the chaos and screams of fleeing maintenance crew members, the horde of creatures advanced relentlessly, their newly formed razor-sharp claws tearing through flesh and bone with savage ferocity. Despite their valiant efforts, Moreau and Gauthier struggled to fight their way toward the safety of the shuttle, only to find that the massive sliding doors leading to it were tightly shut.

"Faster!" Moreau shouted, her fingers racing over the keypad in a desperate attempt to unlock the door. Behind her, Gauthier fired relentlessly at an approaching figure, aiming for its writhing tentacles as it lunged toward them.

The creature slowed but continued its inexorable advance, its flailing arms morphing into deadly weapons. A sharp hiss filled the air as Gauthier emptied his clip into it, but still it came closer.

In one swift motion, the beast lunged forward and wrapped its tendrils around Gauthier's throat, squeezing until he could no longer fight back. "Get on the shuttle!" he managed to gasp before a mass of writhing tentacles engulfed his head.

Tears streamed down Moreau's face as she watched her comrade fall to the ground, his life snuffed out in an instant. With fear and adrenaline coursing through her veins, she made a mad dash toward the shuttle door, trying to block out the sight of other victims scattered like broken dolls on the cavern floor. Each step forward felt like an insurmountable weight, the agonized screams and moans filling her ears.

But even as she fought for her own survival, Moreau couldn't escape the horrific scenes unfolding around her. Men and women writhed in excruciating pain, their faces contorted as tentacles burst through their facial orifices, eye sockets and skin. The sickening stench of blood and death filled her nostrils as she pushed herself onward toward safety.

"Move," she urged herself, using every ounce of strength left in her trembling body to reach the doorway and roll onto the floor. The creature, preoccupied with Gauthier, paid no attention to her as she frantically pressed the button to seal the door behind her.

A woman's piercing scream echoed through the air, shattering the tense silence as Moreau peered through the door's closing gap. Her heart thudded violently as she saw a young woman running toward them, terror etched on her face. But before Moreau could react, a monstrous creature lunged at the unsuspecting woman, its slimy tentacles coiling around her neck in a deadly embrace.

The captain grabbed for the controls to open the door again, but it was too late. The woman's screams were abruptly cut off, leaving Moreau frozen in horror and helplessness. The hatch closed with a soft thud and hiss, trapping Moreau inside, alone. She let out a weak whimper before succumbing to a fit of uncontrollable, gut-wrenching sobs.

Time seemed to stand still as she remained frozen, her mind in chaos and her emotions in turmoil! She berated herself relentlessly, seething with anger at her lack of self-control.

How could she have fooled herself into thinking she was strong-willed? The realization only fueled her self-hatred, consuming her in an endless cycle of regret.

Moreau's body shook with adrenaline as she struggled to regain control of her racing thoughts. With a deep breath, she forced herself to stand, her muscles trembling with the effort. As she made her way toward the cockpit, her heart pounded not only from the physical exertion, but also from the fear of what she might find.

But as she entered the cockpit and looked out through the windshield, all sound seemed to vanish into an eerie stillness. A scene of violent chaos that had previously filled her ears with screams and shouts was now replaced by a haunting silence. And then, as she focused on the terrifying sight before her, Moreau's blood turned to ice in her veins.

The shuttle was now surrounded by figures clad in orange jumpsuits, their bodies twisted and distorted with grotesque tendrils sprouting from every inch. Amidst the frenzied crowd, Moreau spotted people with fatal wounds still standing, their bodies infected by whatever horrid transformation was taking place.

And there, amidst it all, stood a figure in white—Curt. His head crushed and deformed, his body writhing with pulsating tentacles reaching over his shoulders. The sight brought Moreau to her knees as she let out a broken whisper.

"Curt," she choked out before another wave of grief washed over her and she wept once again. The magnitude of the situation crashed over her like a tsunami, engulfing her in a whirlwind of emotions that left her drowning in despair.

CHAPTER ELEVEN

Hope slipped into her blue coveralls. She tied her dark hair back in a tight ponytail, readying herself for the day ahead. With efficient movements, she packed her toiletries and unicorn pajamas into her bag and zipped it shut. As she made the bed that she didn't sleep in, she thought back to the passionate night she had spent with Harris and Gonzalez, feeling a rush of excitement and longing.

With her bag placed on the end of the bed and the tablet device in hand, Hope left the room with a spring in her step. The scent of freshly cooked bacon wafted through the air, drawing her toward the dining area. As she scrolled through emails on her tablet, she passed by various facility staff members in the passage and exchanged quick greetings with them. Some messages from different UN departments caught her attention, and she quickly responded to them before deleting spam.

Entering the dining area, Hope noticed that it was relatively empty except for the busy kitchen staff. She made a beeline for the tea dispenser, grabbing a mug from the bench before tucking the tablet under her arm. She chose English Breakfast tea and smiled as she heard a familiar voice beside her.

"Good morning," Tracey Zelski, the head chef, greeted her with a warm smile.

"Good morning," Hope replied, returning the smile. "How are you?"

"Okay," Zelski answered, glancing at Hope curiously. "Did you sleep well?"

Trying to hide her grin, Hope shrugged nonchalantly. "I can't complain."

"Well," Zelski gestured to the glass cases along the bench filled with an array of breakfast foods. "Breakfast is waiting. We have cereal if you prefer. Our fruit is all canned, unfortunately."

"I'll need some bacon," Hope declared with a grin.

Zelski chuckled. "Get in there before everyone else does. Take an extra rasher or two or pile your plate like that big Aussie who came with you." Hope's thoughts immediately went to Harris, and she scanned the room for him. Zelski pointed to a large figure sitting behind a cluster of ferns. "He's over there."

"And Private Gonzalez?" Hope asked, looking around for her other companion.

"Not up yet, I guess," Zelski replied, gesturing toward the kitchen crew. "Just us foolish early risers."

Hope smiled gratefully at the head chef and made her way down the bench, loading her plate with various breakfast items. "I think I'll grab a bit of everything."

"Living on the edge," Zelski teased before heading back into the kitchen.

Hope piled her plate high with a hearty breakfast—sausage, eggs, a crisp hash brown, a scoop of savory beans, and four strips of bacon. She knew it was more than her small waist could handle, but the smell alone was enough to tempt her. And she figured she could balance it out later with an extra mile or two on the treadmill at her local gym back in Tudor City.

Carefully carrying her plate and mug on a tray, Hope made her way across the empty dining area to join Harris at his table. He reclined in his chair, absorbed in whatever he was reading on a tablet device, as he sipped on a strong cup of black coffee. His plate had already been cleaned down to the last crumb.

"Morning, Lieutenant," Hope greeted him cheerily as she sat down. "That looks like an entertaining read."

Harris briefly glanced up at her before turning his attention back to her loaded plate. "Quite the appetite," he observed.

"I don't normally eat this much," Hope admitted sheepishly. "But everything just smelled so good."

He nodded in understanding before taking another sip of his coffee. "I need to maintain a certain level of professionalism," he explained. "Especially in public. I hope that doesn't offend you."

"No, not at all," Hope replied, trying to play it cool.

Harris' focus returned to the tablet as he sipped his coffee. Curiosity getting the best of her, Hope asked, "What are you reading?"

"The assembly and operations manual for the new M nine-seven-nine-zero," he replied casually.

"M nine-seven..." Hope repeated, cutting into a sausage with her knife.

"M nine-seven-nine-zero," Harris clarified. "It's a new pulse cannon that the Australian military has developed. It uses energy manipulation technology."

"A new laser gun?" Hope asked with fake enthusiasm, trying to impress him. "Like a pulse rifle?"

"It's a bit more complicated than that," Harris replied, noticing a small dribble of bean sauce on Hope's chin. Without hesitating, he grabbed a napkin from the dispenser and reached across the table to wipe it away. "Sorry," he apologized, crumpling up the napkin and placing it on his empty plate. "I should have asked for permission."

Hope could only stare at him, mesmerized. She thought about how close they had been the night before while he was inside her. He didn't need permission to wipe sauce off her face.

"It's okay," she managed to say, still in a daze. She continued to stare at him, momentarily forgetting about her food.

He met her gaze, his brow furrowing slightly as a small smile tugged at the corners of his mouth.

Her mind recalled his words, *I need to maintain a certain level of professionalism.*

"Your breakfast is getting cold, Hope," Harris reminded her.

"Huh?" Hope snapped out of her trance and looked down at her plate. "Oh," she said, quickly stabbing her fork into a piece of bacon.

For a few minutes, she ate in silence. Hope focused on her food while Harris returned to reading the weapon's manual, occasionally sipping his coffee.

Suddenly, there was a burst of static, followed by a woman's voice crackling through the speakers.

"-olonel. It's Moreau. Come in."

Harris reached into a pouch on the leg of his coveralls, retrieving a small hand-held radio.

The sound of static filled the room as Harris pressed the button on the radio. "Colonel?" Moreau's voice came through the speaker.

"Captain Moreau, this is Lieutenant Harris," he said into the radio, his tone serious and urgent. "The colonel is elsewhere at the moment."

"Lieutenant," She sounded excited, frantic. Her voice was tinged with fear and desperation. "Thank God. Is everyone all right? Are you all alive?"

"Alive?" he asked, confused by her question.

Hope, who was sitting nearby, looked up from her meal and stared at the radio curiously.

Alive?

"What's happening?" Harris asked urgently.

"Something happened to everybody," Moreau answered, her voice trembling with emotion.

"Please explain," he pressed.

"Something..." She started to cry, her voice breaking. "They attacked. It was so quick. Everybody is... I'm the only one left."

Hope locked eyes with Harris, sensing his growing fascination and curiosity about what had happened. She felt a knot form in her stomach and a lump rise in her throat as she sat frozen in her seat, waiting for either Moreau or Harris to say something.

"I'm coming up," Harris said into the radio, his voice firm and determined.

"No," Moreau replied urgently. "Lock the elevator down. Don't come up here. They'll take you."

"Take me?" Harris asked incredulously.

There was a brief moment of silence before Moreau spoke again, her voice shaking with fear and disbelief.

"They're all infected with something," she explained frantically. "Like fucking squids bursting from their bodies."

Squids? Hope's curiosity was piqued, but so was her sense of fear.

Harris looked at her for an answer, but she could only shake her head in response, equally confused and terrified by Moreau's words.

"You're not making sense, Captain," the lieutenant said sternly. "I need some clarification. Where's Captain Gauthier?"

"I don't know," Moreau sobbed, her voice breaking again. "They're all infected. They killed him. Crushed his fucking head.... He's one of them. He's one of them."

Hope's heart raced as she listened to Moreau's distressing words. She mirrored Harris' actions as he stood up from his seat and began walking swiftly toward the passageway that led to the rooms of their group members.

"Are you safe?" asked Harris, his voice full of concern.

"I'm in the shuttle," Moreau answered. "Safe."

"Good," he said decisively as he continued on his way. "Lock it down. I'm going to get the colonel and we'll figure out a way to get you out of there."

Hope followed Harris, unable to shake off the feeling of dread that had settled over her.

"Okay," Moreau said shakily into the radio.

"Can you wake the deputy secretary?" Harris asked, glancing at Hope.

"Yes," the assistant replied with determination. "I was already on my way."

"We need to notify Professor Ford," Harris added, his mind already racing with plans and strategies.

"To lock down the facility," Hope interjected, stopping by Tinsley's door as Harris continued along the corridor.

"Exactly," he replied, turning to face her. "I'm sorry you didn't get to enjoy your breakfast."

She shrugged and shook her head, dismissing his apology with a small smile. It's not your fault, she wanted to say, but the weight of the situation was pressing down on her, and words failed to come out.

"I'll meet you back in the dining area," he said, turning away.

***

The entire delegation, led by Doctor Isaac Palmer and Glenn Schwartz, crossed the floor in a synchronized march. Each member of the security detail carried a modified G-36 assault rifle over their shoulder, except for Harris who had two slung across his body, collected from the crate unloaded from the shuttle and stored in Colonel Power's room when they arrived. The glint of metal and size of the weapons drew curious gazes from the breakfast-eating crowd in the dining area. Whispers and murmurs could be heard as they passed by, questioning the need for such firepower.

Hope walked behind Deputy Secretary Tinsley, her eyes flickering to Harris beside her with curiosity.

"Why two guns?" she asked under her breath.

"Corporal Garrett is still in the Med Lab," he replied quietly. "One of them is for him."

As they reached the door to Ford's office, Tinsley knocked firmly.

"I'm in a conference," came Ford's muffled voice from inside. "Please come back in about twenty minutes."

Colonel Powers let out an exasperated sigh and turned the doorknob.

"We need a more direct approach," he said to Tinsley as he swung the door open and entered.

Ford sat at his desk like a stunned fish, watching as the entire delegation filed into his office. On the screen behind him, several faces glared down at them from video conferencing boxes. It was clear that Ford was in the middle of a meeting with executives from Innovative Energy Corporation.

"Apologies for the disruption, ladies and gentlemen," Tinsley said, taking control before Ford could gather himself. "There's an emergency that requires Professor Ford's immediate attention. I'm sure you'll understand the abrupt interruption of this meeting."

"Who is this person, Professor?" an elderly man on the screen wanted to know.

Harris quickly made his way around the desk to stand beside Ford, his fingers deftly moving across the trackpad of the computer.

Tinsley smiled, patting her chest. "I'm Deputy Secretary Sally Tinsley, representing the United Nations Industrial Development Organization in this delegation. Professor Ford will be in contact with you after we've addressed the situation at hand."

"What situation?" one of the executives on the screen interjected.

"Now hold on just a minute, I think we..." another started.

"This meeting is adjourned," Tinsley declared.

With that, Harris pressed a button on the trackpad, closing the display window and cutting off any further objections from the corporate executives.

"Thank you, Lieutenant," Tinsley said with a nod.

Harris returned to his position beside her without a word.

"What...what's going on?" Ford stammered, looking around the room in confusion.

"There has been an incident upstairs," Tinsley informed him calmly.

"An incident?" Ford repeated, his voice trembling slightly. Hope wondered if the word triggered any memories for the professor, given what had happened in the Energy Generation Chamber with Doctor Amy Caldwell.

Pointing to the screen on the wall, Colonel Powers spoke up again.

"Can you project a live feed of the cavern onto this screen?" Powers demanded, gesturing to the large monitor on the wall. "You have a camera down in that shrine of yours. You must have CCTV all over this place, right?"

Ford blinked, as if coming out of a trance, and nodded, pressing a few buttons on his keyboard. The display changed to show a high view of the cavern from above the exterior of the conference room, where they all congregated the day before. It showed the massive metal doors leading out of the cavern, shut, the bustling garage and machine workshop, the large elevator doors and the shuttle with scores of people surrounding it.

"What are they doing down there?" Ford asked, squinting at the screen.

Teresa Jackson, a private in their unit, spoke up with wide eyes. "And what's that strange mass on their heads?"

The others in the room were just as shocked, resembling stunned fish as they stared at the screen.

"Those are tendrils," Lieutenant Harris answered, his voice cool and collected despite the chaos unfolding before them. He reached for his radio at his side. "Captain Moreau, do you copy?"

There was a tense moment of silence before a response came through.

"I'm here," came Captain Moreau's voice.

"We're watching you on a monitor," Harris explained. "What is your current situation?"

"Not good," she replied. "I found some bottles of water and rations in one of the rear compartments."

Powers held out his hand to take the radio from Harris, silently instructing him to pass it over. Harris complied, keeping his eyes glued to the screen.

"Captain?" Powers said into the radio. "This is Colonel Powers. Ration those supplies. Make them last."

"Yes, sir," she responded.

"Are you armed?"

"I have my pistol and a few clips," she confirmed. "But not enough for all of them."

Powers furrowed his brow in concern. "What can you tell me about these creatures?"

"They move fast," Moreau reported. "And they transform quickly."

"Transform?" Powers repeated, his mind racing with possibilities.

"Yes," she replied, her voice trembling. "Curt was attacked and within minutes, he had transformed into one of them."

Powers took a deep breath, trying to remain composed in the face of this terrifying information. "Stay strong, Captain," he said, his voice filled with compassion. "We will find a way to get you out of there."

"Sir?" Moreau's voice sounded desperate now. "I think it would be best for you to come here so we can all evacuate together."

Powers glanced around the room at his team, seeing the fear and concern etched on their faces. With a slow nod, he turned back to the screen. "We're working on a plan, Captain," he assured her. "Just hold tight."

Colonel Powers slowly handed the radio back to Harris, his knuckles white and trembling. But before he could even catch his breath, she called out to him again.

"And sir?" Moreau's voice wavered with fear and urgency.

"Yes, Captain," Powers responded, trying to maintain a calm demeanor.

"I don't think bullets work on them," she said, her voice shaking with emotion. "At least, not all that well."

Powers felt a cold shiver run down his spine at her words. This was worse than he had feared.

"What do you mean?" he asked, his mind racing to find a solution.

"Curt," she answered, her voice breaking into sobs. "One of them killed him before he changed. I think they're already dead."

The room fell silent as everyone tried to process this new information. Professor Ford gasped; his eyes glued to the screen on the wall.

"Dead?" he gasped in disbelief. "How can they—"

But before he could finish his thought, Tinsley interjected with a suggestion.

"I think you should lock this facility down," she said, her voice firm and resolute. "Turn that elevator off so those...things can't find their way down here."

Ford quickly typed commands into his computer, effectively shutting down the elevator.

"Ah..." he stammered, wiping sweat from his brow. "Absolutely. And...done."

Harris turned to look at the Deputy Secretary, her expression grave and determined.

"Is there any other way they could get down here?" she asked.

"The emergency stairwells," Ford answered quickly, pointing to a map on the wall behind his desk. "There are four at the furthest points of the facility from the elevator. They each lead up to the surface, with doors into the cavern and additional passageways leading outside."

Colonel Powers turned to Harris. "We need to barricade those with something heavy," he said firmly, knowing they needed to act fast.

But Schwartz had another idea.

"We need to call in for help, then get up to the shuttle and get out of here," he suggested, trying to keep his voice steady.

"Agreed," Tinsley added, nodding in agreement. "We have over three hundred people here that we need to consider. How long before we can get enough transport vehicles out here to evacuate everyone?"

Ford furrowed his brows, mentally calculating the time it would take to arrange for an evacuation.

"I don't know," he replied honestly. "Hours. A day or two. It all depends on the weather and the availability of the company's shuttles. It might be a few trips for each shuttle. They carry twenty to thirty people max, and I think they've got three based in Edmonton...maybe. We can evacuate them to Isachsen. It's the closest location with an airfield suitable for larger aircraft. The problem will be fueling time for the shuttles."

Powers turned to Ford with a stern expression.

"Can you get back in touch with those suits and push them to do something from their end?" he asked, gesturing toward the wall-mounted screen where they could communicate with the higher-ups.

"Of course," Ford nodded, understanding the urgency of the situation. "I need to in a situation like this, anyway. They'll be able to give a better estimate concerning time."

Tinsley locked eyes with Ford, a sense of urgency and determination in her gaze.

"Please," she said. "Time is of the essence."

Ford nodded, not needing any further explanation as he quickly typed away at his computer.

"Right away," he said.

Colonel Powers turned to the deputy secretary, his voice low and urgent.

"If those things get tired of waiting for Captain Moreau to come out, they might look for ways to get to us," he said quietly. "We need to barricade those emergency exits."

The lieutenant turned to face the professor. "Do you have a gym or workout space with equipment?" he asked.

"In the rec room," Ford replied, his fingers tapping away on the keyboard. "There's some commercial class equipment—leg presses, chest press machines, things like that. They have little rollers on them so they can be easily moved."

Harris nodded, considering their options. "Could work," he said. "Do you have your radio, sir?"

"Yeah," Colonel Powers answered, reaching into a pouch on his thigh to retrieve the device. He turned it on and looked at Harris questioningly.

"Channel four," the lieutenant told him, as if reading his thoughts. "Gonzalez, Jackson, Collier—with me." With that, the four soldiers stood up and started out of the room.

But before they could leave, Schwartz called out, causing them to halt in their tracks. "Wait."

The four troopers turned to look at him expectantly.

"Do you plan to barricade the doors with the gym equipment to stop anyone from pushing them open from the outside?" Schwartz went on.

Harris nodded in confirmation.

But then Schwartz shook his head. "It won't work," he explained.

A small crease formed on the lieutenant's forehead briefly before clarity hit. "Of course," he murmured to himself.

"What?" Gonzalez asked, glancing around the room anxiously.

"The emergency doors are designed to be pushed open from the inside," Schwartz clarified. "They open into the stairwell. So, barricading them from this side is pointless—even if we use the gym equipment. The infected might be able to pry the doors open and then simply climb over whatever obstacle we create. We need to seal these doors completely—prevent them from being opened at all. Maybe even chain them shut."

The engineer turned to look at the professor. "Do you have any chains lying around anywhere?" he asked.

Ford's face fell as he realized the gravity of their situation. "Upstairs, in the maintenance stores," he replied defeatedly.

"Let's take a look at that gym equipment," Schwartz suggested, already moving past the soldiers toward the door. "We might be able to salvage something useful from it."

Palmer hesitated, torn between staying in the room or following the engineer. But eventually, he hurried after them.

Meanwhile, Powers was keeping in contact with Captain Moreau through his radio.

"Captain?" Powers said into his device.

"Go ahead," Moreau answered on the other end.

"Hang in there," Powers told her. "We're working on a plan, but it might take some time."

"How much time?" she asked anxiously.

"We're not sure yet," Powers admitted. "Best case scenario is a few hours."

"And the worst?" she asked.

"It could take even longer," he replied grimly, not wanting to dwell on that possibility for too long.

CHAPTER TWELVE

The group of seven, consisting of a pediatrician, an engineer, and five soldiers, passed through the recreation room where a cluster of sofas gathered before a large flat-screen mounted on the wall. A pool table sat to the rear of the room near a wide doorway leading into another room, a small gymnasium. They cautiously entered the gym, a room roughly the size of a double garage, packed with various fitness equipment and machines. To their right, a large mirror covered the entire wall, reflecting back the image of the visitors in multiple angles. Stands loaded with an assortment of dumbbells, kettlebells, and free weights were carefully arranged before it, gleaming under the bright lights. Several gym benches were placed along the floor, facing the mirror like eager spectators waiting for a show. To their left, more technical equipment was set up to aid with leg exercises and muscle-building, including cable machines and cardio bikes and elliptical trainers. One young woman caught their attention as she vigorously worked out on one of the cross-trainers, casting curious glances at the newcomers.

As they scanned the room, Schwartz's gaze landed on a rack fixed to the very back wall. It held an array of large, colored rubber straps, ropes, and cable machine accessories. He pointed toward it as he moved further into the room.

"What?" Gonzalez asked, following closely.

"Chains," Schwartz replied simply, passing by the young woman without breaking his stride. Dangling from an iron hook beside the colored straps were several long, galvanized chains, looped over so as not to touch the floor. He picked one up and held it high, causing it to jingle musically. "Maybe six millimeters. Should do the trick."

"What?" Gonzalez asked again, eyeing the length of chain that seemed almost as tall as she was. She furrowed her brow in confusion. "Is there something wrong with you? That's definitely longer than six millimeters."

Schwartz gave her a quizzical look.

"He means diameter," Harris chimed in as he pulled alongside Gonzalez.

"This should work nicely," Schwartz continued, ignoring the previous comment. "We can loop these chains through the levers a few times and make it as tight as we can. But we'll need to secure them somehow. Padlocks would be perfect."

"Maybe there's something in the kitchen we could use?" Collier suggested.

"The kitchen?" Jackson scoffed. "Is that where your momma kept all the padlocks in your house?"

"No," Collier replied defensively. "But we had a drawer in the kitchen for things we thought might come in handy. Like batteries and matches. Shit like that."

Harris began scanning the equipment along the mirrored wall, searching for anything they could use to barricade the emergency doors. He considered taking some of the long bars to see if they could help seal the doors shut.

Suddenly, a voice from one of the training machines interrupted them. The young woman had slowed her pace and lifted a towel from the cross-trainer's console as she spoke.

"What are you guys doing?"

The visitors turned to Harris, waiting for him to respond.

"There's a situation," he explained carefully. "I can't give you more details, but we need to commandeer some of the gym's equipment to barricade the emergency doors."

"And you plan on using those chains?" she asked, seemingly unfazed by their request as she stepped off the machine.

"Yes," Harris replied.

"Well—" she turned to Collier. "You won't find any padlocks in the kitchen. Maybe some of those little wire twist ties for garbage bags."

The group exchanged glances before continuing their search for makeshift locks among the gym equipment.

The tension in the room was palpable as Doctor Palmer hesitated, unsure of what to do next. The young woman, with her vibrant red hair tied back in a loose bun and confident demeanor, offered a solution.

"Why not use the biners attached to the cable machines?" she suggested, gesturing toward the nearby gym equipment. "They may not be padlocks, but they should be strong enough to hold your chains."

Harris quickly made his way to the nearest cable machine. He marveled at its design, meant to work out one's upper back muscles. Attached to the top of the machine was a long bar secured by a carabiner clip—a metal loop with a spring-loaded gate that seemed oddly shaped yet perfectly functional.

"Of course," Harris murmured as he lifted the bar to release the clip.

The young woman playfully slapped his shoulder and remarked, "I thought someone who looks like you would know all about this kind of thing, big boy."

Gonzalez clenched her jaw as the redhead strode toward the door. The woman paused for a moment before turning to face them. "Should I be concerned?" she asked, surveying their expressions.

The group felt a sense of dread overwhelm them, except for Harris, who remained calm.

"Yes," he answered simply. "But I'm not at liberty to say more. Thank you for your assistance."

"No problem," she replied nonchalantly as she left the room.

Harris moved on to the next cable machine, removing another carabiner clip while his companions continued to stare in disbelief at the door that the young woman had just walked through. Teresa Jackson furrowed her brow in confusion and exclaimed, "What the fuck?"

"I know, right?" Collier chimed in, turning to look at Jackson. "How can she be so calm? We have guns and everything."

Harris moved with practiced ease to the next cable machine to remove the carabiner clip.

"Perhaps she has remarkable control over her emotions," he said, moving on to the next piece of exercise equipment. "I could use some help here."

"Sorry L-T," the private replied, quickly joining Harris at his side. "I just can't wrap my head around how someone can stay so composed after being told there's something to worry about."

"Everyone handles things differently," Harris replied, removing one more biner from another machine before handing them off to Collier.

"Maybe she's like you," Gonzalez offered, still watching the door.

Harris let out a small chuckle. "I highly doubt it," he responded. "She doesn't seem to be the right age."

A curious expression flickered across Gonzalez's face.

The right age for what? Gonzalez wondered briefly before refocusing on her task.

Harris removed another clip from a different machine before instructing them, "Enough gawking. We have work to do. Let's focus on securing the doors."

The others snapped out of their daze and joined in. Harris split them into teams, and they set off down the various corridors, armed with chains and carabiner clips, each taking a different door to secure. The engineer, Mister Schwartz, and Private Gonzalez took the corridor to the left of the elevators, while Doctor Palmer and Private Jackson headed toward the far end past Professor Ford's office. Harris and Private Collier were left with the task of securing the corridor that ran along the back end of the facility.

***

Schwartz carefully threaded the thick chain through the push bars of the double doors, taking extra care to make sure it was pulled tightly with each pass. The metal links jingled and clinked softly as they dangled from his fingers, creating an eerie melody in the otherwise quiet room.

As he worked, Gonzalez stood beside him, her thumb plucking at the spring-loaded pin of a carabiner clip as she watched Schwartz secure the door.

Suddenly, he spoke up. "I saw your face," he said to Gonzalez, his voice quiet and serious.

Confused, she turned to face him. "What?"

"When the lieutenant mentioned that the girl in the gym couldn't be like him because she didn't look old enough," he clarified.

Gonzalez scoffed. "She doesn't seem to be the right age, is what he said," she corrected him. "What the hell does that even mean?"

"I don't know," Schwartz admitted, threading another loop of chain through the push bars. "How long have you known him?"

She shrugged. "A couple of years," she replied. "We did a few humanitarian missions in Europe and Africa together. There was this one where we were under fire from some militia group trying to steal supplies for a medical unit. Fucking horrible."

"Were you hit or something?" Schwartz asked.

"No." Gonzalez shook her head. "Luckily, those idiots didn't know how to use their assault rifles properly. They took off and, after twenty-four hours, we were pulled back to base. But when we got back, we found out that the militia had returned and wiped out the remaining med unit and their patients and taken everything." She cursed in frustration. "If we had stayed until they evacuated everyone…"

Giving her a moment to collect herself, Schwartz continued threading the chain through the door, sensing that she might be ready to talk more.

"So," he began again as he tugged on the chain once more. "You don't really talk to him about anything personal?"

Gonzalez shook her head. "I wouldn't say that," she answered. "But he never really talks about anything outside of the mission. He's like a machine. When we're on the job, it's all he cares about."

"I see." Schwartz nodded, reaching out his hand for the carabiner from Gonzalez. She placed it in his grasp, and he expertly looped it through two chain links.

He pushed against the push bars with force, testing their strength. The chain was tightly wrapped around the locking mechanism, making it nearly impossible for the doors to budge. The room was now secure, at least as secure as it could ever be. As he stood back to survey his work, Schwartz felt a sense of unease about the strange and mysterious lieutenant.

"Excellent work," Gonzalez praised, her voice echoing softly down the lengthy corridor as they made their way toward the dining area. She glanced at Schwartz with a quizzical expression. "Why all the interest in the L-T? Have you got a hard-on for him?"

The engineer chuckled, his eyes sparkling.

"No, not quite," he replied with a smile. "He's an enigma, a puzzle waiting to be solved. And I do enjoy solving puzzles, but every time I think I'm getting close to figuring out Lieutenant Harris, another layer of mystery presents itself."

Schwartz continued; his curiosity piqued. "Who is he really? Where did he come from? Is he a human or a machine?"

Gonzalez shook her head, her lips curved into a small smile. "I don't think he's a machine. He's *like* one."

"How can you be certain?" Schwartz countered; his playful tone evident.

"Well," she answered with a cheeky grin, thinking back to their intimate moments together. "I've…ah…seen him working out in the base's gym. A machine wouldn't exhaust themselves like he does when he pushes himself."

"He could be putting on a show," Schwartz suggested, his smile widening.

"Maybe," Gonzalez conceded, joining in on the playful banter. "But it's a damn good show."

"Private Gonzalez!" Schwartz exclaimed, mock surprise evident in his tone. "And here I thought you were an innocent, devout Catholic girl."

"You got the Catholic part right," she said, and laughed.

A distinct voice resonating along the walls of the corridor interrupted their light-hearted conversation, growing louder as they approached the dining area.

"That sounds like Professor Ford," Gonzalez noted.

"I believe so," Schwartz confirmed, unable to see into the room from their current location.

"The lock down is only temporary," Ford's voice boomed through the corridor. "The doors are secured for your safety."

"Safety from what?" a voice interjected.

There was a pause as Ford presumably searched for the right words to explain the situation.

"And why are there armed military personnel here?" another voice chimed in.

"Is it because they brought something dangerous with them?" a third person speculated.

After a moment, Ford spoke again. "It's difficult to explain. But it appears that the maintenance crew in the cavern above us have been compromised by something. Perhaps a kind of pathogen."

"A pathogen?" someone questioned as Gonzalez and Schwartz finally entered the dining area. Roughly one hundred people had gathered around tables, including kitchen staff and other personnel. Ford stood at the edge of the room, close to his office, with Deputy Secretary Tinsley and Colonel Powers nearby for support. "We should send a medical team up there to assess the situation," the man suggested urgently.

Ford nodded in agreement. "We should, but we can't."

Confusion and worry spread among the group.

"What do you mean 'can't'?" the man pressed for clarification.

Ford's expression became troubled.

Tinsley stepped forward, placing a reassuring hand on his arm before addressing the crowd.

"I'm Deputy Secretary Sally Tinsley acting for UNIDO," she announced.

"We know," a woman responded, her voice trembling slightly.

Tinsley got straight to the point.

"We can't send a team up to the surface and we can't let the people up there inside the other levels of this facility," she stated gravely. "The pathogen appears to have caused a metamorphosis to all infected; a physical transformation as well as demonstration of aggression resulting in violent behavior."

A murmur swept through the room as everyone processed this unsettling information.

Movement near the professor's office caught Schwartz's eye. He saw Harris and Collier standing by the door, their expressions grave. Suddenly, Hope emerged from the doorway, her normally vibrant face now drained of color.

"There have been fatalities," Tinsley continued, her voice heavy with dread. "And it appears the pathogen enables the deceased to remain animated."

"Fucking zombies?" someone shouted incredulously, causing sudden murmurs to fill the area.

"Bullshit!" another exclaimed.

At that moment, Hope moved closer to Tinsley and whispered urgently in her ear. Schwartz noted the look of fear spreading across Tinsley's features as the two women engaged in a hushed discussion.

"Something's happening," he said quietly to the young soldier next to him.

"I noticed," Gonzalez replied in an equally hushed tone. "I think we should go inside that office and find out what exactly."

"I agree." Schwartz stepped forward cautiously and noticed Private Teresa Jackson and Doctor Palmer emerging from the corridor that ran past the professor's office.

Meanwhile, the rest of the group continued to stir and mutter among themselves as Tinsley spoke quietly to Colonel Powers and Professor Ford. The tension in the room was thick with fear and confusion as they all awaited further instructions.

Finally, Professor Ford broke the awkward silence.

"Okay," he called out, holding up his hands to signal their attention. "You can believe or not believe what we tell you. I can't convince you, except I will say I intend to be transparent throughout all of this. I'm not going to speculate as to why this is happening, only that I can assure you it is. The doors remain secured shut. Please, don't open them. The elevators to the surface are currently disabled, and I'm about to shut them down completely."

A sense of panic began to spread through the group as they realized their confinement on this level.

"It appears this... whatever it is... may have spread to the level beneath us," Ford continued, his expression grim. "You are hereby confined to this level only until further notice. I will keep you informed, but there isn't more I can tell you right now."

With a swift pivot, Ford's boots scuffed against the floor as he turned to make his way back to his office. The tense murmurs of the crowd followed him; voices laced with concern.

"How did the pathogen manage to infiltrate the lower levels?" one voice called out, loud and accusatory.

Ford paused, turning back to face the crowd, taking in a deep breath before responding. "I wish I knew," he replied. "The news has only just reached my ears."

A wave of unease washed over him at the thought of a potentially deadly pathogen making its way through their facility undetected.

A young woman's voice rang out in a shrill cry, sharp and urgent. "There are people working down there," she called. "We can't just leave them there."

Ford, the man in charge, nodded. "I'm about to investigate the matter further," he assured her. "I'll inform the company of our situation and wait for advice. As soon as I know something, I'll share it with all of you." His words were calm, but his expression was tense.

He waited for a moment, expecting another comment. Just as he started toward his office, another voice called out from the group.

"Do you think this is related to the incident?" they asked. "The one that killed Doctor Caldwell?"

Ford's lip quivered, and a lump formed in his throat at the mention of their colleague's death.

With tears forming in his eyes, he prepared to answer.

"I can't speculate on such matters," he managed before his emotions got the better of him, forcing him to turn away to cross the room.

Schwartz and Gonzalez stepped into the office and positioned themselves against the wall by the door. Others continued to gather inside, casting worried looks at the security feed displayed on the large screen on the wall. It showed the maintenance level, where the shuttle waited near the giant iron doors, shutting out the world beyond. A small crowd of infected personnel surrounded the aircraft, their movements jerky and erratic.

Professor Ford, the last to enter, closed the door behind him and moved to his desk with heavy steps.

"So," Palmer started. "I think Private Jackson and I missed something. What's going on?"

Hope shook her head slowly, her face pale with fear. "It's worse than we first thought," she replied, her voice trembling. "Much worse."

Chapter Thirteen

"Worse?" Palmer inquired, his eyes scanning the young assistant with curiosity.

Hope's face was grave as she explained, "Whatever is affecting the top level seems to have spread to other sections of the facility. I started cycling through the cameras placed throughout this floor and the lower levels and... well, it's probably best to just show you." She leaned over Professor Ford's desk, her hand hovering over the keypad. "May I?"

"Of course," Ford replied, gesturing with a wave of his hand toward the keypad.

But before Hope could press any buttons, Gonzalez interjected, drawing all eyes to her. "Wait. Aren't we going to discuss what's on the monitor right now?"

"What?" Collier asked, turning to look at the screen.

"We're missing quite a few people in this picture," Colonel Powers observed.

Hope nodded grimly. "That's why I started cycling through the cameras—to see where they've gone."

"They're not on the maintenance level?" questioned Palmer.

Hope lifted the keypad and pressed a button. The image on the monitor shifted to another angle of the maintenance level, revealing the pod-like structures that served as living quarters for personnel.

"I looked at this image for some time," she told them. "We couldn't see anyone or any movement."

"They may have retreated into the buildings," Jackson suggested.

"No," Hope replied, pressing another button on the keypad. The display changed once again, now showing an empty metal stairwell rising through a wide concrete tube with a line of lights running along its uppermost point, like a glowing spine. "This is the emergency escape passage nearest to the shuttle's position, on the eastern side of the facility."

She pressed a key on the pad bearing a > symbol and the image flickered to show an almost identical vista—only this time, there were clusters of orange-clad bodies making their way steadily down the stairs.

"This view is from ten meters further down the same emergency passage," Hope stated, her voice tight with tension.

"Jesus," Schwartz breathed, his face pale.

Powers quickly lifted the radio from his belt. "Captain?" he called into the device, his expression growing more and more tense with each passing moment. "Captain Moreau?"

The radio crackled.

"Sir?" she replied, her voice soft and shaky. "I'm here."

A look of relief washed over Powers' face, his tense shoulders relaxing slightly.

"Are you okay?" he asked, concern clear in his voice. "How are you holding up?"

"Fine as can be, sir," Moreau answered, trying to sound calm. "Just a bit shaken up."

"Good," the colonel said, running a hand through his hair. "We were getting worried. Several of your friends are using the stairs to make their way down to us."

"I apologize, sir," the captain stated, with a hint of regret in her tone. "I should have been more vigilant and kept watch."

Powers shook his head. "No, Captain. Your safety is top priority. Stay low and hidden, and please inform me if you have any updates."

"Yes, sir," she responded.

"And Captain?"

"Sir?"

"Try using the shuttle's radio to contact the UN base in Quebec," he suggested.

"I've been trying, sir," she informed him. "But I think the cavern doors are blocking the signal."

"Understood," he said, before focusing on the monitor again. "Keep doing what you're doing. We will stay in touch."

Powers returned the radio to his belt and directed his attention back to the screen.

"So, they're making their way toward us," Harris interjected, turning to Hope for information. "The professor mentioned this spreading to lower levels. What do we know about the situation there?"

Hope gave them a serious look.

"All I can say is to be prepared," she warned before pressing a button on the control panel. The display changed to show a corridor outside the elevators on the level directly below theirs. It angled slightly to the left, giving a view of the passage leading toward the medical laboratory.

One of the lights above an open office door, a short distance from the camera, flickered erratically. The rectangular fixture dangled from its wires at one end, as if violently torn away from the ceiling.

Schwartz leaned forward and pointed toward the floor near the office door on the monitor.

"Is that blood?" he asked, his voice filled with dread.

A thin trail of red liquid streaked through the doorway and into the corridor, disappearing into the distance.

"What in God's name!" Collier exclaimed, shaking his head in disbelief.

"There's more," Hope informed them gravely.

She pressed the > button, changing the image to another passage lined with doors on either side. Blood trails and handprints splattered and stained the walls, bringing gasps from those viewing it for the first time. The scene was chaotic and gruesome, a stark contrast to the controlled and sterile environment they saw the previous day.

"This is the corridor that runs along the southern edge of the lower level," Hope explained.

"Where is everyone?" Palmer asked, his voice trembling. "What about the child? Can we see the medical facility on this thing?"

"We're getting there, Doctor," the young assistant assured him, pressing the button again. The display flickered to an intersection with a sign protruding from the ceiling, indicating the directions to various tech labs and the med lab. The floor and walls were awash in glistening blood that appeared to streak and smudge further down the passage, as if pushed toward the direction of the medical laboratory.

Hope pressed the button again.

The screen displayed the exterior of the med lab door.

A disturbing scene filled the monitor.

Hope turned away from the screen, unable to look at it any longer.

Blood covered every inch of the floor, creating a sickening carpet of red. Handprints and smears ran up and along the walls, intensifying as they drew closer and closer to the wide-open med lab doors.

Lying scattered on the floor and propped up against the walls were several bodies, their limbs twisted in unnatural positions. Their clothes and heads were drenched in blood, making it difficult to discern who they were.

"Oh, my God," Tinsley gasped, covering her mouth with her hand. "What is she doing?"

Hope raised her head to look at the screen.

A young woman stood before the door. Hope shook her head in disbelief.

"No," she muttered. "Not again."

On the display, the young woman raised her right hand, brandishing a pair of scissors.

"Did you see this woman before?" Harris asked. "Is she responsible for this?"

"No," Hope managed to say, her words directed more toward the young woman on the screen than to the lieutenant.

With a tremendous thrust, the young woman buried the blade of the scissors into her own abdomen.

Tinsley let out a short, sudden shriek.

"Fuck!" Gonzalez blurted out.

The young woman slid the blade out of the wound slowly, raising the scissors above her head as a thick trail of dark blood ran down her left leg to the floor.

With another thrust, the scissors plunged into her stomach again and again.

"Oh, my God!" Palmer cried out.

"No." Hope shook her head and closed her eyes in anguish.

Harris moved in closer to the monitor, scrutinizing every detail of the horrific event.

"I can't watch." Schwartz turned away.

The young woman continued to stab herself over and over again, leaving everyone in the room shaken and horrified.

Ford's face scrunched up in disgust and distress. "I think I'm going to be sick."

The lieutenant's eyes narrowed as he observed the woman on the screen. "She's not responding," he stated, his tone grim.

"What?" Powers asked, turning away from the screen to look at the others.

"She doesn't appear to feel any pain," Harris explained, his voice tinged with unease. "It almost looks as though she's analyzing, experimenting."

"What are you talking about?" Private Jackson asked, giving the lieutenant a perplexed stare. "The fucking girl is killing herself."

Harris shook his head. "I'm not sure about that. She might already be..."

The woman opened the scissors, revealing a glinting blade, before inserting it back into the wound on her body. With swift, precise movements, she carved a deep line into her flesh, sawing back and forth like a butcher's knife.

"Nope," Collier muttered, averting his gaze to stare at the wall instead. "Nope."

"Perhaps she's in a trance," Harris speculated. "Or more likely, infected like the maintenance crew."

"She doesn't have any squid bits like the others," Collier replied, briefly turning to face Harris before quickly looking away again as the woman's innards splattered onto the floor. "Fucking hell!"

The woman fell to her knees, dropping the scissors beside her. She raised her hands toward the ceiling, holding them there for a moment before collapsing onto her side.

"What was that?" questioned Jackson, still watching in morbid fascination. "With her hands up and on her knees? It almost looked like she was praying or something."

Hope's eyes darted around the room nervously.

"The one I saw before did that too," she whispered shakily. Her whole body trembled, causing the keypad in her hands to rattle softly.

Harris reached over and gently took the keypad from her grasp.

"Do I press this button for the interior of the med lab?" he asked, pointing to the > symbol.

"No," Hope replied, her voice trembling. "The med lab is on a different loop. You need to press F6."

He did as she instructed, and the image changed back to the view outside of the elevator.

"I'm sorry," Hope apologized, her voice filled with self-reproach. "Try F7. I'm so sorry."

"It's okay, Miss Aguilar," the lieutenant reassured her, pressing the button. "That was a lot to handle." The screen flickered to show the interior of the medical facility, revealing more bodies scattered across the floor in violent deaths, like discarded toys in a child's playroom.

Discarded toys, thought Hope bitterly as Harris pressed the > button once again.

The new view showed hospital beds pushed at odd angles, some even lying on their sides. More bodies slumped over equipment, piled on top of each other in a chaotic and gruesome display.

"Where's the boy?" Palmer asked, bringing his attention back to the screen. Ford tensed up in his seat, visibly disturbed.

With a flick of his fingers, Harris changed the view on the monitor once more. The screen now displayed a child's bedroom, the camera angle capturing the scene from high in the corner of the room. In the center of the view was a crisp, clean, white bed, surrounded by mutilated bodies arranged in a circle with their hands outstretched toward the bed. But on the bed itself, untouched and seemingly safe and sound, sat a young boy cross-legged, engrossed in reading a picture book.

"What the fuck is going on here?" Gonzalez cried, her eyes wide with shock.

Doctor Palmer pointed to the screen as he turned to face Colonel Powers. "We need to get him out of there," he said urgently. "He's in danger, and we need to bring him to safety." He scanned the room for support, his gaze landing on Tinsley before shifting to Hope.

"I don't think that's a good idea," Schwartz muttered, barely audible. He shook his head slowly.

"What?" The doctor locked eyes with the engineer.

"I said, I don't think that's a good idea," Schwartz repeated.

Palmer looked taken aback. "That's a child," he retorted.

Ford squirmed in his seat. "Yes," he agreed. "But it's a child who, by all laws of nature, should be a three-week-old baby in a crib or something, wearing a diaper and oblivious to its surroundings." He gestured toward the image on the screen. "Yet here we see a boy calmly reading a damn book in the middle of that mess."

"Exactly," Gonzalez said. "He looks completely at ease down there." She winced as her gaze shifted from the boy to the corpses littering the floor. "And can we please change this fucking channel?"

Harris handed the keypad back to Hope, who fumbled it in her shaking hands before managing to press a button and switch the view to the shuttle on the upper level.

"Thank you." Gonzalez sighed.

Colonel Powers watched intently as the screen now showed a few infected creatures standing around the aircraft.

"I agree with the doctor," he said gravely. "The boy may seem calm, but he likely doesn't understand the danger he's in." Powers turned to face Schwartz. "As you said, he's essentially a three-week-old infant. He might even think"— he gestured at the screen— "what's happening down there is perfectly normal."

"The boy could hold a crucial role in this puzzle," Harris suggested.

All eyes turned to the lieutenant; their gazes fixed on him as he remained focused on the screen.

Jackson tilted her head, attempting to catch a glimpse of his emotions, but as usual, his face remained stoic and unreadable.

"What do you mean?" she asked.

Harris turned his head toward her briefly before returning his attention to the screen.

"None of the deceased appeared to be attacking him," he explained. "In fact, they seemed to have arranged themselves as if worshiping or as an offering to him."

"An offering?" Professor Ford interjected.

"But why?" Deputy Secretary Tinsley added.

"I am unsure," Harris replied. "But all those infected above on the surface attacked indiscriminately, leaving no one untouched."

"Except for Captain Moreau," Hope reminded them.

"She managed to escape," Harris confirmed, nodding toward the monitor. "They didn't let her go. But look. They have left sentries waiting for her. It seems they have no intention of letting her live."

"The individuals downstairs seem to have taken their own lives," Harris continued. "It is possible they were under some sort of outside control."

Powers furrowed his brow in confusion.

"Control?" he questioned.

"Like a puppet master?" Private Collier suggested. "What do they call those?"

"Puppeteers, tonto," Gonzalez corrected him in a hushed tone.

"No, the ones with strings," Collier corrected himself once again.

"Cierra la puta boca," she hissed. *Shut the fuck up.*

Collier held his hands up in surrender.

Doctor Palmer's hands were shaking as he asked, "What could have caused this?"

Harris shook his head. If his own nerves were on edge, he didn't show it. "I'm not sure. But has anyone seen Corporal Garrett?" He turned to face them; the extra pulse rifle still slung over his shoulder along with his own weapon. "The last I saw him; he was headed to the med lab with Mister Wade."

Ford sat up straight in his chair and tilted his head inquisitively.

"Are you suggesting that static electricity is responsible for this?" the professor questioned.

"It's a possibility," Harris replied. "But perhaps it's something more...vestigial."

"Vestigial?" Ford studied the monitor intently. "As in something left over from the previous incident?"

"I don't know," Harris admitted, pacing the room, stopping by the door. "But we have a three-week-old infant who looks like a three- or four-year-old child, numerous infected personnel who have mutated—" He pointed to the screen displaying orange-clad figures with tentacle-like appendages sprouting from their bodies. "Many of them are currently making their way down the stairwell toward us. And now, a mass suicide on the lower level with a center point in the med lab. All of this followed an incident that occurred in your Energy Generation Chamber."

Harris frowned as he added, "I saw something in that footage. Something alive. I can't explain it, but my guess is that all of this has something to do with whatever that thing is."

Hope furrowed her brow, trying to make sense of the situation. "But the incident was weeks ago. Why is this happening now?"

Harris let out a heavy sigh, the only evidence of his inner turmoil. "I think we might have triggered this into action."

The group exchanged confused looks, all silently asking the same question: *What does he mean?*

Harris took a deep breath before explaining, "If I hadn't made the request to investigate the site of the incident, and if we hadn't gone down there, I don't believe we would be in this situation. This happened because, since the incident, no one else has been back in the Energy Generation Chamber until yesterday. It's our fault. It's *my* fault."

Colonel Powers interrupted with a stern voice. "I understand your concerns, Harris. But our top priority right now is getting the boy out of harm's way. You can berate yourself later."

"Sir?" Gonzalez interjected.

The colonel raised his hand, signaling for her to listen.

Powers' voice, laced with authority, cut through the tense air. "You and Harris," he barked out, pointing to two soldiers, "are hereby assigned personal detail to Deputy Secretary Tinsley and her assistant." His gaze then rested on Jackson and Collier. "The two of you will accompany me to the lower level to retrieve the boy. I need you in hazmat suits in five minutes." He turned to Harris; his expression grim. "Those things are coming down the eastern stairwell. Right?"

Harris stood at attention and replied crisply, "Yes, sir."

"Then we'll take the western," declared the colonel, his tone resolute. "Keep the elevators shut down and secure the door after we've entered the stairwell."

The lieutenant nodded; his jaw clenched.

"Sir?" Jackson said. "The med lab is all the way across the other side from the western stairs. We need to pass through all that...mess we just saw."

Powers' face hardened as he took in her words. "We have a job to do, Private Jackson," he said. "Suit up."

***

Harris dangled the chain, looped a few times around his left hand, the carabiner attached to a link near the floor. He pushed the release bars, opening the heavy emergency doors into the dimly lit passage. The creak of metal echoed through the air as he stepped forward, his right hand gripping an assault rifle tightly as he scanned for any signs of danger.

Silence greeted him, broken only by the distant sound of murmuring voices and shuffling feet from behind him, in the corridors of Level A. With a nod to the three soldiers behind him, all dressed in white protective suits and armed with AR90-D pulse rifles, Harris signaled that it was safe to proceed.

"Clear," Harris announced, his voice low but firm.

Moving with caution and precision, they approached the open doors and entered the stairwell.

Their steps were quiet but purposeful, each one trained for moments like this. They moved quickly but cautiously, their weapons at the ready.

"Close and secure the door behind us, Lieutenant," he ordered, as he continued with his two escorts.

"Understood," Harris replied crisply, adrenaline pumping through his veins as Teresa Jackson and Roland Collier slipped past him and headed down the stairwell.

"Lucky bastard," Jackson muttered under her breath as she passed by Harris.

"We'll be monitoring your progress," he reminded them before turning back to close and secure the door behind them.

Using the chain to loop through the bars, Harris carefully secured the door before checking it multiple times to ensure it wouldn't budge. Satisfied with his work, he jogged back down the corridor toward Professor Ford's office.

As he neared the office, Harris slowed his pace and surveyed the dining area where clusters of people still lingered after the professor's speech. Some of them looked up at him with fear or disgust in their eyes before quickly diverting their gazes. He couldn't blame them—his pulse rifle was a powerful and intimidating weapon and the presence of the UN delegation correlating with everything suddenly in upheaval didn't help with public relations either.

Glancing up at the ceiling, Harris made note of all the security cameras trained on the open room. He then turned his attention to the other cameras he had passed on his way down the passage, mentally mapping out their locations.

"All clear to the lower-level doors, Lieutenant," Gonzalez reported from her seat in Professor Ford's high-backed chair, her attention glued to the large, mounted screen on the wall that displayed the live feed from the cameras. The images were sharp and clear, showing every detail of the facility's interior. Harris peered over her shoulder and saw the familiar figures of Colonel Powers, Jackson and Collier slowly descending, their movements cautious and deliberate. Collier had his pulse rifle trained upwards as he took each step, a clear display of his dedication to protecting their important guests.

"Let them know," Harris ordered, his voice confident and commanding. He surveyed the rest of the room, taking in Deputy Secretary Sally Tinsley and her assistant Hope Aguilar sitting side-by-side on a small two-seated sofa. Doctor Isaac Palmer, Glen Schwartz, and Professor Allen Ford occupied other chairs scattered around the room. All of them had their eyes fixed on the monitor, fully engrossed in the live footage of their team's progress. Aguilar clutched a tablet device close to her chest, holding it tightly as if for comfort.

"You're all clear to the next level, Colonel," Gonzalez relayed into the radio with precision.

On the screen, Powers plucked the radio from his belt with practiced ease.

"Received, Private," he replied, before reattaching the device to his belt. They watched as he gestured with his hands and exchanged words with his team. Collier turned, now facing down the stairwell. The group picked up their pace and continued their descent.

"Professor Ford?" Harris spoke up. The professor jumped slightly in his seat, brought out of his intense focus on the screen.

"Yes," he answered, turning from the monitor to give Harris his full attention.

"There are multiple cameras throughout this facility," said Harris, gesturing toward the door. "Is it possible to view feeds from different cameras at once?"

Ford furrowed his brow in concentration. "I believe so. I have a desktop monitor that displays all the cameras in specific zones, but I'm not sure if it can be shown on this screen." He gestured to the wall-mounted display unit.

"Why would you want to do that when we have a team currently engaged in... what was it again?" Doctor Palmer asked with interest.

"An operation," Schwartz chimed in, completing the doctor's inquiry.

"I don't want to display multiple feeds on this monitor," Harris clarified. "I want something more portable, like the device Miss Aguilar has, or the one you lent me earlier." He glanced at Ford.

"That tablet doesn't have access to the CCTV network," the professor explained. "It's only set up for carrying documents and data storage."

Hope looked at Harris curiously. "You need my device?"

"Only if it can be used for what I'm enquiring about," Harris replied. He turned back to Ford. "Can it be done?"

Ford shrugged and shook his head uncertainly. "I'm not sure. I'm not very knowledgeable about that sort of technology. The security personnel or computer tech guys might have some suggestions, but—"

"Where can I find the security personnel?" Harris interrupted.

"They're downstairs," Schwartz said. "The security office is right in the center of the lower level. It's got a room with a wall of monitors, each one displaying footage from a different camera in the facility. They might have been able to link it to a tablet device."

"That must be a lot of monitors," Gonzalez remarked.

"One hundred and fifty, to be exact," Schwartz confirmed. "But only one hundred and thirty-six are operational. They still need to hook up more in the dining area and in the cinema—"

"There's a cinema?" Palmer interjected.

"Yes," the engineer said. "It's located down the same corridor as the rec room, a small room with around a hundred seats. The other two monitors are backups in case of technical malfunctions."

Tinsley's eyes widened in surprise and admiration at Schwartz's vast knowledge of the facility.

"How did you come to know all of this?" she asked, her curiosity piqued.

"I read through the schematics, plans, and reports before we arrived," he explained. "I also spoke with some of the personnel here, asking questions about operational procedures, equipment, and structural functionality."

Tinsley raised an eyebrow at him, impressed by his thoroughness.

"I came prepared to do my job," he continued, shrugging nonchalantly as he turned his attention back to the large display screen. "And I bet if you go out there, you can find a technician or security guard off their shift who could give us even more information. There were a lot of people out there having breakfast earlier."

"That's right," agreed Ford. "There should be several security and computer technicians stationed here. I can make an announcement for them to come to us."

Harris nodded gratefully. "I would appreciate that, Professor."

Ford rose from his chair and made his way over to stand next to Gonzalez.

"Sorry, Miss Gonzalez," he apologized, maneuvering around her to reach the phone panel sitting on his desk.

"Private," she corrected him automatically as she switched the feed on the monitor to show a camera further down in the stairwell. The image showed three soldiers steadily making their way down the stairs.

"Of course," Ford murmured, before pressing a button on the panel. "Attention," he announced, his voice echoing through speakers placed throughout the facility. "This is Professor Ford. Could I have any available security personnel and computer technicians report to my office? Any available security personnel and computer technicians, please come to my office immediately. Thank you."

He pressed a red button on the phone panel.

Tinsley swiveled in her seat to face Harris.

"Why do you want to view multiple cameras, Lieutenant?" she inquired.

"We have one of our team members trapped above us," he explained. "And we also have a large group of infected individuals making their way down the eastern stairwell. I want to keep an eye on their progress in case we need to divert resources elsewhere. And if either Private Gonzalez or I need to leave this room, it would be helpful to have access to camera feeds on a portable device."

Tinsley nodded in understanding. "That is a wise precaution."

Gonzalez clicked on another screen, displaying the colonel and two privates at the top of the stairs, their pulse rifles trained forward and ready for any potential threats. Above the emergency doors with large, stenciled letters on the surface spelt out the words:

LEVEL-B.

EMERGENCY DOORS

CAUTION: DOORS OPEN INTO STAIRWELL

The static of the radio crackled through the tense silence, as Colonel Powers announced their arrival.

"We're here," he said, his voice sharp and determined.

"We got you, sir," Gonzalez replied.

Powers placed his hand on the cold metal handle. Jackson and Collier positioned themselves on either side of him, their weapons trained on the door.

"Here we go," Powers declared.

Hope leaned forward in her seat, her muscles coiled like a spring, her tablet clutched tightly to her chest like a lifeline.

With agonizing slowness, Colonel Powers turned the knob. The locking mechanism clicked loudly, releasing the door. Slowly, the colonel pulled the doors open, revealing what lay beyond with a creak that sounded deafening in the stillness of the moment.

CHAPTER FOURTEEN

The passage loomed ahead, enveloped in darkness; except for small, circular lights embedded into the ceiling, spaced several meters apart. Their dim glow barely illuminated the surroundings, creating an eerie atmosphere.

"What the fuck?" Jackson's voice came over the radio as Colonel Powers spoke.

"Do you see this, Gonzalez?" he asked.

"Yes, sir," she replied, her voice tinged with uncertainty. "Looks as though someone turned off the power down there."

"Seems so," the colonel agreed. "I'm setting the radio to continuous two-way feed. Suggesting you and Harris do the same."

"Yes, sir," Gonzalez responded, flipping a small switch next to the push-to-talk button on her radio. Doctor Palmer looked at Harris with confusion as he casually maneuvered a similar switch on his own radio attached to his belt.

"It allows constant incoming and outgoing feed over the radios," the lieutenant explained, noticing the doctor's questioning gaze. "Useful for when your hands are full. It would be even better if we had wireless headsets linked to each device to avoid feedback and minimize unnecessary noise."

"And you don't have those?" Tinsley asked incredulously.

"Didn't think we'd need them on this detail," Gonzalez admitted. "Just a quick overnighter babysitting a delegation."

Hope caught sight of movement behind Harris and saw a group of four people approaching from the dining area. Harris turned in response to their arrival, addressing them with a professional demeanor.

"May I be of assistance?" he asked politely.

One of them, a young man with a thin build and long hair hanging over his collar, stepped forward. He wore a loose button-up checkered shirt and tight slacks, and his bespectacled face bore a look of concern. An identification badge affixed to his chest pocket showed a small headshot photograph of the man, along with his name and occupation.

Alonzo Ferengi

Computer Technician

Level B: Section 15-D

Security Clearance: Alpha 09

"Professor Ford called for us," Ferengi announced, his outstretched hand encompassing the others in his company; two young males and one female, all appearing fresh out of high school with their youthful features and casual attire. Harris noticed the identity badges pinned to their chests; Jahangir Sharma and Jiahao Ling had the same occupation, work location, and security clearance as Ferengi. They dressed much more casually than their colleague, sporting cargo pants and long-sleeved shirts adorned with the logos of heavy metal bands. The only female among them was someone Harris recognized from the gym; her identification badge clipped to the front pocket of her jeans.

Sandra Martin

Security Officer

Level B: Section 6B

Security Clearance: Alpha 02

"They're computer technicians," she clarified. "I'm with security."

"I did call," Ford confirmed, rising from his seat to approach them. "Lieutenant Harris has a request that I believe you may be able to assist with."

"We're happy to help," Ferengi replied eagerly.

Harris turned to face Hope and extended his hand toward her.

"Miss Aguilar, may I have your device?" he asked courteously.

Hope glanced at Tinsley for permission before nodding and handing over the tablet to Harris.

"Thank you," he said graciously, before turning to address the four newcomers at the door. "I need access to the security feed from all cameras on this device. Currently, we can view footage from Professor Ford's desktop computer, but it would be beneficial for us to have mobile access throughout the facility."

"We can make that happen," Sharma chimed in, reaching for the device in Harris' hands. "Jiahao and I are responsible for setting up all the tablets used by security personnel for this exact purpose. We even developed an app for it – a small tile on the screen that works seamlessly."

"Why do you need access to the security feed?" Sandra Martin inquired, her tone suspicious.

Harris looked to Ford, then at Tinsley for approval before speaking.

"Clear ahead. Proceed with caution," Gonzalez's voice echoed through the radio attached to Harris' hip.

Martin peered over Harris' shoulder and toward the screen on the wall. The dimly lit corridors of the lower level were visible.

"What's happening?" she pressed.

Tinsley exchanged a nod with Harris before responding, "They need to know."

"Agreed," Colonel Powers' voice affirmed through the radio.

Harris turned back to face the group of four.

"We have a large number of infected approaching from the upper level," he began, scanning the faces of those gathered. "That's why we secured the doors with equipment from the gym and why the elevators are no longer functional. Some infected are still guarding our shuttle on the top level, where one of our personnel is trapped. It appears that most of the people downstairs are dead."

"The team you see on the screen is attempting to retrieve the child from the med lab," Harris added. "As far as we know, he is the only survivor."

Ferengi let out a tense breath at the sight of the carnage on the screen.

"Jesus," he muttered.

Martin pointed to a vending machine on the screen, its front all lit up to display snacks and drinks. "There are five machines like that down there, all hard-wired into the same network as the lights. If someone turned off the master switch for the lights, these machines should be off too."

"And where is this master switch?" Harris inquired.

"In section 6B, the security office," Martin replied. "Right in the center of Level B."

"Is there a chance anyone could still be alive down there?" Hope asked, her voice trembling.

"It's possible," Harris confirmed.

Private Collier's voice sounded over the radio, adding his own thoughts to the discussion. "But why would anyone turn off the lights? That makes no sense."

The group fell silent as they considered this question.

Finally, Colonel Powers spoke up. "I agree. We need to make a detour to the security office and investigate before continuing on to retrieve the boy."

"Understood," Harris acknowledged.

Martin took Hope's tablet from Sharma and turned it over, studying it briefly before looking up at the lieutenant.

"Is this device necessary?" she inquired. "By that I mean, does it need to be this particular device?"

Harris responded with a resigned nod. "Besides the one the professor has, it's the only one we have."

Martin extended the tablet toward Harris, who accepted it with a quizzical expression.

"Our tablets are usually kept in charging cases down there," Martin began. "The cases have cables so they can be plugged into any power socket for charging. Usually, they are stored overnight in a large container in the security office, allowing us to charge up to thirty devices at once. Each case holds five tablets, and we have nine cases in total."

"I fail to see how this is relevant to our current situation," Ford said impatiently.

"We have forty-five devices total," Sandra Martin continued calmly. "Nine charging cases. During the night shift when there are fewer security personnel on duty, we rotate the cases in the container. Two of them are used by the night crew, while those not on duty bring one case to their quarters to charge overnight, away from the others in case of an emergency situation. Fire was the initial thought we considered. Not something like this."

"So, you have five fully charged devices in your quarters?" Harris clarified.

"Yes, and they all have the app for accessing the security feed loaded on them."

The lieutenant smiled appreciatively. "May I have one?" he asked, reaching behind to hand the tablet back to Hope.

"You can have all of them," Martin replied, turning to head toward her quarters to retrieve them.

Harris called out to her before she could leave. "Miss Martin," he said, taking the pulse rifle from Garrett's grasp. "Do you have much weapons training?"

Hope watched uneasily as the lieutenant and security officer exchanged words, feeling a twinge of jealousy stirring inside her.

"A bit," Martin answered cautiously. "I've completed some basic handgun awareness courses required for security accreditation. But nothing that covers the type of weapons you're carrying."

Harris handed the spare pulse rifle over to her.

"Thank you, gentlemen," Professor Ford said, addressing the three computer technicians who had been standing by. "It seems we may not need your services at the moment."

With a nod and a smile, the three technicians exited the room, leaving Ford to take his seat once again. Hope's gaze lingered on them for a moment before returning to the two remaining by the door.

"Well, that was a fucking waste," Ferengi uttered to the other two computer technicians as they moved away, causing Sandra Martin to smirk momentarily.

"This will be a quick run through," Harris instructed Martin. "Sling it across your shoulders to start."

She followed his instructions, lifting the heavy rifle over her head and resting it on her left shoulder. The weight of the weapon pressed against her right ribcage as she adjusted her grip.

"Now, press the recoil pad against your shoulder," Harris said, demonstrating as he lifted his own rifle and aimed it at the door next to him.

Following suit, Martin pressed the recoil pad against her shoulder. "Doesn't seem like much," she commented.

"It's just for show," Harris explained. "This rifle doesn't have much kick when fired. It's not like a traditional gun that shoots bullets. This one discharges energy blasts in single, short, or automatic sequences."

He pointed to a small black switch on the side of the rifle, just above the pistol grip. "You can select your sequence here."

Martin nodded and looked at the switch. A tiny white dot and small writing indicated that the rifle was currently in SAFE mode.

"So, I just turn this?" she asked, pointing at the knob.

"Exactly," Harris confirmed with a nod.

"All clear ahead," Gonzalez announced.

"Received," Colonel Powers' voice came through the communication link.

The image on the screen shifted to another section of the corridor, but Hope kept her attention focused on Harris and Sandra Martin.

"If you find yourself in a situation where you need to use this weapon," Harris continued, "I'd recommend setting the sequence to short bursts. It enables thirty bolts to be fired in rapid succession. If you need more than thirty, you'll have to pull the trigger again. And if you set it to automatic, you can just hold down the trigger and it will continuously discharge thirty bolts per second until the charge is depleted."

"How much charge does it have?" Martin asked curiously.

"The rifle is fully charged and will last for seventy-two hours of continuous firing on automatic," Harris replied proudly.

"That's a long time," Martin commented, cocking her head in amazement. "What kind of damage does it do?"

"Fatal," Harris stated bluntly. "One bolt can kill. And even a short blast can cause serious tissue damage."

"It can basically turn an enemy into mush," Gonzalez chimed in with a hint of excitement.

"Private Gonzalez, stay focused," Colonel Powers snapped.

"Yes, sir," Gonzalez responded quickly.

Martin nodded; her gaze locked onto Harris as he continued his briefing. The low hum of the radio filled the room, punctuated by the occasional static crackle.

"And automatic?" Martin inquired.

"I put a big fucking hole in a brick wall once," Gonzalez boasted with pride.

"Private," Powers reprimanded over the radio.

"Sorry, sir," Gonzalez responded with an impish grin.

"A hole in a wall?" Martin raised a skeptical eyebrow.

"I was there," Harris confirmed. "It was only a training exercise, but it was impressive nonetheless."

"You? Impressed?" Hope blurted out, breaking the tension in the room. A chorus of chuckles and giggles erupted from Gonzalez and the security detail over the radio. Blushing furiously, she turned away and stared at the floor, hoping to disappear into it. "I said that out loud?" she whispered to herself.

"Yes, you did," Deputy Secretary Sally Tinsley replied with a kind smile.

Clutching her tablet tightly, Hope felt everyone's eyes on her.

"All clear," Gonzalez chimed in again.

Sandra Martin leaned forward to get a better look at the rifle in front of her. Her fingers traced along its sleek surface, and she tapped on a small window just below the muzzle.

"What's this?" she asked curiously.

"That's a torch," Harris explained, pointing to a button near the end of the hand guard. "Or a flashlight, if you prefer. It has multiple settings controlled by this button—one press turns it on, another adjusts the beam from wide to narrow, and so on."

The security officer flipped the rifle over in her hands, examining it closely as Harris finished his explanation. She nodded in understanding.

"I'll go and get those tablets now," Martin said as she lowered the rifle to her side.

"Thank you," Harris returned before she set off.

He moved to stand behind the sofa where Hope was sitting, his presence looming over her like a heavy weight. She felt his gaze on her, and every muscle in her body tensed up as she imagined him standing behind her, his piercing eyes drilling into the back of her head.

"I think they need to take the next right," Harris said casually. "If I read the floor plan correctly, the security office is along the intersecting corridor."

"If you read the floor plan correctly," Collier said tauntingly. "You know you read it correctly, asshole."

Gonzalez pressed a button on the keypad, causing the image on the wall display to change. The corridor appeared clear, except for something flickering in the distance and several darkened open doors on both sides of the passage.

"Hold position," Gonzalez said.

"Is that around the corner?" Schwartz asked eagerly, leaning forward in his seat.

"This is the intersecting corridor," Gonzalez clarified.

"What do you see?" Colonel Powers questioned.

"Hmm." Gonzalez squinted at the screen. Hope lifted her head to get a better look.

"It looks like some debris on the ground and a few open doorways further down," Harris reported. "Proceed with caution."

"Understood," Powers replied. "Proceeding."

The gathering was transfixed on the screen as the trio made their way toward the camera's view. Jackson and Collier held their weapons at the ready, scanning each open doorway they passed while Powers kept his rifle pointed forward, prepared for any potential threats.

Gonzalez switched the display to the next camera along the corridor, revealing a toppled vending machine with its contents strewn across the floor. The neon lights from the

SNACKS sign flickered sporadically, casting brief bursts of light across scattered packets of chips and chocolate bars.

Hope's sharp eye caught something on the screen, and she pointed it out to the others. "Wait," she said, gesturing toward the sign as it flickered again. "Did you see that?"

"Where?" Tinsley asked, squinting at the screen.

"Near the 'K'," Hope replied excitedly.

All eyes were now fixed on the sign, waiting for another flicker to catch a glimpse of what had piqued their curiosity before disappearing into darkness once again.

"It's blood," Harris announced after a moment. "Sir, it appears that there was some sort of a violent altercation in this area."

"Thank you, Lieutenant," Colonel Powers acknowledged. "Any signs of present hostiles?"

"Not that I can see," Harris reported. "But I suggest remaining vigilant as there are more open doors ahead."

"Understood," Powers said calmly. "Let's continue."

As the trio walked, Hope heard a faint clinking sound coming from her right. She glanced over at Professor Ford, who nervously chewed on his thumbnail while watching the soldiers on the screen.

Gonzalez changed the image again, revealing multiple open doorways leading into dark rooms. Blood smears and spatters covered every surface, painting a gruesome picture of what had occurred.

"That's the camera above the security office door," Professor Ford informed them.

"Can you rotate it?" Doctor Palmer asked eagerly. "Is there any way to get a view of the security office?"

"Angle it down," Schwartz added.

But Gonzalez shook her head, scanning the keypad for options. All eyes turned to Professor Ford, hoping he could provide a solution.

"I'm sorry, sir," Gonzalez finally announced. "I don't know how to adjust the angle."

"It's okay, Private," Powers reassured her. "It appears all the windows and doors have been smashed in, with glass scattered everywhere. And there's a lot of blood. It's hard to make out much else in the darkness."

"That's the main entryway," Professor Ford explained. "There should be a reception desk with a door right behind it."

"Yeah, I see it," Powers confirmed on screen. The glow of white light spilled onto the floor as the soldiers grouped beneath the camera, their weapons trained on an unseen space, lights from their torches illuminating the area. "Looks like another corridor back there."

"It doesn't extend too far," Professor Ford continued. "Just a few offices, the monitor room, an equipment storage room, and a holding cell."

"A holding cell?" Tinsley raised an eyebrow in surprise.

"Just a precaution," Professor Ford clarified. "It's quite a distance to the nearest authorities, so we keep it empty except for some tech equipment that hasn't been installed yet."

As Collier stepped into the room, his heavy boots crunched on broken glass, the sound echoing through their radio system. The passageway was dark and musty, with a faint smell of chemicals and blood lingering in the air. "Where is the junction box located, Professor?" he asked.

"It's in the back, at the end of the corridor," Ford responded.

Colonel Powers took charge, assigning roles to each member of the team. "Jackson, stay here and keep watch. Collier, take point. I'm right behind you."

Teresa Jackson aimed her rifle down the corridor, her light beam casting eerie shadows on the walls. As Powers disappeared from view, the sound of his footsteps on shattered glass crunched through the radio speaker.

"Stay alert," Harris reminded them.

Hope watched intently as the soldiers made their way through the dark hallway. She felt her heart racing, her chest tightening with each loud crunch under their boots. Her breath became short and shallow as tension filled the room.

Stay in there, Hope.

Suddenly, an explosive thud caused her to jump, and her stomach twisted in anxiety.

"What the fuck was that?" Gonzalez exclaimed.

"My boot hit the desk," Collier replied apologetically. "Sorry about that."

"Watch where you fucking go," Gonzalez scolded. "You scared the shit out of me."

Hope agreed with Gonzalez's sentiment. Her own fear had been heightened by Collier's misstep.

"Moving around the reception desk now," Powers reported over the radio, the sound of crunching glass resounding through the speakers. "Approaching the passageway."

CHAPTER FIFTEEN

The sharp sound of broken glass beneath her boots echoed through the silent corridor as Private Teresa Jackson slowly made her way forward. Gripping her weapon tightly, she scanned each open doorway with her flashlight, revealing overturned desks and chairs, broken framed photographs, and glistening bloodstains on the floors and walls.

"We're in the passageway." Colonel Powers' static-filled voice pierced through their communication devices.

"Copy." Gonzalez's response crackled in her ear.

"Check that door on the left," Powers barked at Collier.

As they pressed deeper into the unknown territory, Jackson stepped away from a shattered window and into the center of the corridor. Her flashlight flickered along the row of doorways on the opposite wall, casting eerie shadows that danced across her skin. A sudden sense of dread washed over her as she caught a glimpse, in the corner of her eye, of the fallen vending machine emitting sporadic flashes of light. The sight sent shivers down her spine, as if someone or something was watching her.

Panicking, she swung around and aimed her weapon toward where they had come from.

Nothing.

Just the toppled vending machine sending out its strange Morse code with packets of crisps and chocolate bars strewn about. But Jackson couldn't shake off the feeling that they were not alone in this hallway.

"Clear," Collier's voice rang out again.

"Clear," Powers repeated in a lower tone, his voice slightly muffled by the hood covering his head. "Check that junction box."

"Sir," the private responded crisply, the sound of his heavy boots scuffing against the floor as he made his way to the designated spot.

A metallic click and ear-piercing whine shattered the tension-filled silence.

"What's that?" Jackson asked sharply, her pulse rifle held steadily in her hands as she turned her head to peer into the security office.

"Opening the cover of the box," Collier's voice came back through the radio.

A quick moment of silence followed before Harris's voice filled their ears. "What's the situation?"

"Fuck!" Collier's curse was loud and clear over the static-filled radio.

"Is there a problem?" Professor Ford's calm voice cut through the chaos.

"It's not the breakers," Collier informed them all, frustration evident in his tone. "They're fine."

"What is it then?" Jackson pressed, her eyes scanning every corner of the room for any sign of danger.

"The wires have been ripped out of trip switches three, four and five," Colonel Powers reported grimly. "All the rest have been left untouched."

"That's…" Professor Ford paused, trying to make sense of this strange development. "I think that's just the lights on Level B."

"Peculiar," Harris remarked thoughtfully. "Why would someone only pull the wires for Level B? Why not shut down the entire facility?"

"And why leave some switches untouched?" Gonzalez added, confusion clear in her voice.

Another length of tense silence fell upon them all. Jackson furrowed her brow and shook her head slowly, trying to piece together this puzzling situation.

"Life support," said Hope suddenly.

"What's that?" Powers asked, his attention now fully focused on Hope's words.

"The heat," she repeated urgently. "The air-conditioning."

"Of course," Doctor Palmer said with a hint of realization in her tone.

"Can someone please explain?" Collier requested, turning to face the broken facade of the security office.

"Estúpido idiota," Gonzalez snapped angrily. "She's talking about staying the fuck alive. Everything would freeze down here without it."

"Right," Collier replied with a sigh, starting back toward the reception desk with Powers following closely behind. "I knew that."

"We're going to have to move on to the med lab," the colonel reported over the radio. "We can't do anything to fix this mess."

A loud THUD echoed through the dark corridor, causing Jackson's heart to race. With trained instinct, she quickly flipped off the safety on her pulse rifle and brought it up to her shoulder, ready to fire at any potential threat. The bright light from below shone out from under the barrel, casting sharp shadows and highlighting the fallen vending machine in front of her. Jackson scanned the area for any signs of movement or danger while Powers called out to her.

"What was that?" he asked.

"It came from back there," she reported, her voice tense with anticipation.

"Gonzalez?" the colonel's voice queried over their communicators.

"Already on it," the private responded from the professor's office. "Checking the feed now."

Powers pulled up next to Jackson, his own weapon at the ready as they both aimed down the dark corridor. Collier stood guard in the other direction, his eyes scanning for anything further down the way.

"Anything?" Powers asked, his question directed at Gonzalez.

"Nothing, sir," she replied calmly.

"Sir?" Harris' voice interrupted.

"Yes, Lieutenant?" the colonel replied.

"It's possible something dislodged in the vending machine. There were items sitting in the dispensers and one of them may have fallen out," Harris explained.

"You might be right," Powers acknowledged. "Gonzalez? Anything else?"

"Still nothing, sir," she confirmed. "I believe Lieutenant Harris is correct."

Powers let out a sigh of relief and lowered his weapon, signaling for Jackson and Collier to do the same.

"Okay then. Stand down, you two," he said before gesturing down the corridor past the security office. "We'll continue along this way and head toward the med lab. Gonzalez, will you check ahead for us?"

"Yes, sir," Gonzalez replied dutifully, her eyes scanning the area for any potential threats as they cautiously moved forward.

Inside the professor's office, the glowing monitor displayed a new image. It showed a series of yawning doors leading to darkened rooms, with a T-intersection and a branching corridor on the left. A sign hung from the ceiling at the center of the intersection, showing the offices of technical advisors and administrative staff ahead. The left side held various computer workrooms, appliance research facilities, and a medical laboratory. The walls and floors were splattered with dried blood, and scattered sheets of paper littered the area.

"Collier, take point," Powers commanded through the radio speakers as the sound of crackling glass filled the room.

"Looks clear ahead," Gonzalez reported.

"Use caution," Harris warned them. "I see many open doors."

"Thank you, Lieutenant," the colonel replied.

The image on the display showed beams of light slowly bouncing and sweeping over the walls and floor. After some time, three soldiers appeared in the lower right corner of the screen.

A soft knock at the door caught everyone's attention in the room. Hope jumped in fright, turning to see Sandra Martin, holding a square carry case with five tablet devices neatly packed inside and a pulse rifle slung across her back.

"Miss Martin," Harris greeted her as he walked toward the door.

"Fully charged and ready to use," she said confidently, holding out the case to him as if it weighed nothing more than tissue paper.

Hope considered the weight of her own device. While it wasn't heavy, it still had substantial mass. But five devices in one case? Could Martin be that strong?

"Come in." Harris motioned for Martin to enter before turning toward Professor Ford's desk.

"What's happening?" she asked, moving closer to stand behind Hope and Deputy Secretary Tinsley.

"The junction box in the security office has been tampered with," Harris explained, placing the case of devices on the desk. "The wiring for the lights on Level B have been ripped out. The rest of the circuitry appears to be untouched."

"Hmm," Martin grunted, her eyes locked on the screen as the three soldiers approached the intersection. "Any sign of the staff down there?"

"No one in the security office," Harris replied. "The window and door have significant damage."

"It's all smashed to fucking pieces and there's glass everywhere," Gonzalez chimed in.

"No bodies?" the security officer asked, her voice devoid of emotion, much like Harris'.

"Only those near the med lab," Harris reported. "We assume most of the personnel down there are deceased and in that area."

With her arms folded tightly across her chest, Sandra Martin nodded in agreement as she lifted a slender finger to tap her lips in deep thought.

Schwartz, the engineer, noticed. "What's on your mind, Miss Martin?" he asked.

"Sandra," she corrected him with a stern tone. "And I was just about to ask if you've checked the med lab cameras recently."

Harris shook his head, unsure of her implied request.

"Could you?" pressed the security officer, her eyes scanning the hallway for any potential danger.

"Sir?" Harris questioned his commander for clarification.

"It might be worth a look," Powers answered with a nod. The three soldiers carefully edged around the corner of the intersection, their weapons at the ready as they slowly moved out of view. "We're heading to the left here."

"We won't be able to see you," Gonzalez warned them from their position behind a nearby wall.

"We'll handle it," Harris assured them confidently, retrieving a small device from his case and pressing a button on top to ignite the screen. "You stay on the colonel. I'll check the med lab."

The display on the wall changed to show an angled view from a camera further down the intersecting corridor, pointing back toward their current location. Three tiny figures with bright lights emitting from their weapons were visible at the top of the screen, likely part of another search team.

As Harris joined Martin's side, he quickly navigated through various screens and menus until he found the app he was looking for. He pressed the icon, causing a new display to appear on the screen—one adorned with the company's IEC logo and a column of buttons labeled with different levels of the facility.

SURFACE

LEVEL A

LEVEL B

LEVEL C

Harris tapped on LEVEL B with confidence and the screen changed once again, revealing a list of locations at that particular level.

ELEVATORS
LEVEL C RECEPTION
ADMINISTRATION
COMPUTER WORKROOMS
APPLIANCE RESEARCH
LABORATORIES 1
LABORATORIES 2
LABORATORIES 3
MEDICAL LABORATORY

"How do I access the camera outside the med lab?" Harris asked, tilting the screen toward Martin for her input.

"Tap here," she instructed, pressing her finger to the listing for MEDICAL LABO-RATORY. Another list appeared on the screen, this time with specific areas within the medical wing.

EXTERIOR
RECEPTION DESK
FOYER
BEDS 1
BEDS 2
OPERATING ROOM 1
OPERATING ROOM 2
QUARANTINE ROOM

"Thank you," Harris said gratefully before tapping on the option for EXTERIOR. Hope observed as the usually stoic lieutenant froze in his tracks, his gaze fixed on the screen as he processed what he was seeing. She could almost detect a hint of confusion in his expression—a rare occurrence for someone like Lieutenant Harris. "Hmm!" he grunted in surprise, almost mimicking Martin's earlier noise of contemplation.

Gonzalez turned to Harris; her eyes wide with confusion as she looked from the screen on the wall to the lieutenant. "What is it, L-T?"

Harris met her gaze. "They're gone," he replied curtly.

"Gone?" Doctor Palmer interjected; his brow furrowed in disbelief. "What do you mean, gone? Who's gone?"

Harris tore his attention away from the device's screen to meet the doctor's bewildered look. "Everyone," he answered gravely. Then he gestured to the large screen on the wall. "Private Gonzalez, if you would be so kind."

"Of course, sir," Gonzalez responded, pressing a button on the keypad in front of her.

Hope felt a surge of anxiety at the thought of taking her eyes off Harris and Gonzalez, remembering the horrific image of the woman mutilating herself that she had previously witnessed on the monitor.

The image on the screen changed to show the exterior of the medical laboratory. The mass of bodies that had littered the corridor just moments ago had vanished. In their place was a dark pool of blood staining the passageway before disappearing out of view.

"What the fuck?" Gonzalez asked in frustration. "Where did they go?"

"Details, please," Collier requested over the radio.

Gonzalez shook her head. "They're all gone," she reported in disbelief. "The bodies are all gone."

Palmer stood up from his chair, his hand instinctively covering his mouth as he trembled with shock. "Could you show us the boy?" he asked, his voice shaking.

Gonzalez looked to Harris for permission before pressing a button on the keypad to cycle through cameras in the med lab.

The foyer, the beds, the operating rooms—all empty. The screen finally settled on a high-angle view of the bed where the boy had been kept under observation. Illuminated only by emergency lighting, the white sheets were now streaked with red stains and handprints around the edges.

"He's gone," Deputy Secretary Tinsley remarked with a shaken voice.

Professor Ford mirrored Doctor Palmer's reaction, standing up from his seat with trembling hands he struggled to hide.

"Gone?" Colonel Powers' voice sounded over the radio once more.

"The room is empty," Harris reported, his tone remaining neutral and detached despite the shocking scene. "As is the rest of the med lab, sir."

"Empty," the colonel murmured in disbelief. A brief moment of silence followed before he spoke again. "Do you have any idea where they might be?"

"Where they might be?" Schwartz echoed in disbelief, turning to look at Doctor Palmer. "We saw one of them die right there on the screen. How could they just get up and go somewhere else?"

Palmer shook his head rapidly, his shaky hand still covering his mouth as he struggled to process what was happening. "Show us the exterior again," Harris ordered Gonzalez.

She quickly complied, backtracking through camera feeds until landing on the door to the med lab.

Harris stepped up to the display; his eyes locked on the image. His finger traced a section of the screen, revealing a distant view of smudges on the corridor floor.

"There are marks here," he explained, his voice low and focused. "Could be footprints. It's difficult to say for sure."

Hope watched as Harris made his way back to his spot behind the sofa, while Colonel Powers responded through the radio.

"We'll investigate when we get to the med lab," Powers said, addressing the team. "Gonzalez, continue to keep an eye on our progress."

"Yes sir," Private Gonzalez replied, dutifully pressing a series of buttons on the keypad to bring up the image on the display of all three soldiers.

"Lieutenant," Powers continued, turning his attention toward Harris. "Use the security tablet to search the facility for any traces of where the bodies may have gone. Our priority is to find the missing boy. Understood?"

"Yes, sir," Harris answered confidently.

"I'll help too," Sandra Martin chimed in, approaching Professor Ford's desk to take a tablet for herself. As she lifted it from the crate, Schwartz stood up from his seat and reached out a hand toward her.

"Give me one of those as well," he said. She handed him a device before taking another for herself.

As the soldiers made their way through Level B, they came upon an intersection that offered three different paths. The sign dangling from the ceiling indicated that the left passage led to the elevators, the right to more offices and tech labs, and the med lab was somewhere straight ahead.

The floor was littered with strewn papers, some carelessly crumpled, and others stained with blood that extended to the surrounding walls. Doors stood wide open, beckoning the soldiers to explore the darkness beyond. But instead, they shone their bright lights into each entrance, revealing nothing but office furniture and more discarded paperwork.

Powers broke the silence by calling for Gonzalez. His voice hushed as he surveyed the passage to the right before turning his attention to the path ahead. Jackson joined him at his side, scanning the left path while Collier pointed his weapon toward the path they had just come from.

"Gonzalez," Powers said softly into his receiver, "Anything about the boy?"

"Nothing, sir," her reply crackled through the speaker.

"What about our path?" Powers pressed on.

There was a brief pause before Gonzalez responded. "You can continue straight on," she reported. "The corridor leads to a T-intersection. The med lab is to the left. Or you could turn left now, and it will take you to the same corridor where the elevators are located. You will then need to turn right to get to the med lab."

Jackson chimed in with a question. "Any advantage in either direction?"

"None," replied Gonzalez solemnly. As they weighed their options, Jackson scanned over each of the open doorways along the left passage, searching for any clues or signs of danger.

Powers pressed on, his boots echoing in the quiet corridor as he strode through the intersection. He took the lead, his eyes scanning for any signs or clues that could lead them to their objective.

"We'll follow the signage," he said, gesturing for his team to follow him. "I'll take point."

They continued on for what felt like an eternity, their footsteps cautious and deliberate as they checked open doorways and scanned each room they passed with a quick swipe of their flashlights. The corridor was long and wide, with large glass walls lining both sides in certain areas. Through these transparent barriers, they could catch glimpses of computer terminals and lab equipment, giving the illusion of a much larger spaces inside each room. However, the blood smears and handprints marred the pristine glass, informing them of horrors that took place here.

"Over there," Jackson announced, her flashlight beam cutting through the darkness and illuminating a computer laboratory on their left.

Powers turned, following the beam of light into the room. What he saw made his stomach turn.

"What is it?" Gonzalez asked, straining to see through the darkness.

"Shit," Collier whispered.

A young man sat slumped in a chair at a computer terminal, his body twisted unnaturally to one side. His arms hung limply by his sides, with one hand clutching a pair of bloody scissors. A deep gash crossed his throat from ear to ear, almost decapitating him.

"How…" Collier trailed off, aiming his light toward the figure's head, which hung loosely over his back.

The young man's lifeless eyes stared blankly ahead at something in the corridor, while his mouth hung open in a grotesque smile with his tongue lolling out.

Powers shook his head in disbelief and disgust.

"You think he did that to himself?" Jackson's voice broke through the silence.

"How…" Collier repeated, unable to comprehend how someone could inflict such a gruesome wound on themselves.

"I can't see a fucking thing," Gonzalez said, his voice trembling.

"You don't want to see this," Powers replied, turning away from the horrifying scene. "We found one of the personnel."

"Fucking hell, how does someone do that to themselves?" Collier muttered, taking one last look before following the colonel and Jackson down the corridor.

"Someone else must have done this to him," Jackson said, her voice filled with unease. "Right, sir?"

Powers cautiously scanned the open doorways and glass barriers that lined the walls of the narrow passage. Each step forward felt like a trap waiting to be sprung. The lingering scent of antiseptic and blood lingered in the air, a sharp contrast to the grisly scene unfolding before them.

"We all witnessed what that young woman did outside the med lab," the colonel said. "She did that to herself."

"How?" Collier's voice was edged with disbelief. "It defies all logic."

Powers nodded in agreement, his gaze following a long smear of blood that streaked along the wall at waist height to his right. It ceased abruptly after a few meters, as if the source had simply vanished into thin air. But Powers knew better; the trail continued along the floor.

"None of this makes sense, Private." The colonel's voice was heavy with frustration. "Not one fucking thing."

Chapter Sixteen

"You're coming up to the med lab," Gonzalez announced over the crackling radio.

"I see it," Powers returned, sighting the open door about fifty meters from his position. The floor and walls were coated in a sickly mixture of bodily fluids and small, unidentifiable particles that clung to surfaces like living organisms. In the low light, they seemed to move and pulsate, giving off a palpable sense of unease.

"Jesus, it stinks," Jackson huffed, trying to adjust her mask. "I thought these suits were meant to keep most odors out."

"So did I," Collier agreed, his voice muffled by his own breathing apparatus.

"Stay focused," the colonel said, stepping carefully over some particularly large smears on the floor. "Anything, Lieutenant?"

"Nothing," Harris reported through gritted teeth. "We've checked every functioning camera on Level B. There's no sign of the boy or any of the missing personnel."

Powers furrowed his brow beneath his helmet. "Functioning cameras? Some aren't operational?"

There was a brief moment of awkward quiet as the colonel waited for an answer, sweeping the walls and open doorways with his torch as he slowly made his way down the corridor. Faint mumbling could be heard through the speaker as a conversation took place in the professor's office.

Suddenly, a different voice came through the static, "Glenn Schwartz here, Colonel. I did some digging earlier and found that a number of security measures are yet to be fully installed around the facility. We have Sandra Martin with us here. She's part of the security team."

"I know who Miss Martin is, Mister Schwartz," Powers interjected impatiently. "Are you telling me that some cameras are not even installed on this level?"

"They're physically installed," Sandra Martin's voice said clearly. "But they are not yet functioning digitally. Our technicians are still working on software updates to cater for the security feed around the facility."

Colonel Powers came to a halt a few meters from the med lab door. The scent of blood and filth hit him like a physical force, causing him to pause and take a deep breath through his mask. As he stood there, surrounded by pools of thick, congealed muck, he recalled the image on the screen in the professor's office—bodies piled upon bodies in this very same spot.

"What cameras are we not able to see?" he asked, his voice echoing off the walls of the dark and eerie med lab.

"The eastern and southern emergency doors, the southern corridor on your level," Harris replied, his words punctuated by the sounds of distant footsteps and muffled voices. "And the eastern stairwell from the Level A emergency door down to the Energy Generation Chamber."

As Collier took in the information, Powers nodded slowly, his gaze fixed on the darkness beyond the med lab's open doorway. The silence was unsettling, broken only by the occasional sound of movement outside.

"Captain Moreau?" the colonel called out. "You still with us?"

"Sir?" came the pilot's answer. "I thought you might have forgotten me up here."

Powers cracked a faint grin. "Never. What's your situation?"

"No change," she replied, her voice strained with effort as a rattling sound emitted through the speaker. "Just getting up to take a look outside." After a moment, she spoke again. "I've still got friends waiting for me out there."

"Okay," Powers said reassuringly. "Hold tight. We'll get to you when we can."

"Take your time, sir," she returned with determination. "I'm not going anywhere."

The colonel then turned to Collier, signaling him to enter the med lab foyer.

"Lieutenant?" Powers called out to Harris.

"Sir?" came the reply.

"What about the rest of Captain Moreau's friends coming down the stairs?"

"They're here," answered Harris. "They're outside the emergency doors."

Powers instinctively glanced over at Teresa Jackson, who stood guard by the med lab door with her weapon pointed down the passageway and her flashlight tracing a path along bloody footprints leading away from their position. Upon hearing Harris' report, she turned her gaze to the colonel, her expression a mix of curiosity and concern.

"What are they doing?" she asked, her voice barely above a whisper.

"Nothing," Harris responded. "They're just standing at the door and on the stairs. Almost like someone waiting to be let in."

Powers raised his rifle in the same direction as Jackson's, studying the footprints with intensity.

"Any chance some of them are making their way down here?" the colonel inquired, his tone guarded.

"Sorry sir," Harris answered apologetically. "We can't tell."

"Let me guess," Powers continued with a sigh, shaking his head slowly. "That's one of the stairwells with no functioning cameras."

"Correct," confirmed Harris. "The eastern stairwell, sir."

Collier let out a frustrated chuckle. "Fucking great," he muttered sarcastically. "What's the odds that those footprints lead straight to the eastern emergency doors?"

"It would appear so," Harris told him.

"Fuck," Collier spat, mirroring Jackson's profanity. Powers turned around to sweep the corridor behind them with his flashlight.

He pursed his lips and furrowed his brow in deep thought.

"Collier, come back out here," he finally ordered. As the private complied and exited the med lab, another voice spoke over the radio.

"What are you thinking, Colonel?" came Deputy Secretary Sally Tinsley's concerned voice.

Powers took a deep breath and let it out slowly, trying to steady himself.

"I'm thinking we're going to go back to you," he replied reluctantly.

"No," protested Doctor Palmer, his tone desperate and pleading. "You must find the boy."

"The boy could be dead," Powers replied with a heavy heart and a hint of sadness in his voice.

"You don't know that," Palmer argued back.

"No, I don't," Powers agreed, his tone resigned. "But I can't help feeling that this is a trap."

"But..." the doctor protested again, but Powers cut him off.

"The safety of my team comes first," he declared, scanning the corridor leading to the elevators for any sign of danger.

"Which way should we go?" Jackson asked, her voice echoing off the walls.

"We'll take the shorter route," Powers replied, his steps echoing as he moved toward the left path. Collier followed closely, his rifle at the ready as they passed by open doors, scattered papers, and pools of blood.

"You take point," Powers said to Collier, tapping him on the shoulder before turning to Jackson. "You cover our rear."

"Yes sir," Jackson responded, her torch casting shadows on the adjacent wall as she stood in the right corner. Her heart raced as they turned into a new passage, scanning for any signs of danger. Suddenly, her light fell upon a young bespectacled woman standing in the doorway of the med lab. "Fuck me!" Jackson exclaimed, her rifle raised, and safety switched off in an instant.

The other two soldiers whirled around, their beams of light illuminating the woman's pale figure. Her body trembled and swayed, as if struggling to support its own weight. Her head tilted unnaturally to one side, while a twisted smile spread across her face. In her left hand, she toyed with the organs spilling out of a large gash in her abdomen.

"Holy shit!" Gonzalez's voice crackled over the radio. "Where did she come from?"

The woman slowly raised her right hand, revealing a long letter opener. Her body continued to shake as she lifted it up to shoulder level.

"Put down the knife," Powers commanded sternly. The tension in the air was palpable as they all waited for her next move.

The woman's eyes fluttered shut and a look of ecstasy crossed her face as she heard the colonel's voice. Slowly, she lifted the letter opener to her face, running the tip of the blade along her cheek before pausing at her temple.

"Put the knife down," Powers repeated, his voice firm.

But the woman only opened her eyes, staring back at him with a wicked grin. Without hesitation, she plunged the letter opener deep into the side of her head, nearly burying it in her skull.

"Fuck!" Jackson shouted in horror.

Still smiling, the woman wobbled unsteadily on her feet as she yanked the blade out of her head and dragged it across her cheek, tearing a jagged line from her temple to the corner of her mouth. She dropped the bloodied letter opener to the floor with a clang and used her left hand to touch the fresh wound on her face while keeping her right hand firmly on the gash in her torso.

With a frenzied determination, she dug her fingers into the fresh cut on her cheek and tore at it, revealing bone and teeth beneath. Her other hand scraped and clawed at the skin around her temple until it too, was ripped away, exposing raw flesh beneath. A sickening sound filled the room as she pulled at her forehead and eyelids, revealing a bulging eyeball swiveling and turning in its socket.

Grunts of disgust, screams of terror and strange noises from Professor Ford's office crackled through the radio as Powers quickly readied his weapon. He flipped off the safety and switched to rapid-fire mode before pulling the trigger.

Thirty bolts of energy per second erupted from his weapon like blinding white light, each one slamming into the woman's face with an intense force. Flesh sizzled and burned under the onslaught as bones shattered and tissue disintegrated.

Jackson's finger twitched on the trigger, her adrenaline-fueled instincts matching her commander's swift action. She aimed her blasts at the woman's chest, unleashing a barrage of destructive energy that tore through her flesh and ripped open her ribcage. Collier struggled to catch up, fumbling with his weapon as he switched off the safety and toggled the selector. Finally, he fired into the woman's torso.

Within seconds, the once-human figure crumpled to the floor, a grotesque mass of shredded meat and bone resembling roadkill more than a person.

Collier sucked in deep breaths, his entire body trembling as he tried to regain control of his nerves.

"What the hell was that?" he gasped. "Did you see what she did with that knife? What the fuck?"

Jackson could only shake her head in stunned disbelief.

"Nope," she said. She pursed her lips. "Mmm-mmm. That shit... Nope! No fucking way that shit happened."

Powers cautiously approached the corpse, his gun trained on it and his finger ready to pull the trigger at any moment. He noticed a letter opener on the ground, not far from the woman's outstretched hand. Using the toe of his boot, he kicked it away from her and sent it flying across the floor toward the bloodied footprints leading away to the emergency exit. The metal blade clanged against the wall before falling into silence somewhere in the darkness.

With his gun still pointed at the lifeless body, Powers gave it a gentle nudge with his foot, prepared for any sudden movements.

But there were none. The figure remained motionless.

Collier's hand trembled as he gestured to the mangled pulp of flesh lying on the floor. "I think she's dead," he said, his voice shaking with fear and disbelief.

"Dead? Do you mean before or after we pumped her full of bolts?" Jackson's voice was laced with adrenaline and panic.

Powers backed away from the woman, his body tense and ready for action. "We need to get back to Level A and get as many out as possible," he barked, scanning their surroundings like a hawk.

"What about the creatures on the surface level, sir?" Harris asked.

Powers took a moment to consider their options before coming to a decision. "We fight our way out," he declared, determination hardening his features. "We turn them into mincemeat like this one here, so they can't harm us anymore. Then we secure the emergency stairwell doors up top. We'll use the shuttle to evacuate as many as we can and call for backup."

"Sounds like a plan, sir," Gonzalez chimed in, her voice filled with both fear and admiration for her leader.

With a nod from Powers, the group made their way toward the elevator corridor again.

"I know this isn't the best time," Tinsley put in. "But we have a protocol issue with evacuating corporate personnel on a UN transport. There will be consequences."

"I'll use my position to make the call. Then, they can have my fucking job," Colonel Powers replied before turning to Collier and Jackson. "Come on, let's go,"

But before they could get far, a sickening, wet slapping sound echoed behind them.

SLAP!

The sound made them freeze in their tracks; their lights trained on its source.

SLAP!

"You've got to be fucking kidding me!" Collier exclaimed in horror as they watched the supposedly dead woman dragging herself across the floor with her one remaining arm. Her other arm dangled loosely, grotesquely by her side as she struggled forward, reaching out with her claw-like hand and slapping it down with each step.

She was smiling through torn flesh and half a face, inching closer and closer to the group.

Jackson lifted her pulse rifle, ready to take a shot.

But Powers stopped her. "Forget it," he commanded, his voice rising in panic. "We need to get out of here."

The three turned to continue down the passage, only to find themselves facing more obstacles.

From open doors emerged more figures, wobbling on unsteady legs and snarling with vicious intent.

Colonel Eric Powers took in the scene and summed it up with one word.

"Shit."

Captain Dona Moreau, leaning heavily against the cockpit console, wiped the drying tear streaks from her cheeks. The radio crackled and warbled beside her, excited and elevated voices calling through the little speaker. It was a cacophony of chaos and fear, each voice trying to be heard over the others.

"They're everywhere," she heard Teresa Jackson shriek, her voice loud and frantic. The whirring sound of the AR-90D's rapid fire followed in quick succession. Roland Collier swore, resulting in a sharp reprimand from the colonel.

"Stay focused," he said sternly. "Watch that door."

Moreau sat up, lifting the radio, and holding it closer to her ear as she listened intently to the panicked voices on the other end.

"Fuck," Collier barked. "Two more."

More shooting.

More cursing.

"They just keep coming," Jackson hollered, her voice hysterical. "Fucker has no head, and they just keep coming."

Rising to her feet, Moreau felt her heart racing in her chest, neck, and ears. Hearing the fear in her friends' voices caused an intense knot to tighten in her stomach.

"Keep firing," Powers commanded urgently. "Keep moving."

The captain stepped out of the cockpit and entered the main cabin of the aircraft. There, she paced back and forth along the short aisle between the seats, holding the radio up to her ear as rapid fire filled the speaker.

"Fucking die," Collier screamed with a mix of anger and terror.

"Gonzalez," Powers called out urgently. "Any clear way out?"

"Nothing," she replied, sounding terrified. "They're in every fucking corridor."

"It's as if they were hiding in most of the rooms you passed," Harris remarked calmly. His voice sounded composed and passive despite their dire situation. "Waiting for you to reach the med lab before they attacked."

"Fucking trap," Powers said, as if confirming his previous hunch.

"It would appear so," Harris agreed.

"We're near the elevator," the colonel reported. "Can you see us?"

"Yessir," Gonzalez answered through heavy breaths. "It doesn't get any better ahead of you."

"Not any better back there, either," Collier shouted, his voice strained and frantic.

THUD!

Moreau stopped in her tracks at the loud sound that came from the hatch. She stood frozen in place, staring at the door with wide eyes, feeling her heart galloping in her ears and throbbing in her temples.

THUD!

Someone or something out there was trying to get in.

Another thud followed immediately, accompanied by another on the side of the craft, near the rear of the cabin. Within moments, consistent knocking, tapping, and banging ensued as the creatures struck the side of the aircraft relentlessly.

I'm under attack, she thought, fear and dread creeping up within her.

The pummeling sound spread across the wall, growing louder and more intense as it extended into the cockpit.

I'm under attack.

She could hear the noise growing and growing as it seemingly enveloped her from all sides. It felt like an unstoppable force bearing down on her, and Moreau felt a sense of impending doom.

"I'm under attack," Moreau said into the radio, her hand shaking as she brought it to her mouth. She heard the chaos and shouting behind her, the sound of metal hitting metal and heavy footsteps echoing through the narrow halls.

"A little busy right now," Collier's voice replied, strained and tense.

"I'm here, Captain," Lieutenant Harris chimed in. "Checking your situation."

Moreau sat in a seat at the back of the cabin, previously occupied by one of the security detail during the flight in, her knuckles turning white as she gripped the armrests.

"I don't know how many are out there," she said, trying to keep her voice steady.

"You have fifteen," Harris began before pausing briefly. "Make that sixteen individuals on your port side. The shuttle is coated with reinforced titanium, and they would need high explosives or military grade weaponry to break in. You're perfectly safe."

She knew all this, but still felt threatened, scared, and alone in the face of such an attack.

"Hang in there, Captain," Harris told her with a poor attempt at compassion in his voice.

The thumping, knocking, and smacking continued to reverberate through the cabin like a relentless thunder that wouldn't subside.

"I'll try," Moreau replied through clenched teeth. "But the noise is starting to get on my nerves."

"I understand how you feel," Harris replied with forced empathy.

But Moreau didn't believe him. In this moment of crisis, she was acutely aware of just how alone she was.

Harris gently tapped a small icon on the top of his device's screen, causing the image to shrink and return to the main menu of security camera listings. Beside him, Sandra Martin glanced quickly from her own device to his and back, her brows furrowed with concern.

"You should keep an eye on her," she said softly, nodding toward the tablet in Harris' hands.

"I need to check the eastern stairwell feed on this level," Harris replied, pressing the tab for Level A on his device.

"I'm already there," Martin told him, tilting her tablet for him to see. On the screen, several grotesque creatures pounded on a metal door with their fists and tentacled heads. "They started this just before you got the call from your pilot."

Lieutenant Harris peered across the room to Private Gonzalez. She appeared fixated on the large display mounted on the wall where three soldiers were engaged in a fierce battle against a horde of undead creatures.

He watched as Colonel Powers and Private Jackson aimed their weapons at one particularly threatening creature that had emerged from below the camera's view. With precise synchronization, they fired simultaneously, blasting chunks from the attacker's torso and legs. An arm fell to the floor and flopped around like a fish out of water while the creature continued its relentless march toward them.

Meanwhile, Collier stood guard at the rear, firing into a small crowd approaching from along the passage. Suddenly, he turned and fired directly into the head of another approaching figure, watching with satisfaction as it exploded into a mess of flesh and bone. But there was no time for celebration as Colonel Powers urgently yelled for the team to push forward, disappearing from sight at the bottom of the screen.

Gonzalez, too preoccupied by what she witnessed, fumbled with her keypad before finally managing to switch the display to the next camera along the corridor. "Estúpido idiota," she huffed frustratedly.

"Private Gonzalez," Harris called out, drawing her attention away from the screen.

"Sorry, sir," she apologized, flustered by her delayed response in changing the display. Clearly, she was feeling overwhelmed by the intensity of the situation.

"We need to go," Harris told her firmly.

"Sir?" Gonzalez offered a curious expression, wondering why they were leaving their posts.

"They're trying to break in," Martin chimed in, turning her tablet device to show the others in the room.

"What about…" Private Gonzalez started, gesturing to the wall-mounted display with a nod.

"Miss Aguilar," said Harris, addressing Hope, who had been intently watching the events unfold on the large screen. "Would you mind taking over for Private Gonzalez?"

"Uh…" Hope timidly stood up and nodded. "Of course."

"Hurry, grab your rifle and leave the radio," Harris commanded as he turned to Gonzalez.

"Yes sir," she replied, as she quickly followed his orders.

She handed the keypad to Hope, their fingers briefly brushing against each other before Gonzalez retrieved her AR-90D from its resting place against the wall. Giving one last affectionate look toward Hope, she nodded and joined Harris and Martin in exiting the room.

As they left, Hope made her way around Professor Ford's desk and settled into his high-backed chair. Placing her tablet device on the desk beside her, she slid the keypad across the desk until it was directly in front of her. With practiced ease, she dragged the small radio closer to her and activated it.

"I'm here," she announced. "This is Hope Aguilar."

"Good to hear your voice, Hope," Powers responded through the static-filled radio. On screen, he stepped forward with his rifle raised, firing down at a fallen body that reached out for him with clawed hands. "There's not much you can do for us at the moment. We can see the emergency doors from our position. They appear shut, but could you check the stairwell to see if any of these things made it out?"

"Checking," Hope replied without hesitation, quickly pressing a series of buttons to change the image displayed on her tablet.

As she ascended the stairs via the camera feeds, both Collier and Jackson cursed loudly over the radio.

The western stairwell appeared empty beyond the closed doors. Hope continued to switch between camera views until she reached Level A.

"All clear, all the way," she reported back to the colonel.

"Fuck you!" Collier's voice jerked through the radio. "Fuck you, bitch!"

Hope's fingers flew across the keypad as she hurriedly switched the camera feed, back to show the three soldiers fighting for their lives.

"Oh my God," Glenn Schwartz gasped in shock as he took in the gruesome scene before them.

A decapitated man lay on the ground, his arm missing from above the elbow, and his body split open down the middle. His organs spilled out onto the floor, twitching and writhing like giant, wet worms as they slithered over his feet. His spine stood stiff and upright, tendrils extending from each vertebra and scraping against the walls and ceiling.

Closer to Collier, another creature, a woman with her lower jaw hanging awkwardly open, crawled over his legs toward his waist. A cluster of slimy feelers expanded from her mouth to lap hungrily at his crotch, causing him to thrash and scream in terror.

Jackson's hand shook with fear and adrenaline as she unleashed a barrage of energy bolts into the woman's back, each one ripping through her flesh and exposing her ribcage in a gruesome display. The creature convulsed under the force and collapsed onto Collier, who screamed in agony as his body was crushed beneath its weight.

With an unearthly strength, slimy tentacles burst forth from the creature's mouth and plunged deep into Collier's stomach, piercing through his hazmat suit with ease. His screams turned to choked gasps as the creature pulled out his insides like twisted playthings.

In a blur of movement, the woman scurried backward on all fours like a grotesque spider, dragging Collier along with her by his entrails. Powers and Jackson frantically fired their assault rifles, the deafening sounds blending with the sickening squelches of flesh being shredded. But no matter how many bolts they pumped into the creatures, they seemed unstoppable.

The room suddenly brightened with blinding flashes as gunfire and energy blasts filled the air, but it did nothing to deter the relentless beasts. In a desperate struggle for survival, Powers and Jackson knew they had to keep fighting.

The grotesque mass of the split man slammed onto Collier, smothering him, engulfing him in a writhing sea of churning tissue.

Powers gripped Jackson's shoulder as he shouted above the chaos, pulling her toward the emergency doors.

"We can't save him," he yelled into their radio. "We need to get out now." Without hesitation, Jackson followed her commander's lead.

"Private Collier is gone," Colonel Powers reported over their radio. "Me and Jackson are heading to the stairwell."

"Understood," came Harris' response. "I'm approaching the east door on this level with Gonzalez and Sandra Martin. Do you need us to come to you?"

"Negative," Powers replied as they ran. "Secure that door. Just get someone ready to open the door for us when we get there."

"I'll do it," Schwartz chimed in. "On my way."

"Not yet," warned Colonel Powers as he raised his AR-90D and let loose a barrage of energy bolts at a man emerging from an open doorway ahead of them. "Wait until we're close to the door. We can't risk letting any of these fuckers inside."

Jackson rained bullets upon the approaching horde, but they seemed unfazed by the barrage. Limbs were blasted off, bodies fell to the ground, but still they crawled toward them.

In a moment of panic and disbelief, Jackson's gun fell silent.

Powers tore his gaze away from the fighting to check on his comrade. To his horror, he saw Jackson staring blankly, her body twitching uncontrollably.

"Private?" Powers yelled, trying to snap her out of it. She was unresponsive, though seemingly unharmed despite the chaos surrounding them. "Private Jackson! What's wrong?"

With trembling hands, she pointed down the corridor behind them, her chin quivering with fear.

Powers turned just in time to see a figure clad in a hazmat suit sprinting through the throng of creatures toward them.

Collier.

A flicker of hope surged through Powers' veins, his heart beating wildly as he saw Collier still alive. But in an instant, that glimmer of optimism was extinguished by a wave of horror as he witnessed tentacle-like appendages squirming out of Collier's stomach and face.

Reacting with lightning speed, Powers spun around and aimed his weapon at the rapidly approaching soldier. With one blast, he managed to hit his target before Collier tackled him to the ground. The colonel felt tendrils wrap tightly around his throat, crushing the air from his lungs and squeezing mercilessly. A sickening crunch filled the air as even more tendrils emerged from Collier's body, reaching out to grab Jackson and pulling her closer and closer with each passing moment.

She let out a guttural scream that pierced through the chaos as Collier tore through her uniform, his monstrous appendages ripping into her flesh. Powers could only watch in horror as his comrade was mutilated before his eyes, before the world turned black.

CHAPTER SEVENTEEN

A deafening silence fell like a thick blanket, smothering any sounds beyond the thudding against the emergency door. The lack of communication through their radios seemed to stretch on for an eternity as Gonzalez and her team waited for some kind of response. Harris checked his radio, the power level display showing a full bar. It was at that moment that the speaker crackled to life.

"What the fuck just happened?" Captain Dona Moreau's voice came through loud and clear.

"Ugh," a woman's voice groaned, followed by a slight pause. "They're gone."

"Who's gone?" Moreau demanded. "The colonel? Teresa? Roland?"

"All of them," Tinsley answered, with sorrow in her tone. "I'm sorry."

Harris spoke up. "Why can't we hear the colonel's radio?"

Gonzalez gave him a questioning look, her eyes beginning to well with tears.

"It, ah," Tinsley started before pausing again. "It looks like it was smashed against the wall when the colonel..."

Silence fell once more as the deputy secretary's voice trailed off.

Harris nodded to himself. "I understand. Have the personnel from Level B entered the western stairwell?"

"Come on, L-T," Gonzalez whispered. "Our people just died."

"No," Hope's voice cut in. "They're just there. Not moving."

"Thank you, Miss Aguilar," Harris said. "Keep me updated if there are any changes."

A loud thud at the doors snapped Gonzalez back into focus. She wiped her eyes on her sleeve and took a deep breath to steady herself.

"I suggest we call for a facility-wide lockdown," suggested Sandra Martin, dragging a heavy two-seat sofa along the passage with ease, maneuvering it to block the passage directly in front of the emergency door, positioning the back of the seat to face the door.

"Where did you get that?" Harris asked, surprised by Martin's strength.

"Rec room," she replied, seemingly unfazed by her action. "There were people down there. They should all be in their rooms behind locked doors."

Gonzalez looked at her in awe. Martin hadn't even broken a sweat.

"You're like him," Gonzalez commented, staring at Sandra in admiration.

"That can't be possible," Harris interjected, kneeling on the sofa, using the backrest to steady his weapon aimed at the door.

"Of course she is," Gonzalez argued, gesturing toward Martin. "Dragging that thing over here as though it's nothing."

The lieutenant straightened his back, his sharp gaze assessing Sandra Martin with calculated scrutiny. She stood before him, appearing like any other athletic woman her age.

"She's not old enough," he stated firmly.

"Cryopreservation, big boy," Martin retorted coolly.

Suddenly, Schwartz's voice crackled through the speaker.

"I fucking knew it!" he exclaimed.

Martin calmly pulled down the collar of her shirt to reveal a small tattoo peeking out from under her left clavicle. There, etched in precise lines on her skin, was the number 1759.

"What do you know?" Harris inquired, while Gonzalez kneeled onto the sofa behind him, also resting her rifle on the back of the seat.

"About this?" Martin questioned, releasing her shirt collar to fall neatly back into place. "Not much. Only what my parents told me."

"Parents?" Harris echoed.

As if on cue, the doors thudded once again.

"The people who raised me," Martin clarified, glancing quickly at the door. "Surely you had a set of those."

Harris nodded slowly, his expression contemplative.

"A geneticist and a teacher," he revealed. "But they weren't my parents."

"Which was which?" Martin asked curiously.

THUD!

The chains securing the door jingled musically for a brief moment before falling silent again.

"My mother was a geneticist at a research facility in Norway," Harris explained. "My father was a science teacher at a high school in Hobart until his retirement. And yours?"

"Mine came from Ottawa," Martin replied with a trace of sadness. "My father was also a geneticist who worked in Norway. He passed away a couple of years ago."

THUD!

"He told me they cultured me from a stem cell sample," Martin continued, her tone matter of fact. "Just like all the other engineered specimens."

"How many were there?" Private Gonzalez interjected, her grip tightening on her rifle.

THUD!

"I don't know for certain." Martin shook her head, her gaze fixed steadily on the door. "My father believed there could have been as many as five thousand of us."

"The tattoos?" Private Gonzalez pressed. "Are they some sort of product number? Assembly line detail?"

"I suppose so," Martin replied thoughtfully.

"They were inscribed using lasers while we were still developing," Harris added, his eyes locked on the door. "That's what my mother told me."

THUD!

The sound of chains rattling against metal made Gonzalez tense up involuntarily.

"Professor Ford?" Harris called urgently. "We need to initiate a complete lockdown immediately."

Ford moved decisively to his desk. He pressed a button on the phone panel and spoke with a calm authority.

"Attention all personnel. Please move quickly to your accommodations or the nearest safe location to your current position. This is a lockdown."

As he made the call, Hope quickly changed the image on the screen from the gruesome scene of Level B to the western stairwell outside the emergency door on Level A.

"What did you mean when you said you knew it?" Her curious gaze shifted to Glenn Schwartz, who sat across the office space.

He tore his attention away from the monitor and turned to face the young woman at the professor's desk. The call for lockdown repeated, giving him time to gather his thoughts before answering.

"In 2023," he began, "scientists conducted a project where they created synthetic embryos from stem cell samples. It wasn't widely publicized at the time due to conflicts in other parts of the world taking priority in the media. But various labs continued their research and development, until pressure from leaders with strong religious beliefs shut it down in 2040."

"Actually, it was 2037," Tinsley interjected. "But even then, it didn't fully stop. Certain corporations continued their research under the radar. The official reason given was that there were concerns about using genetic alterations to create super soldiers."

"Which is exactly what happened," Schwartz chimed in. "But by then, government bodies had transitioned into corporations and that became the main focus in the news. Not much else was known about these projects, except for speculation that engineered embryos were being grown into infants whose whereabouts remained a mystery."

"Until now," Hope added.

"Well..." Tinsley tilted her head slightly. "Not exactly. Many of us knew of their existence, but the evidence was carefully covered up, making it impossible to prove anything. Some claimed that the infants and embryos were destroyed, while others believed they were being trained as security personnel or raised by kind-hearted individuals working for the companies involved. What we did know for sure was that these projects were real, and the infants were grown. But there was no concrete proof of anything."

"Except for the fact that we have two of them here," said Hope.

"Exactly," Schwartz said before turning to glance over his shoulder. "I'm surprised you're not adding your expertise to all of this, Doctor."

"Doctor?" Schwartz called out, his voice bouncing off the walls of the small room as he stood and pivoted, scanning the area for Palmer.

But the doctor had vanished.

All eyes darted around the cramped space.

"Lieutenant?" Tinsley's voice trembled slightly as she spoke up.

"Harris here," came a response through the radio resting on the desk.

"We've lost Doctor Palmer," the deputy secretary announced, her voice strained with worry.

"Lost? As in, deceased?" Harris's voice remained calm, but curious.

"No," Tinsley clarified, her brow furrowed in confusion. "He's disappeared."

There was a moment of tense silence before the speaker crackled again.

"Maybe he's just gone for a shit," Gonzalez suggested naively, earning a sharp reprimand from the lieutenant. "I know I could go for one right now."

"Private!" Harris reprimanded her.

"I'll check his quarters," Schwartz offered, already moving toward the door with determination.

"I'll search the bathroom near the dining area," Ford added eagerly.

"No," Harris commanded firmly. "You two need to remain in lockdown. It's not safe."

Hope's gaze flicked between the monitor on the wall and the others in the room.

"Uh, guys..." She pointed at the screen nervously.

On the screen, the emergency door slowly closed as Doctor Palmer descended the stairs in a frenzied hurry.

"Jesus," Schwartz hissed under his breath, his heart racing. "He's in the western stairwell."

"What could he possibly be thinking?" Ford asked, shaking his head in disbelief.

"He's going downstairs," Hope observed, her voice laced with fear and worry.

"He's going for the fucking kid," Gonzalez added.

"I'm on my way there now," Harris declared over the radio. "I'll secure the door."

"But those things down there," Hope protested frantically. "They'll kill him."

"Most likely," Harris admitted grimly, his determination clear in his voice.

With a burst of speed, Harris reached the wide-open emergency doors in less than a minute. The sound of distant footfalls echoed through the stairwell. He stepped over a discarded chain and carabiner clip, evidence of Palmer's hasty descent.

"Doctor?" Harris called out, aiming his weapon down the dark passage. "I need to secure this door. You won't be able to get back in."

Silence greeted his words, except for the fading sound of Palmer's footsteps continuing downward.

"Doctor, please come back," Harris shouted into the abyss. Still, there was no response. Frowning, the lieutenant retreated back through the emergency doors and pulled them shut behind him.

After ensuring the doors were secured, Harris hurried back along the corridor to where Private Gloria Gonzalez and Sandra Martin were waiting.

"You weren't gone long," Private Gonzalez remarked.

"The door is secure," Harris reported, taking up position next to her and resting his pulse rifle on the chair's back. "Anything to report?"

"Not really," Gonzalez replied.

"They've stopped banging on the door," Martin added.

Harris gazed at the tightly wrapped chain around the release bars. "Have you checked if they are still outside?" he asked, gesturing toward the tablet device in Martin's hand.

She flipped it over to show him the screen, revealing a mass of tentacled faces and orange coveralls stretching up the stairwell as far as the camera could see.

"Perhaps the lockdown announcement distracted them?" Gonzalez suggested.

"Perhaps," Harris agreed with a slight frown. "Or maybe something else has their attention."

"There's nothing else out there," Martin assured him.

"And I've checked the feed from the surface," Private Gonzalez chimed in. "The ones up there haven't moved."

Suddenly, a sharp crackle pierced through the silence on the radio.

"I concur," Captain Dona Moreau's voice said in agreement. "They've all ceased their assault on the fuselage and are now simply standing around. It's as if they're waiting for their next set of instructions."

Taking a deep breath, Harris turned his attention to Hope.

"Could you please search Level B and report back if you see any movement?"

"Yes," her reply came through the speaker, her voice shaky with fear. "I have been going through the surveillance footage, trying to locate Doctor Palmer."

"Any luck?" Gonzalez asked anxiously.

"No," Hope replied. "But I can see Colonel Powers, Private Collier, and Jackson standing upright."

Private Gonzalez picked up the tablet device resting on the sofa beside her. She deftly navigated through the menu and camera feeds, pausing when she found the trio in the corridor. They stood motionless, their hazmat suits torn and blood-stained, bearing fatal wounds. But around them, others loitered like grotesque mannequins. Some were missing limbs and lay lifeless on the floor. Others had chunks of flesh hanging precariously from their bodies.

Waiting.

Waiting.

Waiting for their next set of instructions.

"I've located the boy," Glenn Schwartz exclaimed with excitement. "I've found him!"

"Where is he?" Deputy Secretary Sally Tinsley demanded.

"He's in the Shrine," the engineer replied breathlessly. "There are others with him."

"What are they doing?" Harris questioned urgently.

"Most of them are just standing there," Schwartz answered. "But the boy is on a raised platform next to a woman who appears to be operating a computer terminal."

"Let me see," Professor Ford requested.

Harris motioned for Gonzalez to change the feed on her device. She quickly switched to the menu and pulled up the camera from Level C.

"It can't be," Ford gasped. "It can't possibly be."

Gonzalez opened the feed for the Energy Generation Chamber. The familiar image of the massive room filled the screen, with long rods protruding from the walls and ceiling, almost meeting in the center. In a corner of the screen sat the computer terminal, and there on the platform next to it stood the unmistakable sandy-haired boy. On a chair, perched at the terminal, was a young, naked woman, her skin a sickly pale hue.

"Who is that?" Gonzalez asked, perplexed. "And why isn't she wearing any clothes?"

"Because she came from the morgue," Sandra Martin explained. Her words met with curious looks from Private Gonzalez. "That's the boy's mother. Amy Caldwell."

CHAPTER EIGHTEEN

Sandra Martin cautiously approached the emergency doors, her weapon raised and ready.

"Why her?" Martin asked, listening for any signs of danger.

"What do you mean?" Hope asked. "Everyone who is dead is…"

"That's what I mean," the security officer replied. "Any of them could sit at the terminal and push buttons."

With a gentle push, she pressed her palm flat against the door. It quivered slightly in response, the chains rattling and jingling like distant chimes. Despite the assault from the beasts outside, the door remained firmly in place.

"Fucking quiet out there," Gonzalez said uneasily.

"Perhaps it's something like past memories," Hope replied. "Maybe she's the only one who holds the knowledge to use that terminal?"

"No," Ford told her. "There are others who have clearance to use that terminal."

Martin returned to the sofa.

"Tell me we're all thinking the same thing," she began, her voice steady despite the tense situation. "That the dead are all under the influence of one species."

"I'm thinking puppets," Schwartz added, his voice barely above a whisper. "So, that's a yes from me."

"Influenced by who?" Tinsley asked, her voice tinged with disbelief. "The boy?"

Harris frowned; his jaw clenched tight as he stared at the closed door.

"I think the boy is a part of the thing," said the lieutenant, his voice grim. "I think, perhaps, the creature that reached through the portal is the mastermind behind it all."

Silence descended upon the group as they let this sink in.

Harris turned to Gonzalez, who nodded slowly in agreement.

"Nothing else makes sense," she said, her tone laced with frustration. "Fucking squid heads out there, dead people running around and shit. Nothing, except some weird shit like that."

"But," Ford said, his voice hesitant. He paused for what seemed like an eternity before finally speaking up again. "For what purpose?" he eventually asked. "And how? We shut the generator down."

"Something residual," Schwartz stated matter-of-factly, reminding everyone of something Harris had told them earlier. "That thing lives in the boy. A part of it got left behind in that chamber and infected both Corporal Garrett and Mister Wade."

"That still doesn't explain the purpose," Harris remarked with a furrowed brow.

Gonzalez pursed her lips and cocked her head, deep in thought as she tried to piece everything together. Her brow furrowed as she searched for a solution.

"What if..." she began, before shaking her head and trailing off.

Harris and Martin exchanged a confused look, their eyes filled with questions.

"What if what?" Hope asked.

"Nada. Es estúpido," Gonzalez replied, running a hand through her hair in frustration.

"Sólo di lo que piensas," urged Hope. *Just say what you think.*

Reluctantly, Gonzalez answered. "Okay. Pero es estúpido. I'm just thinking...what if it needs to be together?"

"Together?" Tinsley repeated, furrowing his own brow in confusion. "What do you mean?"

"Like..." The private took a deep breath, carefully choosing her words before speaking. "Like how ants or bees need to be together in their hives and shit. Except, instead of being hundreds of different little insects, all of these fuckers are part of one thing. Right now, they're all apart. Separated. But they need to be together."

"So," Ford said slowly, trying to understand the soldier's theory. "What? They're in the chamber to..."

"Open the portal," Harris interjected with sudden realization. "And re-join with the source."

"But I don't think it wants to simply *re-join* with lost parts," Schwartz chimed in. "Remember what the boy said? Mother will come."

"Mother will devour," Tinsley added, his gaze fixed on the screen showing the boy and his birth mother. "Mother is hungry." The gravity of their situation weighed heavily upon them as they realized the true intentions of the mysterious entity they were facing.

Hope's breath caught in her throat as she watched Doctor Palmer stride into the chamber, entering through a door to the left of the elevator. Her heart thudded painfully against her ribs as he hurried past three figures standing nearby, seemingly oblivious to his presence. He gestured urgently toward the central platform where the towering rods almost converged, appearing to talk or plead with someone.

"Can we get sound on that?" Schwartz asked, rising to his feet, and nervously bringing a hand to his mouth.

"No," Professor Ford replied, shaking his head. "The consoles have microphones for inter-sector communication, but the operator needs to press a button."

His explanation was cut short as Amy Caldwell reached out and placed her hand on a touchpad. Suddenly, bright orbs of light sprang forth from the tips of the giant rods, bathing the entire chamber in a blinding white glow.

Palmer fell to his knees as jagged beams of electricity crackled and snaked between the rods, forming a cage of energy around the central platform. Hope tore her gaze away from the monitor on the wall to see a pen rattling slowly across the desk, tiny vibrations coursing through the floor.

"Oh no," Tinsley whispered, her hands trembling as she watched the screen on her tablet device.

"What's happening?" Harris' voice inquired through the radio.

"The generator's starting up," Ford informed him.

Hope narrowed her eyes as the monitor briefly flashed white before revealing bolts of electricity swirling around a massive, dark circle—the singularity. Despite its potentially catastrophic consequences, there was something almost mesmerizing about its beauty.

Movement at the edge of the screen drew her attention away from the spectacle. Doctor Isaac Palmer remained on his knees, speaking earnestly to a sandy-haired boy who approached him with arms outstretched. The knot in Hope's stomach tightened as she watched Palmer reciprocate by reaching out to embrace the boy.

And for a brief moment, he did.

As the boy and Doctor Palmer held each other tightly, a grotesque transformation began to take place. The sandy-haired head split open like a flower blooming, revealing a mixture of thick and thin tendrils that eagerly wrapped themselves around Palmer's head, covering his face.

Hope's eyes widened in horror as the knot in her stomach tightened with every passing second. She could only watch helplessly as Palmer's arms flailed wildly before the doctor clenched his outstretched hands into fists. He struck the boy's body again and again in protest, trying desperately to escape. But the boy didn't budge. Instead, the tendrils wrapped around Palmer's face squeezed tighter and tighter until the doctor's head burst open at the crown, spilling thick flesh and dark blood onto the boy before cascading onto the floor below.

The young assistant let out an earsplitting scream as she witnessed the boy tear what remained of Palmer's head away from his neck. The doctor's body fell to the ground, limbs twitching uncontrollably as the lad used his tentacles to toss the severed head toward the large elevator doors, where it rolled and collided with the wall.

"Fuck," Schwartz barked in shock and disgust. "Fuck!"

The boy turned back to Caldwell, revealing his still-open head with twisting and dancing tendrils reaching out excitedly toward the singularity.

The others in the chamber gathered together at a safe distance from the giant, ominous orb that pulsated with an otherworldly energy.

"Are you watching this, Lieutenant?" Tinsley asked through trembling lips, her emotions getting the best of her.

"Yes, Deputy Secretary," Harris replied calmly through the speaker.

Hope shook her head instinctively, tears streaming down her cheeks as she watched Palmer's body convulse and writhe on the ground with increasing violence.

Stay in there, Hope.

The knot in Hope's stomach tightened even more until she thought she might be sick. She couldn't believe what she was witnessing.

Palmer's body went still. For a moment, there was a small sense of relief. But then she saw his body stand up on its own accord.

Still crying, she wiped the tears from her eyes and looked away from the screen to the Deputy Secretary.

Tinsley's chin quivered, and the tablet device in her hands trembled as she stood shakily to her feet, her gaze fixed on the screen.

"Dear Lord," she whispered.

Hope turned her attention back to the monitor, just in time to see Doctor Isaac Palmer's body stand all the way to its feet.

Uncontrollable fear flooded Hope's being, bringing forth tears and a strange guttural sound. "I want to go home," she repeated over and over, her mind unable to fully comprehend the nightmare unfolding before her. All she wanted was to be back in her tiny one-bedroom apartment in New York, surrounded by her huggable plushies. But instead, she was trapped deep underground with dead people walking and the walls closing in on her, trapping her, suffocating her.

Stay in there, Hope, a voice shouted in her mind. *Stay in there.*

It's your turn now, bitch, roared another.

Tears cascaded down her cheeks like a waterfall, and she let out a small, heart-wrenching whimper. "I just want to go home."

Palmer's body strode across the floor to join the others who stood near the pulsing singularity.

Sandra Martin, mirroring Harris' stoic demeanor, asked, "What are they doing?"

"Waiting," the lieutenant answered, his voice devoid of any emotion.

"Waiting?" Sandra repeated incredulously. "Waiting for what?"

Harris looked at her with unflinching eyes, his expression solemn.

"Mother."

Perched in the shuttle's cockpit, Captain Dona Moreau sat askew in her pilot seat, her body tense and coiled as she surveyed the cavern outside. The thick glass of the canopy provided a clear view of the stillness that surrounded her, broken only by the unsettling sight of twisted creatures gathered around the craft.

Their faces were contorted and deformed, giving way to alien appendages that writhed and extended from their flesh, teasing and testing the air. Moreau's stomach clenched at the sight, her mind struggling to comprehend these otherworldly beings.

Suddenly, one of them broke away from the group and made its way toward a large orange panel recessed into the rock wall. Etched onto it was a symbol of a lightning bolt with a warning:

CAUTION: MAIN ELECTRICAL CONDUIT WITHIN.

As the creature reached for the panel with its twisted fingers and smaller tendrils, Moreau realized what it was about to do.

"Lieutenant?" she called into her radio, sitting upright, and planting her feet firmly on the floor. "Harris, are you there?"

"Captain?" came the response through static.

"I think you're all about to lose power down there," she warned. "One of those things is opening an electrical panel in the wall."

"That seems counterproductive," Sandra Martin chimed in. "They just turned on a generator downstairs. Wouldn't shutting off the power also affect their chamber?"

"No." Professor Ford's voice replied through the speaker. "The singularity provides its own energy. It's what this facility was built for—a never-ending power source."

Moreau watched as the creature pried open the panel with its tendrils, revealing five thick black conduits running vertically within. Next to them was a touch panel with an unreadable display screen.

"We could try to change the code here," Martin suggested. "Make it harder for them to shut down the power."

But Moreau shook her head, her eyes fixed on the creature as it reached inside the access point with its arms and head, wrapping its tendrils tightly around the conduits.

"I don't think they care about the code," she said grimly as the creature braced itself against the wall and pushed off with its legs. The conduits bent and stretched under its weight before finally...

Explosions of sparks burst forth from the wall as the monstrous creature crashed to the ground, its twisted appendages clutching broken conduits. The lights attached to the cavern's ceiling flickered wildly before finally dimming, plunging the area into near-total darkness.

"Fuck," Gonzalez barked over the radio, informing Moreau that even the power down in the lower level was out. A loud clunk echoed through the space as all eyes turned toward the giant metal doors leading to the outside world. With a metallic whirr, the doors began to slowly open, revealing a beam of blinding daylight that illuminated the dark expanse. Drifting snow followed suit, floating gently into the maintenance level on a chilly breeze.

"The main doors are opening," the captain reported, her fingers flipping switches on the console before her. "I'm going to try to send a message."

"You should leave, Captain," Harris urged her.

"Leave?" she repeated incredulously. "What do you mean?"

"You have a chance to escape," he explained. "We're trapped down here for now, but you could get out on that shuttle and survive."

She understood his words, and as she peered at the widening door and considered her options, temptation tugged at her mind. But then she shook her head.

"No," she replied resolutely.

"Why not?" Harris pressed. "You have an opportunity to escape. Take it."

"I am still your ranking officer, Lieutenant," she reminded him sternly, watching as the creature rose to its feet near the electrical access point, sparks still sporadically bursting from the wall behind it. "I will leave when you are safely aboard this shuttle and not a second before."

After a brief moment, Harris responded with understanding.

"Yes, Captain."

"Until then," Moreau declared firmly. "You do what you need to do. I'll make a call."

CHAPTER NINETEEN

Inside the professor's office, the large display on the wall flickered intermittently between a blank, blue screen and static, casting eerie shadows in the dimly lit room. The emergency lighting slowly illuminated the dining area outside, casting an orange glow through the windows. Hope wiped her tear-filled eyes as she took in her surroundings. Tiny LED globes, recessed into the ceiling, emitted a dull light that did little to dispel the darkness pressing in on her.

The once spacious office now seemed cramped and suffocating, as if some unseen force were closing in around her. She felt it wrapping around her shoulders and arms, confining her movements. Her breath came in rapid, shallow gasps and she could hear her own heart beating loudly in her ears.

It's your turn now, bitch!

Suddenly, the monitor sprang to life, displaying the company logo in stark white against a black background.

IEC

Innovative Energy Corporation

Hope wiped her eyes again and focused on the screen. She saw people gathered in the Energy Generation Chamber, all facing the dark orb with jagged bolts of electricity dancing across its surface. Among them was Doctor Isaac Palmer's body, standing with the other creatures.

Not far from him stood Amy Caldwell, her naked form eerily still as she gazed at the singularity. Beside her was the boy—his sandy hair matted with blood and his skull split open to reveal snake-like tendrils writhing above his shoulders.

Waiting.

Waiting.

"Lieutenant Harris?" Hope's voice, delicate and trembling, reached out to him. It was as if the weight of her words were too heavy for her to bear.

He responded with a crisp, "Yes, Miss Aguilar."

"We lost the feed from the Shrine for a moment," she said, trying to steady her voice. "But it's just come back and nothing new is happening down there."

"Thank you for the report," Harris replied calmly.

A pained expression crossed her face, like a sharp jab of realization. She corrected herself, "No, that's not what I mean. When we watched the footage of Doctor Caldwell and that creature attacking her, it was only moments after turning on the generator. But now, it has been operational for some time, and nothing has happened."

"Well, isn't that a good thing?" Glenn Schwartz offered optimistically.

"Maybe it's on its way," Gonzalez suggested hopefully.

"On its way?" Professor Ford questioned. "What do you mean?"

"I'm just thinking," the private's voice said through the radio speaker. "That singularity is like a doorway to somewhere else. Maybe that creature lives in a really big place and is out shopping or some shit."

"A portal to another world or galaxy." Schwartz nodded in agreement. "Or even another dimension."

"Whatever it may be," Deputy Secretary Tinsley interjected, "I don't think any of us want to know what will happen when that thing returns."

"Is there no way to shut down the generator remotely?" Harris asked urgently.

Professor Ford shook his head. "No, there isn't. The failsafe protocol requires someone to physically access the terminal that controls the miniature hadron collider."

"In another room?" Tinsley added, her voice full of concern.

"Correct," Ford confirmed, pointing to a screen displaying the layout of the facility. "It's through a door just to the left, out of view here. You can't shut down the generator, but you can realign the rods, causing energy displacement and ultimately dissipating the singularity."

"And what exactly will happen when that occurs?" Schwartz asked, his tone laced with doubt.

"Theoretically, it will rupture or break apart," Ford explained. "The chamber is designed to contain energy bursts, so the surrounding walls and floor will absorb the power displacement and the generator will shut down."

"Hypothetically," Schwartz added cynically.

Ford pursed his lips in contemplation, offering a noncommittal shrug in response.

"And, if the terminal is out of order?" Harris questioned; his voice tainted with faint concern. "Is there another plan?"

The professor's eyes flicked to the screen; his brow furrowed in deep thought. "Ah—" He paused, as if trying to come up with a solution on the spot. "One of the rods would need to be manually loosened and adjusted."

"That sounds like a big task," Hope interjected, taking in the giant rods protruding from the wall around the orb.

"It is," Ford agreed with a heavy sigh. "It's a job that requires at least five people and a mechanical hoist."

"Let me guess," Gonzalez's voice said through the radio. "Those people are probably outside this door, and that mechanical hoist is upstairs."

"Correct," Ford confirmed. "As are the tools needed to unhook the rods."

Gonzalez let out a string of curses.

"What's that?" Tinsley interrupted, pointing at the screen. "Is that normal?"

All eyes in the room turned toward the mounted display. A bright, pulsating disk of light had appeared on the surface of the orb directly in front of the boy and those gathered around him. It expanded, forming a perfect circle and giving off an eerie glow resembling that of an iris with a dark pupil in its center.

The iris continued to pulse, sending waves of energy over the orb and throughout the chamber. It washed over the ceiling and floor, causing everything to vibrate in its wake. The beings in the Shrine shook with excitement, their long tendrils reaching out to touch the energy as it passed over them.

Hope felt her stomach tighten and a lump form in her throat. She fought back the urge to throw up as her mind whispered words she didn't want to hear—*You're going to die down here. Deep underground, where you can't see the sky or taste the air. You're going to die.*

The shadow of a familiar, imposing figure loomed over her, triggering a rush of memories. Images of alcohol and smoke flooded her senses as the figure in her mind descended upon her with a heavy weight. A cruel laughter echoed through the air as she felt its presence grow closer.

It's your turn now, bitch, it sneered, voice dripping with malice. The weight of the memory alone was suffocating, closing in on her like a vise. It pulled her down into an uncontrollable spiral, dragging her deeper and deeper into the depths of despair. Each breath was a struggle, as if she were being dragged under water and struggling to reach the surface for air.

A tear escaped her eye and rolled down her cheek as she watched the pulsating light increase in intensity.

Faster.

Faster.

A pen on Professor Ford's desk vibrated, slowly inching its way from the edge of a faux leather desk mat onto the smooth surface of the timber.

"Jesus," Schwartz hissed, jumping to his feet. "I can feel that through the floor."

"That's impossible," Ford denied, shaking his head. "The structure is designed to absorb shock waves."

"Well, I don't know what to tell you, Professor," the engineer retorted. "But right now, your design doesn't seem to be working."

From outside the eastern emergency stairwell door, the three guardians heard an otherworldly commotion of guttural calls, high-pitched squeals, and inhuman grunting and snorting. They stood frozen, their bodies tense and ready for whatever might burst through the door.

"What the fuck?" Gonzalez spat as she tightened her grip on her rifle, her heart pounding as she positioned herself against the back of the sofa, aiming directly at the door. A sudden thud from outside made the chain to rattle, sending shivers down their spines.

Harris and Sandra Martin raised their weapons at the ready, their eyes scanning the room for any sign of danger. But there was no escaping the incessant thuds that grew louder and more frenzied with each passing moment.

The door began to buckle and bend at its center under the force of whatever was trying to break through. Gonzalez felt her fear intensifying with each passing second.

"They're gonna get through." Her voice trembled with terror.

"Control yourself, Private," Harris told her sternly. "We've been in sticky situations before."

But this time felt different. The barrage of thuds continued without pause, filling the small room with a deafening cacophony. Tears welled up in Gonzalez's eyes as she shook her head in disbelief.

"Not like this," she whispered, wiping her tears on the back of her sleeve.

Harris turned to her, placing a gentle hand on her back.

"Maybe you're right," he said. "But I'm here with you. And you're here with me."

She looked at him, her chin quivering as she realized that this could be the end. But in that moment, all fear and uncertainty melted away as Harris leaned in and kissed her hard on the lips.

Hope's eyes focused on the monitor, her heart racing as she watched the pulsing light. The items on the professor's desk and surrounding bookshelves shook violently, creating a cacophony of sound in the otherwise silent room. A low hum reverberated through the air, adding to the tension that filled the space.

"Lieutenant?" Captain Dona Moreau's voice crackled through the radio. "I can feel tremors up here. And those creatures are going wild, attacking our shuttle."

Harris responded, his words strained with urgency. "We're experiencing something similar down here. It seems something is happening in the Energy Generation Chamber."

On the display screen, Hope saw the energy iris open wide, expanding and growing as if it had a life of its own.

The pulse quickened, becoming a continuous glow that enveloped the entire room.

"What's happening?" she asked, but her question was met with static from the speaker. "Merde!"

"Captain?" Harris called out. "Are you all right?"

A figure appeared from the iris, emerging slowly from the darkness beyond. It was a towering tendril, thick and smoky colored, reaching toward those gathered near the orb.

"One of those creatures just hit our shuttle above my head," Moreau explained. "I'm fine. What's going on down there?"

"We believe something is trying to come through the singularity," Harris replied.

Hope attempted to speak, to warn them of what she saw on the screen, but no words came out as she stared in disbelief.

Out of the corner of her eye, she saw her teammates rising to their feet, equally spellbound by the sight before them.

"And they want to help it," Moreau added in a hushed tone.

"They are a part of it," Harris explained.

Another tendril appeared, emerging from the iris with a sinuous grace. It was thinner than the first, but still impressive in size as it reached out toward the energy orb hovering in mid-air. Like a hand on a table, it wrapped itself around the orb, its movements otherworldly and mesmerizing.

Before long, five more tendrils joined the first one, slithering through the iris and coiling themselves around the orb in a display of power and control that seemed almost sentient.

"It's here," Hope managed, her voice barely above a whisper.

"Miss Aguilar?" Harris's voice crackled through the radio. "Was that you? It's hard to hear you."

"It's here," she repeated, more confidently this time. "It's here, and it's huge."

A moment of tense silence followed as another thick tendril emerged from the iris, adding to the already captivating scene.

"Fóllame duro," Gonzalez's voice warbled excitedly. "Take a look at this."

Another moment of silence passed as Hope presumed the soldiers were viewing the image on their tablet devices.

"Shit," said Harris, his usually composed voice laced with surprise and concern.

Hope raised her eyebrows, surprised to hear the lieutenant curse for the first time.

The radio erupted with chaotic sounds—bending metal, splintering timber, clinking chains and the deafening blast of pulse rifles. It was clear that whatever they had been observing had broken through into their world.

"They broke through," Harris's voice reported grimly over the chaos.

With a swift motion, Harris unzipped Gonzalez's protective coveralls down to her sternum, revealing a flash of her black undershirt. She let out a surprised yelp as he deftly slid a tablet device between the layers of fabric before zipping the coveralls back up. The tension in the air was palpable as Sandra Martin fired rapidly at the door, her shots striking the creatures with relentless precision. The beasts, attempting to break through, exploded into a shower of gore, torn apart by energy bolts, leaving behind a gruesome scene of blood and scorch marks on the walls, ceiling, and floor.

Meanwhile, Gonzalez struggled to adjust the tablet nestled within her coveralls, trying to find a comfortable position for it. Harris trained his rifle toward the door and pulled the trigger, aiming for direct headshots rather than random targets.

The result was a grotesque display of bone, brains, skin, flesh, teeth, and tendrils splattering onto the floor. But for Harris and his team, this was just routine as they focused on taking down any new targets, pushing their way through the horde of creatures at the entrance.

Gonzalez's voice cut through the din with one of her typical crude retorts.

"Mierda de puta!" she shouted. "Esa cosa está viva."

Squirming chunks of flesh wriggled into the corridor, while various sized tendrils snaked their way toward them from the emergency exit. Other detached body parts crawled like worms or caterpillars, some even sprouting new limbs and moving like grotesque cephalopods.

"Fucking hell," Harris cursed, continuing to fire at the ever-growing crowd at the door. "We've got a big problem here."

"Something worse than what we're already facing?" Deputy Secretary Sally Tinsley asked urgently.

"It's possible," Harris replied. As he shot down a severed hand, missing its fourth and fifth phalanges crawling toward him, he explained, "Body parts are reanimating and finding ways to slip past us."

"Body parts?" Tinsley sounded incredulous.

"Mostly smaller pieces," Harris confirmed, his rifle still trained on the doorway. "There's too many of them for us to chase them all."

As the women beside him continued to fire into the chests and heads of their advancing foes, Harris aimed low and unleashed rapid bursts of fire, slicing through legs, feet, and anything else that dared to creep forward.

"These small portions you mentioned," Professor Ford's voice asked through the radio. "Could they potentially fit through closed doors? Like under them? Through the cracks?"

"It's possible," Harris replied, never taking his eyes off the door as he squeezed the trigger. "I think if even a drop of infected blood gets into any of the rooms where your personnel are currently located, we'll have even more of these things to deal with."

Moreau shifted from her seated position on the floor to a squat, her body tense and ready for danger. Slowly, she lifted herself to peer out through the small canopy window. The once incessant thudding and thumping had ceased, piquing her curiosity, and drawing her gaze outside to see where the infected creatures had gone.

Through the window, she caught sight of two figures sprinting on all fours through the door to the eastern emergency stairwell, disappearing into the darkness beyond. Pressing her face against the cool glass on the left side of the cockpit, she attempted to scan her immediate surroundings.

The port side appeared clear. She darted to the other side and glanced out.

Still nothing.

"Lieutenant?" she called into the radio, but there was no direct response. Instead, she could hear faint sounds of gunfire and muffled voices between Harris, Gonzalez, and Martin coming through the speaker. "Lieutenant Harris?"

"I think they're a little busy, Captain," Sally Tinsley responded calmly. "Is there something I could help you with?"

Moreau hesitated for a moment before replying. "I don't know. It looks as if all the infected have left."

"Left?"

"Yes," Moreau confirmed. "I think they're heading down toward your location."

Her words were met with a brief pause before Tinsley responded again. "The CCTV view is limited, but it does appear to be clear there."

Leaning over the instrument panel, Moreau strained to look up through the windshield to the top of the aircraft where she had heard banging earlier. There was nothing in sight.

"Why do you think they left you?" Professor Ford asked.

"I don't know," Moreau admitted with a slight frown. She peered toward the giant doors at the mouth of the cavern, now open wide to the outside world. A strong breeze blew in, carrying with it frost and snow that scattered across the floor near the workshop. "Maybe it's too cold up here."

"Or maybe these fuckers called for reinforcements," Gonzalez chimed in, her tone grim.

Suddenly, Moreau's heart jolted. If the private had overheard her conversation with the Deputy Secretary and the Professor, surely Lieutenant Harris was also aware of their dire situation.

"Private?" she called out anxiously. "Is Lieutenant Harris there?"

"I'm here, Captain," came the swift response.

"Did you hear what I said?"

"Yes," Harris replied tersely. "You think it's all clear up there?"

Moreau glanced toward the shuttle door, contemplating her next move.

"I could go out and make sure," she suggested hesitantly.

Before she could fully form her plan, Harris's stern voice cut through her thoughts.

"Negative," he barked. "Stick to Colonel's orders. Stay inside the shuttle."

With a defeated nod, Moreau agreed. It would be unwise to leave the safety of the shuttle, and she felt foolish for even considering it.

"Understood," she responded.

Frantically scurrying on a strange arrangement of appendages, the small creatures looked like a peculiar fusion between insects and cephalopods. Their partially charred bodies navigated through the back corridor of Level A, away from the deafening sounds of gunfire. With tentacle-like pieces wriggling along the skirting and snaking around corners, they made their way into an empty passage lined with numerous closed doors.

A herd of diminutive chunks of flesh soon clustered and began sliding and scuttling along the corridor. Every now and then, a few would break off from the group to venture toward one of the doors along the way. As they reached the base of each door, they flattened themselves as much as possible to squeeze into the tiny crack between the floor and the panel.

Before long, piercing screams echoed through the passageway.

Alonzo Ferengi hissed and tried to muffle his own breath in an attempt to stay quiet. Pushing his glasses up his nose with his middle finger, he glanced nervously at the door he was sitting by. Perspiration caused them to slip down his nose repeatedly. Across from him, Jahangir Sharma sat cross-legged on his bed, seemingly unperturbed as he casually read a book.

"What was that?" Ferengi whispered, still trying to keep his voice low.

"It's nothing," Sharma replied nonchalantly, lowering his book to his lap. "Just chill. The soldiers will take care of it."

Ferengi furrowed his brow and shook his head.

"We should have made Jiahao come with us," he said worriedly. "He shouldn't be alone out there."

"He prefers being on his own," Sharma countered, raising his book again. "What good would it do to drag him in here?"

"I don't know," Ferengi admitted with a nervous scratch of his beard. "I just don't want to be alone. I thought everyone else felt the same."

"You're a strange one," Sharma remarked, shaking his head with a small chuckle. "Personally, I wouldn't mind being on my own right now."

Ferengi's jaw dropped in surprise at his friend's words.

"What's that supposed to—" He stopped, feeling an odd tickling sensation flow over his ankle. "Hey, what's that?"

Confused, he stretched out his leg and rolled up the fabric of his trousers to reveal tiny maggot-like organisms crawling over his skin. Disgusted, he tried to brush them off, but more appeared, climbing higher and higher up his legs.

Panicked, he jumped to his feet and frantically stomped and flailed, trying to rid himself of the small invaders. His friend Sharma watched from the bed, lowering his book in confusion.

"What the fuck are you doing?" Sharma queried as Ferengi froze in place. His hands went to his crotch as he gawked wide-eyed at his friend on the bed.

"I think they're in my dick," he said, sounding terrified.

"What's in your dick?"

"I think they crawled in through the eye of my dick," Ferengi's voice trembled as tears welled in his eyes.

"What did?" Sharma asked, sliding off the bed. "What's in your dick?"

Shaking with fear, Ferengi stared at Sharma, silently pleading for help.

"Oh God," he whispered, lifting one hand to his stomach. "They're inside me."

"What's insi—" the other started to ask.

Sharma's brow furrowed in confusion as he tried to understand. Before he could ask more questions, he saw movement at the base of the door. A mass of tiny creatures had gathered, crawling over each other like ants and maggots on decaying flesh.

Sharma's heart pounded as he watched his friend, Ferengi, convulsing violently against the wall. Horrific cracking sounds echoed through the room as Ferengi's body contorted and twisted in unnatural ways, bones snapping and breaking with each agonizing movement.

Sharma felt utterly helpless, unable to do anything to stop the unfolding nightmare before him. As a computer engineer, he was used to solving problems with machines, not with human bodies. Give him a malfunctioning computer and he could diagnose the issue in an instant, but when it came to his friend's health, he was lost. He had no idea how to repair a broken body.

Despite his extensive knowledge and diplomas in computer science, Sharma felt woefully out of his depth as he watched Ferengi suffer. He could program complex algorithms and troubleshoot intricate technical issues, but there was no code or algorithm that could save his friend.

The chaos came and went in a flash, leaving behind a scene of devastation. Ferengi's lifeless body lay twisted and mangled on the ground, his once vibrant presence reduced to a mere shell. Sharma felt his stomach tighten and bile rise in his throat before he vomited all over himself. His hands shook uncontrollably, and his legs threatened to give out beneath him.

Tears streamed down his face as he called out, "Alonzo."

He knew it was futile.

He's dead, he cursed himself bitterly.

Something stirred amidst the wreckage; a slight movement that caught Sharma's attention. Slowly, cautiously, he approached his fallen friend.

"No," he sobbed. But there was no denying the truth as he kneeled beside Ferengi's broken form.

Tears continued to fall from Sharma's eyes as he took hold of his friend's hand, the bones crushed and bent under his touch. He stayed there for what seemed like an eternity, lost in grief and disbelief.

It wasn't until something tickled at his legs that Sharma snapped back to reality. The tiny creatures at the door had finally reached him, and he knew that his fate would be the same as Alonzo's.

Just when all hope seemed lost, Ferengi's contorted body moved once more. Thick tendrils burst forth from his chest with lightning speed, engulfing Sharma in their grasp. A shrill cry escaped him as they squeezed tighter and tighter, crushing every bone in his body.

Amidst the agonizing pain, Sharma heard the sickening sound of breaking bones and felt the warmth of blood spewing from his lips. Yet even in this state, as strange as it was, he couldn't help marveling at the terrifying beauty of the monstrous appendages constricting around him.

As another tendril wrapped around his head, blocking out his vision, Sharma knew this was the end. Before he could fully comprehend it, there was a loud snap and then a rush of water in his ears. And then... silence, as everything faded to black.

Chapter Twenty

In the professor's office, the display showed a monstrous mass of writhing tendrils bursting through the singularity. Like a twisted creature from a nightmare, the tendrils snaked over the energy orb and gripped onto the rods protruding from the walls with a vice-like grip.

Then, from the darkness within the orb, emerged a colossal figure. At first glance, it appeared to be a serpentine head, but upon closer inspection, Hope realized it was more like a bud on a plant. The thick neck seemed endless as it continued to push through the singularity.

Countless strange creases covered the bulbous head-like object, spreading from its tip to the base where it met with the neck.

Hope gasped in disbelief as the giant bulb rose on its thick neck, swaying like a cobra. With her mouth agape, she couldn't tear her eyes away from this bizarre intruder. It swung left and right in search of something.

And then, suddenly, the creases parted, and the bulb pointed upwards toward the ceiling of the Shrine. Slowly, it opened up like petals of a grotesque flower, revealing a horrifying mix of fleshy tissue and razor-sharp white teeth.

But in the center of this horrific display was a pulsating bulge of membranous flesh that seemed to throb faster and faster.

"What is it doing?" Tinsley asked, edging closer to the screen.

Hope's heart pounded furiously in her chest as she watched the pulsing speed of the monstrous being increase with alarming intensity. She felt an icy wave of fear and confusion wash over her as she realized that whatever lay within this creature was about to burst forth into their world.

"I-I want to go home," she stuttered, thoughts of her cozy bed and comforting plushies flooding her mind.

A flap suddenly opened at the bulge's edge, revealing a dark, gaping opening inside the bulbous head-like object. It quivered with an ominous energy before closing and swaying menacingly from side to side.

"What the hell was that?" Schwartz demanded.

Before anyone could respond, the ground shook violently beneath them.

"Earthquake!" Ford shouted, gripping onto the arms of his chair for stability.

But it wasn't just an earthquake. A deep, guttural sound, like a deafening horn, echoed through the air, rattling their bones.

"Fucking hell!" the engineer cursed, covering his ears as the windows shattered into tiny shards and the lights flickered manically, casting the room into darkness for a terrifying moment.

Hope could barely breathe as the air seemed to constrict around her, suffocating her with its oppressive weight. Her heart raced faster than ever before, pounding and drowning out all other sounds.

The air became a crushing vice, constricting her throat and stealing her breath. She struggled against the suffocating grip, feeling the weight of the world press down on her until she was gasping for air like a drowning victim. No escape, no relief, just an endless cycle of tightening agony.

Stay in there, Hope.

Cowering in the corner, Hope's body quakes uncontrollably as an overwhelming darkness engulfs her. She bites down on her trembling lip until she tastes blood, desperate to stifle her cries and avoid detection from the monstrous entity lurking in the shadows. But her mother's voice breaks through the silence, a feeble plea amidst the haunting thuds and agonizing groans that permeate the air.

"Stay in there, Hope," her mother's words echo, barely audible over the menacing growls and snarls of the aggressor. It is a futile attempt to protect her child, offering little comfort in this nightmare-inducing moment.

Another voice slices through the air, harsh and guttural, drowning any semblance of hope. "Don't you dare move, bitch," it seethes with malice. "Keep your fucking mouth shut."

Hope's cries intensify into shrill screams as she begs for her mother's rescue. But her pleas fall on deaf ears as her mother can only repeat the same phrase over and over again.

"Stay in there, Hope." Each time, the words sound more desperate and filled with terror, instilling a sense of dread and despair in both captives' hearts.

The lights flickered back to life as the unsettling resonating sound subsided, leaving a deafening silence. Schwartz trembled, his arms outstretched as he scanned the walls and shattered windows for any sign of danger. His gaze settled on the screen, where the large bulb-like appendage hovered over the small group near the orb, sending thin tendrils snaking out from the singularity.

"It came from that thing," he stated, voice trembling with fear. But how? How could something pierce through hundreds of meters of solid rock with sound?"

"The stairwells?" Tinsley suggested, trying to rationalize the inexplicable phenomenon.

Schwartz shook his head adamantly.

"They're too far away for the sound to reach us like this," he insisted.

Hope's gaze darted nervously around the room, her heart pounding. "It...it made the earth shake," she stammered, her words sounding foolish even to herself.

Tinsley placed a comforting hand on Hope's shoulder. "Are you all right?" she asked gently.

Hope tried to nod but ended up shaking her head instead. *No.*

Tinsley wrapped her arms around the young woman, holding her close against her chest.

"It's okay," she whispered reassuringly. But Hope knew it wasn't. With infected corpses attacking from one side and a colossal creature emerging from an event horizon on the other, nothing was even remotely close to being okay. She longed for the comfort of her plushies, for the safety of her own bed and books back in her little apartment.

"Miss Aguilar?" Harris' voice interrupted Hope's thoughts. She frowned and furrowed her brow upon hearing his concerned tone.

"I'm here, Lieutenant," she responded, reaching for the radio on the nearby desk.

"Are you hurt?" he asked, his voice filled with worry. "I heard Deputy Secretary Tinsley ask if you're okay. Are you?"

Hope's heart skipped at the sound of his voice. "I'm fine," she managed, trying to keep the fear out of her voice. The sound of rapid gunfire in the background made it nearly impossible.

"Get ready to run," Harris warned, the noise drowning out his words. "There's too many for us to hold here. They're pushing through and we'll be overrun soon. Private

Gonzalez is on her way to you. As soon as she gets there, I need all of you to make a break for the western stairwell."

"What about you?" Hope called out desperately.

"I'll be right behind you," Harris promised before the radio went silent again.

Professor Ford placed his hands on the desk, leaning toward the assistant, directing his voice to the radio in her hands.

"What about the people here?" he asked. "My staff hiding in their rooms? What about them?"

"I'm sorry, Professor," Harris replied in his usual emotionless tone. "My orders are to escort and protect the UN detail. With luck, Captain Moreau has made contact with the outside world and a rescue mission is underway as we speak."

"With luck?" Ford returned, spinning around in frustration to look out toward the empty cafeteria.

"I did get a message out," Moreau interjected. "The United Nations office in Quebec relayed my request for emergency assistance to IEG."

"Why'd they do that?" Schwartz asked, turning his attention from the display to the radio. "Wouldn't it be quicker for them to just order that themselves?"

"Something to do with Order of Precedence," the captain answered.

"Order of what?" the engineer replied, sounding irritated.

"It's protocol," Tinsley answered. "The UN takes care of UN concerns, meaning us. The company must take care of company concerns, meaning them." She pointed toward the broken windows, out to the facility.

"That's ridiculous," Schwartz said, shaking his head.

"I agree," the deputy secretary said. "But it's the system we have to follow."

"Surely, we could squeeze a few people onto the shuttle with us," the engineer grumbled.

"We could," Hope interjected. "But we may face disciplinary action for interfering with the operational procedures of the corporation."

"What sort of disciplinary action?" asked Schwartz.

"Fines following legal proceedings," the young assistant replied. She then gestured to the deputy secretary. "Possible disbandment of high-level UN personnel involved. Potential loss of employment for the rest of us if it's proved we went along with the decision."

"Even me?" he queried. "I'm contracted in for inspections like this. My main employment is at NYU."

"They'll drag you through the mud," Tinsley told him.

Schwartz shook his head.

"Think of it like documentarians of natural history," Hope said. "When an animal is in danger, they can observe and record only. They can't interfere, no matter how much they want to. At least, they're not meant to. That's how it is for us."

"But the security detail is out there blasting away at the infected right now," the engineer argued. "We've already interfered."

"Defense," Professor Ford broke in. "Their job is to provide security for the deputy secretary and those accompanying her. Lieutenant Harris and Private Gonzalez aren't protecting me and my staff. They're protecting you, the deputy secretary and Miss Aguilar." He turned his head toward the radio. "Isn't that right, Lieutenant?"

"Correct," Harris answered.

"Interference, in this case, is justifiable," Ford continued.

"There is a loophole to the rules," the lieutenant said, gunfire resonating behind his voice. "But you're right. We can't take everyone on the shuttle."

"Loophole?" Tinsley enquired, creasing her brow. "What loophole?"

"It's a little irregular," he returned. "Best not to discuss over the radio."

"What do you mean, *irregular*?" Moreau's voice warbled through the speaker of the radio, now hooked to Harris' hip.

"Sorry, Captain," he replied, aiming quickly at the next creature clambering over the growing pile of charred, twitching pieces of flesh at the doorway. "I'm a little busy at the moment."

Harris fired and struck the beast in the head, blasting a cluster of small tendrils away from where an ear existed previously. A fine spray of blood splashed over the throng gathered behind the brute.

Together, the creatures pushed through the narrow passage as one, bursting into the corridor, some spilling onto the floor in an untidy heap as more clambered through the door.

"There's too many," Sandra Martin exhaled, firing into the horde.

Harris nodded as the beasts fanned out with their backs against the wall, appearing unwilling or afraid to approach the soldier and security officer.

The lieutenant cocked his head.

"Peculiar," he uttered.

A few creatures sprinted into the adjacent passageway, toward the recreational room and living quarters.

"What's peculiar?" Moreau asked.

Harris fired a few shots toward the escapees, hitting one in the back. It tumbled and rolled before correcting itself to continue on its way.

"They're not attacking Miss Martin or me," he answered. "I would say, based on how they're trying to avoid us, they're afraid."

"Afraid?" Schwartz put in.

"I'm here," Gonzalez cut in, her breath coming in quick gasps. Then suddenly, "Oh fuck!"

Hope watched as Gonzalez pivoted, turning to face away from the office door where she stood, swinging her rifle toward the dining area. Thirty or so individuals raced through the kitchen, and even more tore through the corridor to the right of the dining area toward their position.

At a quick glance through the window, it appeared they were in varied stages of transformation. Some had thick tentacles spreading from their heads, protruding through clothing. Others looked no different from ordinary people, except for obvious mortal wounds they bore.

"What is it, Private?" Harris asked.

"I got hostiles here," Gonzalez answered, firing into the approaching crowd. "Coming through the kitchen and from the corridor to our rooms."

"On our way to you," the lieutenant informed her. "Can you gather the detail and make for the western door?"

"I can try," Gonzalez answered. Between shots, she turned her face to glance into the office. Hope saw fear in her eyes, causing the knot in her stomach to tighten more. "You heard him. Get your asses out here and head for the door."

Deputy Secretary Tinsley led the way out of the office with Schwartz close behind, still holding a tablet device. Professor Ford followed, unable to take his eyes off the display until he was out the door. Hope watched him curiously, glancing back to the screen momentarily, to see what might have held his attention so intently before exiting the room.

She saw nothing different; nothing new.

The gathering around the singularity continued to stand in place as the great beast stretched more tendrils through the portal and the giant bulb swayed to the left and right.

Hope frowned and shook her head as she tailed the professor into the corridor, moving westward. Looking over her shoulder, she noticed several infected personnel leaping over tables and planter boxes, some scampering on all fours around the obstacles.

Gonzalez took care with her shots, quickly blasting a limb or two from each of her targets, hoping to slow them down.

"Wait," Hope blurted before darting back into the office and dashing across the room to the desk.

Gunfire rang out as the soldier returned her attention to the approaching crowd.

"Hurry up," Gonzalez shouted.

Hope snatched the radio from the desktop and returned to the door.

"Here." She offered it to the private.

With a quick glance, still focusing on the creatures, firing her weapon into the throng, Gonzalez jutted her chin toward her waist.

"Attach it to my belt," she said, continuing to fire her weapon.

Hope bent low and hooked the clip on the back of the radio over the belt just to the front of Gonzalez's left hip.

"Do you want it here?"

"I don't give a fuck where," the soldier answered. "Let's go."

Hope started forward, hastily stepping toward Tinsley, who was already a few meters into the western corridor.

"Not too fast," Gonzalez called to the group. "I don't know what's up ahead. Stay close." She reached out and gently squeezed Hope's shoulder. "Estas conmigo." *You're with me.*

Hope nodded, her body quivering with terror. "Okay."

"I need you to hold my shoulder," the private told the assistant as she turned away to continue firing into the oncoming crowd. "Guide me through the corridor. I'll keep shooting these fuckers and you keep watch ahead. Tell me if something gets in our way. Understand?"

"Yes," Hope said, placing a firm hand on Gonzalez's shoulder. The soldier backed up, pushing against Hope, forcing her to hasten into the passage. She kept her hand firm on the other's shoulder, tightening her grip as the recoil of rapid fire reverberated through her arm and into her body.

Looking forward, she saw Tinsley and Schwartz, slowly increasing the distance between them.

"Not too fast, Sally." Hope's voice croaked as tears spilled over her cheeks.

Deputy Secretary Sally Tinsley turned quickly upon hearing her name. Hope didn't realize until that moment she reached toward Tinsley with her other hand. Tinsley took it and started forward, keeping pace with Hope and the soldier.

"I'm sorry," the deputy secretary said, fighting back tears of her own. "I didn't mean to leave you."

"I know," the assistant replied, ducking her head to wipe her eyes on the upper sleeve of her coveralls.

Hope's heart pounded as she turned to see the mass of mutated creatures crawling over their fallen, closing in on them, their distorted forms writhing and twisting with unnatural movements. Among them stood Tracey Zelski, her once-familiar face now contorted into a nightmare of tentacles and torn flesh.

Zelski's transformation was one of the most grotesque and horrifying, with a long tentacle protruding from her eye socket and her jaw hanging by a thin flap of skin. In one hand, she wielded a sharp carving knife, ready to strike.

With a bloodcurdling scream, Hope froze as Zelski burst past the other beasts and into the passageway with incredible speed. Before she could reach them, Gonzalez unleashed a barrage of bolts at her knees, tearing through flesh and sending the head chef crashing to the ground in a writhing heap. Zelski let out an inhuman shriek as she thrashed on the floor, her once-human form now twisted beyond recognition.

"Keep moving," the soldier barked as Zelski, unperturbed, pushed herself up on her hands and bloodied leg stumps to chase on all fours, scuttling like an animal. The knife, still clutched in her hand, clinked softly on the floor with each stride.

Gonzalez ripped through the woman with another volley of rapid fire, tearing the creature in half along its spine and through the right shoulder.

Frantically thrashing and flailing, Zelski's severed body parts sprayed a gruesome mixture of blood, feces, and tissue over the already stained floor and walls. The overpowering stench of bile filled Hope's nostrils as she tried to look away from the horrifying scene unfolding before her. Despite being split in half, both portions of Zelski continued their pursuit, using their remaining appendages to drag themselves forward. The chef's head, still attached to one half of her remains, hung limply as a grotesque blend of thin tendrils and viscous white liquid oozed from her open throat, resembling a revolting bowl of noodle soup. With determination, the other half of Zelski clutched onto a knife with its remaining hand, inching closer and closer toward the assistant in a twisted display of macabre determination.

The horde of creatures charged, crawled, and slithered closer, their grotesque forms moving through the carnage on the ground. The head chef's organs snaked through the mess, entwined with the legs and feet of the other monsters as they approached.

"We have to move faster," Gonzalez bellowed, pushing hard against Hope's grasp as she fired relentlessly into the advancing mob.

The monsters poured into the passageway, their relentless march slowing only slightly as they reached the narrow entrance of the corridor near the professor's office. Despite her best efforts, Gonzalez could only momentarily knock down those in the front of the crowd before more emerged, some of them armed with deadly weapons such as kitchen knives, forks, and meat mallets.

As the sickening stench of death filled her nostrils, Hope realized that this was a fight Gonzalez, or anyone for that matter, could not win. They were unstoppable, and she felt her own inevitable slaughter creeping closer with every passing second. There was no stopping them now.

CHAPTER TWENTY-ONE

Frantic creatures burst from the throng, their movements wild and erratic as they lunged toward the soldier and assistant. With the frenzied crowd quickly closing in, Hope's heart raced with fear.

Gonzalez reacted swiftly, unleashing a rapid fire that tore through the advancing mass and sprayed the walls with chunks of charred flesh and blood. The stench of death and burned flesh filled the air, threatening to overwhelm Hope's senses.

She fought back the urge to retch, turning away from the gruesome sight to see Schwartz and Ford a pace ahead, their faces grim with determination. Tinsley gripped her hand, pulling her along the passageway.

I want to go home, Hope thought desperately. It was more than just a wish; it was a desperate plea to escape this nightmare. She longed to be on the surface, far away from this hellish place.

The recoil of Gonzalez's continuous gunfire sent painful vibrations up Hope's arm and into her shoulder.

"We need to move faster," the soldier called out to the others, pushing against Hope's grasp to urge them forward.

As Hope scanned the seemingly endless corridor, she caught sight of the emergency escape door in the distance. To her, it appeared as though countless doors lined the walls on either side, stretching on for miles. In reality, it was less than fifty meters away, but to her, it might as well have been an eternity.

To the left of the emergency door, an intersection led to another passageway that wrapped around the back of the living quarters. It continued past more emergency exits and eventually reached the eastern stairwell on the other side of Level A.

"The tablet," Hope said suddenly, her voice cutting through the chaos.

Tinsley swiveled her head to look at the young assistant, sweat glistening on her brow from the heat and adrenaline of the situation.

"Don't you have it?" Tinsley asked urgently.

"No," answered Hope. "I left it on Professor Ford's desk. But Mister Schwartz has one."

The deputy secretary followed Hope's gaze to Schwartz, who turned briefly to acknowledge his name and lifted the tablet high above his head.

"To tell you the truth," he said with a sheepish grin. "I plumb forgot I had it."

Ford shook his head, his gaze darting past the soldier still firing into the approaching horde.

"Shit," he spat. "They're getting closer. We need to hurry. We can discuss our technological devices later."

"Maldito estúpido idiota," Gonzalez barked in frustration. "Use the damn device to see what's ahead of us!"

The jaws of the two men dropped open.

Schwartz quickly composed himself and turned on the tablet, his fingers deftly navigating through the various camera feeds for Level A.

On the screen, a high-angle view of the cafeteria greeted him, the once bustling space now stained with blood and littered with bodies. In the bottom corner of the image, he saw a few straggling individuals making their way into the passageway in pursuit of them.

Upon switching to another camera feed, Schwartz saw a group of creatures scurrying through yet another corridor. Sweat beaded on his forehead as he frantically scrolled through more feeds, all showing the same terrifying scene.

"They're everywhere," he said breathlessly.

"What about ahead?" Gonzalez asked, her voice strained as she fired bolts at a few tentacled beasts trying to make their way toward them. "Keep moving."

Schwartz quickened his pace, not realizing that he had slowed down while checking the device. He eventually found a view of the adjoining corridor up ahead, with the western emergency door just visible on the right side of the screen.

"I think I found it," he said, adrenaline coursing through his veins as he glanced at the distant door. His eyes caught a glimmer of something dark protruding from the wall to the right of it. A camera. "There! That must be it."

Gonzalez's grip tightened on her weapon as she waited for Schwartz's confirmation.

The engineer's heart raced as he searched the screen for any signs of danger. His hands trembled as he saw an empty corridor stretching out before them, seemingly endless. Relief washed over him, and he shook his head in disbelief.

"Nothing," Schwartz said, still in shock. "It looks clear."

"Then we run for the door," the soldier commanded, firing a spray of bolts over the throng of monsters chasing them. She turned her body, forcing Hope to release her shoulder, and quickened her pace. "Run putas!"

Tinsley squeezed Hope's hand tighter and pulled with all her strength, almost causing the assistant to trip. But she quickly regained her balance and matched the deputy secretary's speed. Schwartz and Professor Ford pulled ahead of them, glancing down at the device's screen every few steps.

Gonzalez turned back occasionally, firing a burst of energy bolts into their pursuers. The sound of flesh and blood exploding filled the air as the lead creatures tumbled to the floor, only to be replaced by those right behind them.

"Someone get the door," Gonzalez shouted, her voice strained with exertion.

Ford picked up his pace, eyeing the carabiner clip holding a looped chain in place. Schwartz checked the display on the device as he struggled to keep up with the professor.

"Something's coming," he called urgently. "Real fucking fast."

"Fuck," cried Gonzalez as a creature leaped out from between two others and grabbed onto her ankle with a twisted, tendril-covered hand. She rolled onto her back and fired into its face wildly.

"Gloria," Hope screamed, turning to see the soldier on the ground behind her, about to be overwhelmed.

"Keep running," Gonzalez hollered from her position on the floor, firing fiercely at anything in reach as she pushed herself back to her feet. "Get to that fucking door."

Tinsley pulled Hope's arm with all her might, fear and desperation fueling her actions.

"Come on," the deputy secretary cried, urging them forward with all her strength.

With every push and twist, Gonzalez fired her weapon, the sound of gunfire echoing in the narrow passageway. But her boot slipped on something slick, and she fell onto her back yet again. She scrambled to get back up, her right arm still clutching her weapon while she used her left to steady herself.

In that moment of struggle, the creatures closed in, their wet footsteps and squelching noises surrounding her. Panic set in as she realized they were within arm's reach.

"Shit," she hissed, turning to crawl away, knowing it was futile.

Then she saw Hope and Deputy Secretary Tinsley running hand in hand ahead of her, with Professor Ford and Glenn Schwartz not far behind. They were almost at the emergency door—so close yet so far.

Suddenly, two figures emerged from a side passage, blocking their path. Harris' voice sounded through the radio attached to Gonzalez's hip, announcing their arrival just as he ran toward them. He passed the two men with a flurry of rapid-fire shots down the passageway, just above Tinsley and Hope and around Gonzalez, as she continued to scramble.

"Get up, Private Gonzalez," Harris ordered as he raced past them all.

"What do you think I'm trying to fucking do?" Gonzalez spat back, feeling frustration bubbling inside her just as a thick tendril wrapped tightly around her ankle. "Shit!"

She flailed on her back just in time to see a knife swinging down toward her with terrifying speed. Bracing for impact, she squeezed her eyes shut—but instead of piercing pain; she heard a sharp clank and felt a jolt through her body. Opening her eyes cautiously, she saw the headless half of Tracey Zelski's body holding the blade pointed toward her stomach. The knife swung down again and again, slicing through her coveralls and creating a small hole in the abdomen of her outfit.

But then, a series of explosions tore through the attacker's body, sending its arm flying. Harris barked at Gonzalez to get up and run, and she wasted no time in doing so. As she ran toward the door, she felt the tablet device Harris had slipped into her coveralls earlier, providing her with some much-needed protection.

Sandra Martin blasted the thick metal chain and sturdy carabiner clip holding the emergency door shut with a powerful burst of gunfire before throwing it wide open. The loud metallic clang echoed through the dimly lit stairwell, revealing the steep stairs leading to the exit.

"Let's go," she said calmly.

The two men rushed past her and onto the metal platform beyond the doors, turning to wait for the others. The floor shook slightly under their feet as they eagerly awaited their escape from the underground facility.

"You should begin climbing the stairs," Martin instructed them in a firm tone. "It's a long way to the top."

"Not without Sally and Hope," Schwartz replied.

Martin clenched her jaw, appearing slightly annoyed by the engineer's words. She turned and gestured for the two women to hurry.

"Quickly," she called out. "The sooner we can get to the surface, the sooner you can get out of here."

Hope glared at the security officer. "We're not leaving without Dean and Gloria."

Martin shook her head.

Tension filled the air as they all waited for Gonzalez to catch up. Meanwhile, Harris stood his ground on the metal platform, firing his weapon into the horde of creatures that had been pursuing them.

As they watched in confusion, they noticed that instead of attacking Harris; the creatures seemed frozen in place, as if they were afraid of him.

"What is he doing? Why are they just standing there?" Ford questioned incredulously.

Martin cocked her head to the side and gave a small shrug.

"We noticed this strange behavior at the other entrance before," she explained. "I think they're afraid of us."

"Us?" Ford pressed further. "I don't understand. They've been relentlessly chasing us this entire time."

"The lieutenant and me," Martin clarified, her expression serious and grim.

Ford shook his head in disbelief.

"But why? What could have caused them to fear you?"

Sandra Martin shook her head.

"Start climbing," she said as Gonzalez rushed by her, straight into Hope's embrace.

"Are you okay?" Hope asked the soldier.

"I'm fine," she answered before placing her attention on the deputy secretary. "I'll take point. I need you and the rest of the detail right on my ass. Got it?"

Tinsley nodded.

Gonzalez glanced at both Schwartz and Hope, who mimicked the deputy secretary's gesture. "We're going to move fast. The L-T and Miss Martin will follow to guard our backs."

As she spoke, the private unzipped the front of her coveralls with a quick tug, revealing a sleek black tablet nestled inside. The screen was littered with impact points and delicate spiderweb-like cracks across the glass surface, stretching from one end to the other.

Just as she freed the device from its confines, Harris burst through onto the platform and forcefully slammed the doors shut behind him. The locking mechanism clanked loudly into place, but he didn't release his hold. Instead, he pressed his hands against each panel, straining against them as if trying to hold back an impending force.

Hope watched him standing in the doorway, his back rigid and his hand gripping the handle. "I'm not coming with you," he said, his voice low and pained.

Hope felt her heart shatter, her stomach twisting into knots once again. She struggled to find words as panic flooded through her veins. "What?" she choked out.

"L-T?" Gonzalez's voice broke through the heavy silence as he stepped toward Harris, the broken tablet slipping from her grasp and clattering to the floor.

Harris tensed as his gaze fell to the thin tendril snaking its way under the door. His heart pounded, matching the sudden thud that echoed through the stairwell. Something heavy slammed against the door from the other side, trying to break through.

"I'll need to hold them here," he explained urgently. "At least until you are close enough to make it to the shuttle."

"Lieutenant," Captain Moreau's voice called through the radio with urgency. "They could already be on their way up the eastern stairwell. We need you up here."

"Sorry Captain," Harris replied, locking his tear-filled eyes with Hope's determined gaze. "I need to go downstairs to dislodge one of those rods. Or, at least, to try to."

"You can't," the captain returned sternly. "I just received a message from Quebec. IEC is sending one aircraft in response to the request for emergency evacuation."

"One?" Ford wrinkled his brow incredulously. "There isn't an aircraft built for landing here that's big enough to take all the personnel."

"They know that," Moreau answered gravely. "They know what's happening here. They've known the whole time. They can access the cameras and have been watching."

"Watching?" Tinsley asked. "Since we arrived?"

"According to the major-general I've been speaking to," the captain answered, "they've been constantly observing the facility since the incident that killed Doctor Caldwell."

"How does the major-general know this, Captain?" Harris queried, pushing hard against the door as another heavy thud reverberated through the panels.

"I asked him the same question," Moreau replied. "He said the UN security sector has been monitoring IEC communications and operations closely ever since the deputy secretary agreed to this assignment."

"They company and the UN knew this whole fucking time?" Schwartz said, a scowl forming as he turned to face Tinsley. "And they didn't cancel the evaluation; didn't even alert us of what happened here?"

Tinsley shook her head, holding her hands up apologetically. "I didn't know," she told him. "I really didn't."

Harris nodded slowly as he contemplated the new information, his mind racing as he processed this new information. "They're sending a bomber."

"Correct," the captain confirmed grimly. "It should be here within the next thirty minutes. But that may not be enough time…"

"What's the payload?" queried Harris, a hint of fear creeping into his voice.

"Two tactical thermonuclear missiles," Moreau replied, her words hanging heavily in the air like a death sentence.

A thick, heavy silence enveloped them as they processed the captain's words. Hope felt as if her brain was being squeezed by her skull, the walls of the stairwell closing in on her. The air seemed to thin, and her breathing turned into quick gasps.

"I'm going to die down here," she whispered, feeling a cold fear wash over her.

Stay in there, Hope, her mother's voice echoed in her mind.

It's your turn now, bitch, the monster taunted from deep within.

Two arms wrapped around her from behind, providing a sense of comfort and protection. Gonzalez's warm breath tickled her ear as she spoke softly in Spanish. "I won't let that happen. We're gonna get out of here, you and me."

"Okay," Hope said, steadying her breathing.

"On my ass," the private instructed, turning toward the stairs. The other members of the group followed suit, except for Professor Ford, who started descending further down.

"I'm staying," he declared.

"Professor, please come with us," Tinsley urged.

Ford stood his ground. "I can't. I'm not part of the delegation."

"Lieutenant Harris has a plan to make it work so you can come with us," Deputy Secretary Tinsley interjected urgently.

"I do," Harris confirmed as another thud reverberated through the door. He looked at Gonzalez. "Private. When I give you a specific order, I want you to follow it without hesitation. Do you understand?"

"What order, sir?" she asked.

"I can't tell you yet," he replied.

"Understood," Gonzalez said before turning to lead the group up the stairs.

"Professor?" Tinsley called after Ford.

The professor hesitated before looking down at the floor. "I'm sorry, Deputy Secretary," he finally said. "Perhaps I can access a terminal in the control room near the hadron collider. If I can adjust the angle variations for the rods, it might help Lieutenant Harris dislodge one of them and potentially override the singularity. Good luck to all of you."

With that, he turned and started toward the lower levels.

"Let me know when you get to the shuttle," Harris instructed Gonzalez. He turned to Deputy Secretary Martin and gave her a nod. "And when I give it, follow my orders exactly."

"Yes, sir," Gonzalez acknowledged before continuing up the stairs with the rest of the group.

As they climbed, Hope stole a glance back at Harris on the next platform. She saw a single tear glistening in his eye before rolling down his cheek as he silently mouthed "go". Clutching onto the rail, she wiped away her own tears and focused on the task ahead. Staying close to Gonzalez, she felt a heavy weight in her heart as they left Lieutenant Harris behind. Every step upwards felt like a burden on her chest, but she pushed forward, refusing to let her emotions get in the way of their escape.

CHAPTER TWENTY-TWO

Harris pushed against the doors for an eternity. The tentacle tips reaching from the other side increased in number, searching relentlessly for any weakness or opening in the barrier. Each thud against the door reminded the soldier of the creatures' determination to break through.

He listened for any sign of the delegation, hoping they were still moving quickly above him. But as he peered upwards, all he could see was the never-ending stairwell stretching on and on. The sound of their footsteps had faded into the distance, leaving him alone with his thoughts and the eerie presence of the creatures below.

"Keep up," Gonzalez's voice came through the radio attached to his hip. "On my ass."

Harris cracked a small smile. She was a strong soldier, and he knew she would get them all to safety. For now, he needed to buy them some time.

The sound of Professor Ford's steps had also faded, leaving Harris wondering if he was waiting for him or had met a more sinister fate at the hands of the creatures below.

"Captain?" Harris called softly, his gaze shifting down toward the writhing tendrils inching closer to his boots. He stomped down hard on one, causing it to recoil under the door. In response, the creatures slammed against the door with another heavy thud.

"Lieutenant Harris," Moreau responded. "Please tell me you're on your way."

"I'm still here at the emergency escape door on Level A," Harris replied, trying to keep his breathing steady despite the increasing pressure from their relentless attackers. "Private Gonzalez is leading the delegation up to you. They've been climbing for about two minutes now."

"How much progress have they made?" Captain Moreau asked urgently.

"I can't see them now," Harris reported, his eyes straining to catch a glimpse of their progress.

"Private, can you hear me?" Moreau addressed Gonzalez directly.

"Yes, Captain," the soldier responded confidently.

"This is a matter of urgency." Moreau's voice sounded strained. "Can you climb any faster?"

"On my own, yes," Gonzalez replied without hesitation. "But with the delegation…"

"I understand." Moreau sighed. "Just do your best."

Harris stomped on another tendril that was inching too close to his foot, causing it to split and sending a small spatter of blood onto the grated platform.

"What's the situation up there, Captain?" he asked.

Moreau's response was delayed, as if she were moving or sitting up in her seat. "It's clear up here. No sign of those things."

"Any news about the incoming bomber?" Harris pressed.

Moreau let out a heavy sigh before she replied, "Nothing. I've been listening to chatter from the UN. They're closing shipping lanes between the Beaufort Sea and Baffin Bay and holding vessels at the Northwestern Passage, but nothing about a bomber."

Harris felt increasingly anxious at the lack of information. He sensed Moreau's need for conversation after being confined in the shuttle for so long, but he knew his own interpersonal skills were lacking, especially in a high-stress situation like this.

"It can't be a pre-emptive strategy for the initial impact of detonation and potential fallout," he mused aloud. "Could it?"

He cursed himself for always defaulting to work-related content. Even during the rare moments when he allowed himself to relax with Gonzalez in his arms, their conversations inevitably turned back to tactics, weaponry, and operational procedures. It wasn't until he was lying next to Hope that his mind had finally quietened down and focused on something other than his job.

She speaks with a genuine passion about her love for Thai cuisine, describing the intricate flavors and spices of her favorite dish—green curry chicken from a small take-out shop located in Tudor City. She mentions how it's just down the block from her apartment, which she proudly reveals is not too far from the prestigious United Nations Headquarters in New York.

In addition to her love for Thai food, Hope also shares a personal detail about herself—a collection of plushie toys that wait for her on her bed in her tiny apartment. She admits that she can't survive without them, smiling shyly as she confesses this quirky part of herself.

At this moment, Harris feels his heart flutter as he watches Gonzalez fall in love with the young woman.

As they lie together in bed, recovering, Hope opens up even more. She tells them about her phobia of small spaces and how it makes it hard for her to relate to others. This has resulted in a small circle of people she trusts, mostly made up of colleagues—but no real friends.

Tears cascade down her cheeks, leaving glistening trails on her skin as she mutters, "I don't know what made me come here tonight. I've never done anything like that before." Her voice quivers with a mix of embarrassment and vulnerability, the weight of her words heavy in the air.

But Harris and Gonzalez respond with unwavering compassion and understanding, their expressions soft and empathetic. "It's okay," Gonzalez consoles, reaching across Harris to stroke Hope's arm.

Everything seems to stop as Hope gathers the courage to continue. "My father... he raped me when I was nine years old," she blurts out.

Harris' eyebrows furrow with shock and anger, while Gonzalez's jaw drops open in disbelief.

After a moment, Hope speaks again. "He used to beat my mother all the time. But this one time, he came home drunk. Really drunk. She hid me in the closet. I clung to my pooky bear for dear life. I was so scared."

Her voice shakes as she recounts the horrifying memory. "She fought him off for a little bit," she continues. "But then he hit her so hard... she started repeating the same thing over and over. 'Stay in there, Hope. Stay in there.'"

Hope pauses, tears streaming down her face and onto Harris' chest.

"It's okay," he whispers, tightening his arm around her shoulder in a comforting embrace. "You don't have to say anything else."

With shaky breaths and ragged sobs, Hope forces herself to keep going. "When he finished with her," she chokes out through her tears, "he opened the closet door and told me... 'It's your turn now, bitch.'"

Gonzalez weeps openly beside them. It's the first time Harris sees her cry.

Hope's voice trembles as she recounts the terror of her past. "My pooky bear saved me," she tells them, her compact frame huddles against Harris's chest. "I hugged him so close; he covered my face so I couldn't see and my mouth so he couldn't hear me scream. I know he would have beaten me like he beat her if I made a sound. I know he would."

Harris's grip on her tightens, his jaw set in a hard line as he listens to the horror she endured.

"I don't know where he is now," Hope says, wiping her eyes with her palm, the memory fresh and painful. "Probably dead... I hope. I lived with my grandparents and mother in Pueblo after that." The weight of her words hangs heavy in the air, each syllable carrying the burden of her trauma.

But in this moment, safe from harm, Harris whispers reassurances to her.

"You're safe now." His lips gently touch her forehead. His arms wrap around her shoulders, offering comfort and protection.

Safe, he thought.

He told her she was safe.

Now, she ran for her life from something far worse than any of them could imagine.

"I don't know," Captain Moreau said with a slight sigh, answering the question that Lieutenant Harris had posed to her. "It's better to keep people at a distance, just in case."

Harris considered the captain's words.

"I don't think it will make a difference if that thing breaks through the singularity," he replied.

A moment of tense silence hung in the air.

"Well, that's one way to bring some gloom into the conversation, L-T," Gonzalez said.

Moreau added her own input, her tone laced with concern. "I really wish you would reconsider, Lieutenant. Surely the bombs will do their job."

"Maybe," Harris conceded. "But I need to be absolutely certain that we've exhausted all measures to stop that thing."

***

The act of climbing the seemingly endless stairs was a grueling and exhausting task. Hope, who prided herself on her physical fitness and dedication to the gym, felt her heart pounding in her ears as she pushed herself to keep up with Gonzalez's relentless pace. The soldier pushed the group to their limits, determined to get them to safety as quickly as she could.

"On my ass!" Gonzalez called out, urging the others to keep moving. Looking back down at how far they had come, Hope couldn't see Harris anymore. Tinsley offered an encouraging smile, while Martin appeared completely unfazed by the climb, effortlessly walking backward and keeping a vigilant eye on their surroundings.

"We're almost there," the deputy secretary huffed, peering up at something above them. Sweat dripped from her forehead, just as it did for Schwartz, Gonzalez, and Hope.

"Thank Christ." Schwartz sighed heavily.

Turning her gaze upwards toward the next flight of stairs, Hope spotted the door that would lead them to the surface level. But there were still about twenty platforms between them and that door, each representing another arduous climb.

But we're almost there, she thought with renewed energy.

"L-T?" Gonzalez called out over their radio communication. "Are you still down there?"

A moment of silence filled Hope with dread as she feared for Harris's safety.

"I'm still at the door," he finally responded. "How are you all doing?"

"We can see the door to the surface," Private Gonzalez replied. "We should be able to make it in three to five minutes."

"Good work," Harris praised them. "Try to move faster if you can. I need to reach the Energy Generation Chamber and I don't know if those creatures will follow me or come after you."

"Understood," Gonzalez acknowledged, turning to urge the others to pick up their pace. "We need to move as quickly as possible. We're almost there."

"Private?" Captain Moreau's voice burst through their radios.

"Captain," Private Gonzalez responded.

"Notify me when you reach the shuttle door," the captain ordered. "I'm standing by to open it."

"Yes, ma'am," Gonzalez replied, her determination and sense of urgency driving her forwards as she climbed the last stretch of stairs. "On my ass."

Harris pressed his hands against the thick metal doors, taking in a long, deep breath before finally exhaling. He felt the thin, noodle-like tendrils snaking their way around the sides of the door panels and through the doorjamb, twisting and stretching like desperate claws searching for prey. His grip tightened on the rifle slung over his shoulder as he mentally prepared to descend the stairs behind him.

With a quick step back, Harris retrieved the pulse rifle and aimed it toward the quickly approaching doors that seemed to swing outwards with intense speed. As soon as they burst open, a horde of grotesque creatures lunged forward, their twisted forms pushing the doors wider and wider.

Harris's finger hovered over the trigger as he braced himself for their attack. But to his surprise, the beasts stopped in place upon seeing him. Without hesitation, he unleashed a rapid-fire blast toward them before he darted down the stairs at remarkable speed.

Chunks of burned flesh and spouting blood erupted from the throng as Harris ruthlessly mowed them down. Tendrils, fingers, arms, and organs flung in all directions, painting the walls and floor with gory splatters.

Releasing the trigger, Harris leaped onto the next platform and quickly pivoted to take a glance back at the door before preparing to leap down the following flight of stairs. The horde burst through the door, briefly pausing when confronted by the determined soldier before charging after him.

Harris's heart raced as he glanced up and saw a portion of the horde splitting off to climb up the stairwell toward his comrades.

"Private," he called, his feet carrying him swiftly to the next platform. "Some of them are heading your way. Secure the door after you get to the surface."

"How will you get through?" Gonzalez asked.

"I'll figure it out," Harris replied, scanning the creatures rapidly descending the stairs above him. "Just make sure that door is secure for now."

"We'll leave it open for you," Hope called out.

"No." Harris frowned as he leaped again. "Private, I order you to secure that door as soon as you're through it. Understood?"

There was a moment of silence over the radio before Private Gonzalez reluctantly responded with an affirmative.

"Yes, sir."

Harris pushed forward, using bursts of energy bolts to thin out the horde as he leaped from platform to platform. The gap between himself and the attackers widened with each jump, giving him some breathing room by the time he reached the open doors of Level B.

As he cautiously peered through the gaping passageway, a horrific sight met his gaze—pools of blood and scattered body parts squirming and twitching on the floor. Yet, there was no sign of any creatures inside. He couldn't forget the fate of his colonel and two comrades who had entered before him, disappearing into this gruesome scene. Bracing himself, he continued down, occasionally stealing a quick glance upwards to determine the distance between himself and the throng descending the stairs just above him.

Hope's legs burned as she climbed yet another flight of seemingly endless stairs, her breaths coming in ragged gasps. Each step felt like a mountain to conquer, the walls closing in around her, making her long for a moment's rest. But Private Gonzalez was moving too quickly for that.

"Keep up with Private Gonzalez," Sandra Martin urged the delegation, but it seemed an impossible feat.

"On my ass," Gonzalez muttered under her breath.

With a deep breath and sheer determination, Hope pushed herself onward. Her muscles trembled and her joints ached with each step. As they finally reached a platform, Gonzalez was already halfway up the next set of stairs.

"It's right there!" the private exclaimed excitedly. "Hurry!"

Wiping sweat from her forehead and struggling to control her heavy breathing, Hope glanced back at the deputy secretary and engineer behind them. They looked just as exhausted, gripping onto the railing, and heaving themselves up each step.

"Shit," Martin cursed, staring down the seemingly never-ending stairwell.

"What is it?" Gonzalez asked.

"I can see them," Martin replied through gritted teeth. "They're getting closer."

Tinsley whimpered as she forced herself to pick up speed. Tears glistened in her eyes and Hope felt her fear and pain. She reached out and took Tinsley's hand, mirroring the gesture the deputy secretary had made when she needed comfort.

"We'll make it," Hope soothed, though her own voice betrayed a slight tremor.

Nodding bravely, Tinsley followed Hope across the platform to join Gonzalez on the next flight of stairs.

Up they climbed, their footsteps ringing out on the metal grating beneath them. Martin paused momentarily to fire energy blasts down at their pursuers, but Hope couldn't look back—too focused on reaching the door ahead.

"Faster!" Gonzalez barked, crossing another platform before the final set of stairs.

"We can do it," Hope muttered, her determination growing with each step.

"Almost there," Tinsley panted.

"For fuck's sake," Schwartz gasped as he joined them on the platform, clinging to the railing for support.

Martin followed, unleashing another barrage of blasts down at their enemies.

The sound of approaching heavy footfalls echoed through the narrow stairwell, reverberating off the walls and growing louder and more menacing by the second. But Gonzalez reached the door to the surface first, her hand gripping the cold metal knob and pulling it open with a determined strength. A cool rush of air greeted them as she peered into the space beyond, quickly scanning for any danger that might lurk in the shadows.

"Looks clear," she called back to her team, beckoning them forward. "Quickly."

From midway up the flight of stairs, Hope's gaze swept over the cramped space, taking in the side of one of the pod-like structures on the surface level. Her heart swelled with a mix of relief and hope as she realized how close they were to safety.

"Look," she said excitedly to Tinsley. "The cavern is just ahead."

The deputy secretary nodded, barely able to stand, let alone climb the remaining stairs.

Martin fired her weapon again and again, shots ringing out as they ascended the last flight of stairs toward the last platform before the door. Just as the team reached the opening, Gonzalez bolted to Martin's side and held the door open with one hand while aiming her rifle down the stairwell with the other.

Hope noticed how fatigued Gonzalez looked, struggling to catch her breath and maintain her composure under this intense pressure.

"We'll be home soon," Hope whispered.

Gonzalez nodded and managed a small smile before leading Tinsley and Schwartz through the threshold into the cavern.

Exhausted and relieved, the team collapsed onto the ground against a nearby pod, using it as support for their weary bodies.

"Find something to secure this door," Martin ordered, reminding Gonzalez of Harris' command. She quickly pulled the door shut behind her and locked it with a loud clank as the mechanism slid into place. "We're not out of the woods yet."

The soldier stood up, wiping the sweat off her face with the back of her sleeve as she surveyed their surroundings.

"I'll help," Hope offered.

"Check inside the pods for anything useful," Martin suggested, her eyes scanning the area for potential threats. "I'll stand guard."

Gonzalez nodded and started along a short path toward another pod.

"You check this one," she directed Hope, pointing to the pod that Tinsley and Schwartz were leaning against. "I'll check over here." Her voice was steady and resolute, but Hope saw the worry etched in her features. They were still far from safety, and they needed to stay alert and focused if they wanted to make it out alive.

Harris leaped with a desperate determination, landing hard on the unforgiving cement floor below. His heart thudded as he sprinted toward the emergency doors, their gaping maw beckoning him into the unknown darkness beyond. The dim LED lights lining the ceiling inside offered little solace, casting eerie shadows on the walls that were streaked with dried blood.

Mounted on the wall just inside the doorway was a large sign directing readers to the Energy Generation Chamber to the left and the Terminal Control Room and Hadron Collider Access to the right. Harris followed an unmistakable trail of glistening blood leading toward the Energy Generation Chamber with his eyes. He hesitated and turned toward the Terminal Control Room and Hadron Collider Access in the opposite direction.

With a clenched jaw, Harris forged ahead, his feet pounding against the concrete floor as he rounded a sharp curve to find a door directly in his path. He braced himself for what lay beyond and reached for the handle.

A deafening crash reverberated through the corridor from behind him—a chilling reminder that time was running out and the creatures were closing in on him.

Without hesitation, Harris turned the handle and slipped silently into the pitch-black room. The only source of light came from a row of computer terminals lining one wall and displaying the company's logo:

IEG, Innovative Energy Corporation.

Their tagline read "The Future's Bright. The Future's Energy." The desks were arranged neatly with dividers separating each workspace, resembling an office setting.

The lieutenant closed the door behind him with a soft click, the only sound breaking the tense silence that filled the room. As his eyes adjusted to the darkness, he saw a familiar figure hunched over a terminal in the far corner. The professor's fingers flew across the keyboard, scrolling through lines of code and CCTV feeds from the Shrine. On one screen, a massive tentacled entity thrashed its bulbous head around, accompanied by another similar form that must have recently emerged through the singularity.

"I thought you'd be here," Harris said quietly, approaching the professor. "Is there another way into the chamber?"

"Ah," Ford replied, pointing to a wall on the left side of the room. "There's a door just there that leads to the hadron collider. If you pass the ladder and keep going straight on, you'll come to a panel that opens into the Shrine."

"Ladder?" Harris asked, confused.

"Yes, it leads up to the hadron collider access tunnel," the professor clarified.

"We need to barricade this door," Harris said, surveying his surroundings. He spotted six more terminals clustered together in the center of the room, grabbed one and dragged it across the floor as quietly as possible, pushing it against the door. He repeated this process with another desk, placing it against the first.

"What have you been doing down here, Professor?" Harris asked as he continued dragging terminals for their makeshift barricade.

"I'm running a program to realign the rods by ten degrees," Ford explained. "It should throw off the stability of the singularity, but I can't guarantee it. I'm also attempting to reboot the hadron collider."

"Why do you want to reboot it?" Harris asked as he pushed another terminal into place.

"Rebooting acts as a reset for all programs associated with the Energy Generation Chamber," Ford answered. "Essentially, everything will shut down and then run a diagnostic before starting back up. It may not be enough to kill that thing, but it might stop the rest of it from coming through."

Harris finished placing the last terminal in their makeshift barricade, his hands trembling with doubt. "You don't think we can kill it?" he asked, looking up at Ford.

The professor shook his head as they both turned to watch the creature on the screen. "Everyone in this facility is dead, Lieutenant," he said grimly. "And yet, there they are—moving around, infected or affected by that monster. Even in its absence, they respond to its presence. It's as you suggested. They're a part of it."

Ford paused, then added, "It made me think perhaps we can't kill it by simply shutting off the singularity. Perhaps if we cut a limb off that thing, the limb continues to survive as a separate part of that entity. Perhaps each of those people is a separate part of the one thing."

Harris frowned, processing this new information as he adjusted the terminal desks against the door. "Then why should we even try to stop the singularity if it can't be killed?"

"I think this thing might be like a cephalopod," Ford replied, gesturing toward the screen. "Like an octopus. Have you ever seen the way an octopus can squeeze through the narrowest of passages to get to its prey?"

"Yes," Harris answered, walking across the room to stand beside Ford and gaze at the screen.

"Well," Ford continued, his voice tinged with fear and awe. "I think we're looking at something much, much larger than what we can see here. And perhaps it doesn't need to bring its entirety through to our world. Just a portion. Just enough to devour its prey."

"Us," Harris interjected.

"Our world, Lieutenant," Ford corrected him. "I believe this entity has tasted the fruits of our world and now wants more."

As they watched the monitor intently, another tendril burst through the singularity, grasping onto one of the rods protruding from the chamber wall.

Chapter Twenty-Three

The ceiling lights inside the pod flickered relentlessly above Hope's head as she navigated through the debris of strewn clothes and overturned appliances. The bed lay on its side at a twisted angle, one end propped against the wall while the other corner dug into a recliner chair, turned on its back.

As she took in the scene before her, Hope was overcome with a sinking feeling of dread. It looked as though a bomb had gone off inside this room, but the gruesome chaos that greeted her eyes was far more sinister than any explosion could create.

Bloodied handprints smeared the walls, leading away in long, red trails. A large dent marred the short kitchenette counter, evidence of a violent struggle, its surface adorned with chunks of flesh still glistening in the dim light.

A thick pool of blood at the base of the counter grabbed her attention, staining the floor with wet footprints leading out the door she had just entered through.

A chill ran down her spine as she realized someone had died in this very spot where she now stood. The amount of blood was staggering.

Desperate to leave this macabre scene behind, Hope turned to make her way out, following the trail of bloody prints. But as she approached the door, something caught her eye near the impact dent on the counter.

An extension cord dangled over the edge, still plugged into the wall socket.

Instinctively, she remembered the chains used to barricade doors shut on Level A and grabbed hold of the cable near the socket to pull it free. But her hand slipped along its length, coming into contact with sticky liquid.

Blood.

Her stomach churned as she fought back a wave of nausea and disgust. She couldn't believe what she was seeing and experiencing.

But she couldn't afford to dwell on it for long. With determination, she gripped the cable and ran outside, clutching the bloodstained cord as she sprinted toward the emergency exit.

Sandra Martin's knuckles turned white as she clung to the release bars of the locking mechanism, her muscles straining against the force of whatever was trying to break through the doors. Hope noticed tendrils and fingers snaking their way beneath the panels, searching, twisting, and clawing at the edges.

"What did you do?" Deputy Secretary Tinsley demanded, noticing Hope's blood-stained hand.

"It's not mine," Hope insisted, rushing to Martin's side to thread a cable through the locking mechanism.

"Make it tight," the security officer barked as the doors rattled with increasing vigor.

Hope frantically passed the cable through again and again, leaving just enough length on either end to tie it off.

"That's the best I can do," she gasped.

"Can I help?" Schwartz offered.

"I've got it," Martin replied with fierce determination.

Releasing the bars and gripping onto either end of the cable, she pulled with all her might until it stretched another few inches. With trembling hands, she looped the ends over each other three times before tying them securely beneath the release bars.

"Let's move!" she shouted to the delegation, leading them toward the pod that Gonzalez had entered moments before.

Just as they reached it, Private Gonzalez emerged from within, shaking her head in disbelief. Her lips moved as if trying to form words.

"Private Gonzalez?" Tinsley called out. "Are you okay?"

The soldier's expression was one of shock and horror as she locked eyes with Hope.

"Es una puta pesadilla ahí dentro," she whispered hoarsely. *It's a fucking nightmare in there.* She turned to look at the delegation. "It's unlike anything I've—"

"We've barricaded the door," Hope interrupted. "We need to go."

Gonzalez's grip on her rifle tightened, adrenaline coursing through her body as she steeled herself for the inevitable chaos waiting outside. With a deep breath, she turned to face the delegation and spoke with determination. "Stay alert and keep your eyes open for anything."

As they followed her lead, walking between rows of pod structures, Gonzalez felt a sense of foreboding wash over her. They took a sharp left turn, then a quick right, and the cavern opened before them.

The sight of the common room to their left and the shuttle just beyond brought a mix of emotions for Hope; relief at being so close to safety, but also apprehension at the carnage surrounding them.

The shattered windows of the common room littered the ground in shards, bloodstains marking the floor in all directions. But what was most unnerving was the eerie silence that hung heavy in the air.

Harris slowly opened the heavy door, revealing the entrance to the hadron collider access tunnel. The dimly lit passage stretched before them, ending abruptly at a menacing hatch-like door. A bright yellow ladder stood ominously against the wall in the middle of the passage, leading up to a dark rectangular portal.

"How do you plan to get out of here?" Harris asked, his voice laced with urgency.

Ford, still focused on the terminal screen in front of him, replied calmly, "I'm not sure. I wasn't expecting to make it out alive."

Harris turned to look back at the barricaded door and realized there was no way they could escape that way. He turned back to Ford. "Can we access the emergency exits from here?"

The professor shook his head. "They're located through the hadron collider access tunnel. It's too far and we won't make it before that bomber reaches us."

Frantically, Harris thought of other options as lines of code scrolled across the monitor in front of them. Suddenly, everything froze as a deep vibration reverberated throughout the room.

"What's happening now?" Harris asked.

"The hadron collider is rebooting," Ford answered with a sense of relief. "The system is trying to restart itself."

Harris bolted to the professor's side, his heart racing as he watched the scientist clapping his hands with manic excitement.

"This could actually work?" he asked, desperate for a glimmer of hope.

Ford's eyes were wild with determination as he nodded fervently. "It should have reset the Shrine by now."

As Harris frantically checked the CCTV feed from the Energy Generation Chamber, his stomach dropped when he saw the active orb still functioning. The creature's slimy tendrils remained wrapped tightly around every long rod, holding them in a death grip.

"Is it—".

"It's holding onto the rods. Fuck!" Ford exclaimed in frustration, his voice straining with fear. "The singularity won't close!"

"But you reset the program," Harris pleaded, pointing desperately to the ceiling. "That should have fixed everything, right?"

"The program works in a never-ending loop," the professor explained grimly. "The power from the hadron collider flows through the rods, creating the energy initially needed to create the singularity. Then the rods act as an anchor, sustaining and holding it in place. And as long as that aberration keeps those rods locked in place, the singularity will continue to thrive."

"And it seems that the creature inside has figured this out," Harris observed as he studied the image of the monster gripping onto the rods with malicious intent.

Ford clenched his jaw and turned to face the terminal, his fingers hovering over the keys.

A deafening and unearthly roar ripped through the room, shaking the very foundations of their reality. The professor shot up from his seat in terror as the barricaded door thudded violently, signaling the relentless pursuit of whatever creatures lurked outside.

"Don't worry about them," the soldier snapped, his gaze darting to the open door and the increasing clicks that echoed through it. "You'll want to cover your ears." Harris pressed his trembling hands tightly against his head, bracing himself for what was to come.

"Why?" Ford asked, his features twisted in confusion and fear.

But before he could receive an answer, a guttural and resonant cry reverberated all around them. The ground shook with a violent force, sending clouds of dust cascading down from the ceiling like a sinister fog. Harris winced as the sound pierced through him, rattling his bones, and vibrating his very core. Ford collapsed to the ground, writhing uncontrollably as he clutched at his head in agony.

One of the terminal monitors crashed to the ground, shattered into pieces by the sheer power of the sound. Struggling to remain upright, Harris rushed to reinforce the barricade with every ounce of strength he had left. The tremors surged up his legs and through his body, causing waves of nausea to crash over him. From Harris' perspective, Ford appeared to be screaming in torment, mouthing unheard words as he locked eyes with the soldier in desperation.

Feeling utterly helpless and unable to ease the professor's suffering, Harris could only endure the unbearable assault on their senses and pray that it would soon pass.

"What the fuck?" Gonzalez gasped as a deafening roar echoed through the cavern. The ground trembled, threatening to give way at any moment.

"That thing down in the Shrine," Martin offered, her voice shaking as she aimed her pulse rifle at the shattered windows of the conference pod. The monstrous creature could be heard even from this distance, its trumpeting cry filling them with dread.

"Jesus," Schwartz hissed, horror etched on his face as he watched dust and debris rain down from the ceiling. He felt the weight of the solid rock above them, ready to collapse at any moment.

"Dean's down there," Hope said, meeting Gonzalez's gaze with a mixture of fear and determination.

"I'm sure he's all right," Gonzalez replied, trying to sound confident. She turned and motioned for them to follow him toward the shuttle. "Come on. We're almost there."

The deafening roar finally faded, replaced by the ominous clicking that gradually slowed to a stop. Ford and Harris cautiously lowered their hands from their ears, breathing heavy sighs of relief that it was over.

Before they could fully relax, they heard high-pitched squeals and crying coming from behind the barricaded door. The soldier instinctively reached for his gun, ready to defend against any potential threat.

"Fuck me," Ford shouted as Harris pulled him to his feet. But as suddenly as they had started, the cries abruptly ceased, leaving the professor bewildered. "What was that all about?"

"I don't know," replied Harris sternly. "Maybe an announcement of victory."

"Victory?"

"You failed to shut down the singularity," reminded Harris coldly.

Ford nodded, returning to the terminal with Harris by his side. After quickly scanning the CCTV feed, the soldier pressed his index finger against the screen.

"Is this still operational?" he asked urgently, his finger tracing over the large elevator doors on the display.

"Ahh," Ford replied, typing furiously on the keyboard as he sat back in his chair. A new window popped up, displaying a list of features in the facility. He scrolled down and clicked on a tab labeled "ELEVATORS."

Then he clicked on another sub-tab for "SERVICE ELEVATOR."

The screen flickered to life, displaying a digital schematic of the elevator shaft. Red lights flashed frantically, showing the current status of each level: INACTIVE.

The schematic zeroed in on the four doors of the elevator, labeling them with their designated levels in bold letters.

SURFACE.

LEVEL A.

LEVEL B.

LEVEL C.

But it was the flashing red box at Level C that caught their attention—the presence of the elevator sitting idle.

"Is that where the lift is located right now?" Harris demanded.

"Yeah," Ford answered, sweat beading on his forehead. "The safety features will automatically take the cars to the lowest point in each shaft. It's designed so that if we have a power outage or need to shut them down, the system will bring them all the way down before shutting off completely."

The soldier's gaze darted back and forth between the barricaded door and the open entrance to the hadron collider access.

"We need to turn this one back on," he stated.

The professor hesitated. "I can...but why?"

Harris's gaze shifted from the potential escape route on the screen to the dark depths of the hadron collider access passage.

"I have a feeling that's our only way out of here," he said. "And I refuse to die trapped underground with those fucking things out there."

"Captain," Gonzalez barked, ripping the radio from her belt and holding it up to her face. "We're here."

"Okay," Moreau replied. "I'm opening the hatch."

With a hiss, the door slid open, and the ladder extended toward the ground like a mechanical tongue. Martin and Gonzalez raised their weapons, ready for any movement in the dark expanse of the cavern. "You first, Deputy Secretary," Moreau said, one hand outstretched toward Tinsley while her other hand gripped her weapon. The deputy secretary reached up to grab Moreau's hand, feeling the cold metal against her skin. Behind them, Gonzalez nudged Hope with her elbow, silently urging her to keep moving.

"It's your turn." Gonzalez's voice was gruff and commanding as she barked out her order.

Hope hesitated, glancing nervously at the engineer before speaking up. "I really think Mister Schwartz should go next."

Schwartz raised an eyebrow in surprise.

"What sort of gentleman do you take me for?" he asked, gesturing to the open door of the shuttle. "Ladies first. I insist."

Hope turned to Gonzalez. "I don't want to leave you."

"Do as you're told," Gonzalez ordered, pointing to the ladder that led up into the shuttle. "And be quick about it."

With a defeated sigh, Hope climbed the ladder. She reached the top rung and took Moreau's hand for support as she stepped onto the shuttle's floor. She made her way across the aisle and settled into the seat next to Tinsley, giving herself a good vantage point to watch the others as they entered through the open door.

"There's no time for chivalry, Mister Schwartz," Gonzalez barked at the engineer. "Get on the shuttle now."

Schwartz hesitated, his gaze shifting between Gonzalez and Sandra Martin, who stood nearby, her attention fixed on the vehicles clustered together near the giant door leading to the outside world.

"What about—" He returned his gaze to Gonzalez.

Hope recalled the brief conversation they had about protocol. Once Schwartz boarded the shuttle, the entire delegation would be on board. But unfortunately, Sandra Martin wouldn't receive the same courtesy.

"Get on the fucking shuttle," Gonzalez growled.

With a heavy heart, Schwartz lowered his head and climbed the metal ladder into the shuttle. The soldier watched him pass through the door before lifting her radio to her face once more.

"Lieutenant Harris," she said into the device. "You there?"

After a moment of static, Harris' voice crackled through the speakers.

"Here. What's your status?"

"The delegation is safely on board the shuttle," Gonzalez reported. "I'm outside the hatch with Sandra Martin."

"I see," Harris acknowledged with a hint of relief in his voice. A pause followed before his next words came through, clear and commanding. "Listen carefully. This is an order. Take careful aim with your pulse rifle and shoot Sandra Martin in the foot."

Chapter Twenty-Four

Every person within earshot of the radio froze in shock.

Gonzalez gasped and wrinkled her brow, unable to believe what she had just heard.

Martin turned, her face contorting with disbelief as she locked eyes with the private.

"Are you fucking crazy, Harris?" Moreau interjected, her voice laced with confusion and anger.

Harris remained unfazed by the outburst. "Private," he called through the speaker. "I gave you a direct order. Execute that order."

The private's hand tightened around her weapon as she quickly turned and fired one bolt into the toe of Martin's left boot. The sound of sizzling flesh filled the air as Martin cried out in pain and jumped back, dropping to the ground in agony. The rifle slung over her shoulder swung to her side as she gripped at her injured foot, smoke rising from the tip of her boot.

"Fuck," Martin spat through gritted teeth, still gripping her foot in pain. "Fuck, that hurts."

"Did you injure Miss Martin?" Harris asked calmly.

"Yes, I fucking injured her," Gonzalez yelled into the radio, her own response filled with frustration and anger. "What do you fucking think I did?"

"Good," he replied.

"Good?" Tinsley's voice rose in confusion. "What do you mean, good?"

"You should know better than the rest of us, Deputy Secretary," Harris began coolly. "We are unable to offer assistance to anyone but the delegation and members of our security detail. That is, unless a civilian requires medical treatment, whereby we—"

"Whereby we are obligated to assist using reasonable measures befitting the circumstances at hand," Tinsley finished, her expression shifting to one of understanding.

"I believe Miss Martin requires medical assistance," Harris offered, his tone still calm and collected. "And since the medical facility here is non-functioning, would you agree it is reasonable to offer her transport on the shuttle to a functioning medical facility?"

Tinsley's head nodded slowly, her mind still reeling from the shocking tactics used by Harris. Her hand shook slightly as she reached up to brush a stray strand of hair away from her face.

"I would," she agreed, her voice strained, before turning to Moreau. "Following protocol, Captain. As the primary delegate, I must insist we take Miss Martin onboard for transportation to a medical facility."

Moreau's expression shifted between disbelief and frustration.

"Acknowledged, Deputy Secretary," the captain replied, her tone clipped and professional, before leaning out of the hatch and extending her hand toward Martin. "Help her on board, Private."

Moments later, all members of the party were sealed inside the shuttle. Martin sat rigidly in a seat by the hatch as Hope and Gonzalez carefully removed her boot to assess the wound. The tips of the security officer's big toe and index toe were missing, leaving behind bright red skin with traces of charring.

"Shit," Martin grunted through gritted teeth as Tinsley frantically searched through a first aid kit for bandages and salve.

"I'm sorry," Gonzalez murmured repeatedly, her voice filled with genuine remorse. "I'm really sorry."

"You followed your orders," Martin said. "Not your fault."

"No, it's not," Moreau interjected sternly. "It's yours, Lieutenant. You better make it out of there so I can chew you a new asshole."

"Working on it," Harris replied.

Professor Ford stood next to the ladder in the access tunnel, his eyes fixed on the hatch at the end. The tension in the air was palpable as he turned to face Harris.

"So," he began, his voice echoing off the bleak walls. "We run for the elevator. I press the panel while you shoot your gun. The doors open, we get on and we ride to the top. That's it?"

Harris nodded grimly. "It won't be that simple," he replied, adjusting his grip on his pulse rifle. "But, yeah, that's the plan. Are you ready?"

The soldier started toward the hatch, with Ford following. Adrenaline surged through their bodies as they prepared for what lay ahead.

"Not really," Ford answered honestly.

"Just get ready to run," Harris replied, scanning the instructions stenciled onto the hatch's surface—PULL—with two arrows pointing in opposite directions and instructions to turn and open or close.

"Planning on shooting me in the foot to get me out of here?" Ford joked nervously.

Harris gave a small grin. "Whatever it takes."

The soldier and professor took a deep breath and braced themselves. Harris pulled the lever and pushed open the heavy metal door, emitting a loud metallic screech.

As they stepped into the Energy Generation Chamber, their senses were immediately overwhelmed. The air was thick with a loud humming, emanating from the singularity in the center of the room. Strange vibrations shook through Harris' core, making him feel off balance.

Giant tendrils stretched out in all directions, pulsating and twisting. Many wrapped around long rods protruding from the walls while others slithered across surfaces, searching and testing their surroundings. Two massive bulbous appendages resembling heads swung above them on long necks, adding to the surreal scene.

Despite the grotesque nature of the monstrous creature before them, Harris was awestruck by its impressive size and strange beauty. He quickly noted the gray, splotchy complexion of its skin and how it shifted with a sickening elasticity beneath the surface.

His attention was drawn to a large elevator door on the far side of the room, a little over a quarter of the way around from where they stood. Between them and their destination many figures awaited them, crowding together with twisted bodies and grotesque appearances.

Some were inflicted with tendrils growing from and through their flesh, and others bore deep wounds from sharp instruments carving into their skin. There were even some whose flesh peeled away, revealing bone and sinew or gaping cavities in their abdomens.

Harris couldn't shake the memory of the haunting footage he had seen earlier—a woman outside the medical lab cutting herself with scissors.

The lieutenant's sharp gaze flickered to a terminal on his right, sitting on a raised platform and now abandoned amid chaos. The once pristine screen was now smudged with dirt and dust.

"Where's the boy?" he asked Ford; his voice strained with urgency.

"Father," a voice murmured, chorused, and echoed. The word was spoken by all in the room, resounding around the walls and sending shivers down Harris' spine. The two giant bulbs in the room moved together, drawing themselves to hover directly over the scientist and soldier.

Harris felt his stomach tighten as the crowd of creatures slowly parted, revealing the boy standing in their midst. Gray tentacles protruding from his disfigured head and spine stretched and swayed, reaching and coiling as the boy stretched his arms out in a welcoming gesture.

"Father," the voice came again, oozing from all the infected beings surrounding them.

"No," Ford gasped, shaking his head in disbelief.

The corpse of Amy Caldwell stepped into sight behind the boy, her body contorted and twisted into an unrecognizable form.

Ford's eyes filled with tears, spilling over his cheeks as he cried out in agony.

"God, no."

"Father," the creatures called in unison. "Join us."

"Please God," the professor sobbed.

Harris clenched his jaw and stepped forward, raising his pulse rifle. The creatures recoiled at the sight of the soldier.

"The soulless one," they hissed.

Without hesitation, the soldier pulled the trigger. The sound of gunfire echoed through the room as Harris aimed at each infected being with precision. Reacting quickly, they dispersed and ran in all directions, but a few were too close to escape. They fell into pieces, their bodies flipping and flopping wildly on the floor like fish out of water.

"Come on," Harris' voice boomed through the chaos, urging the professor to pull it together and stick to the plan. Ford wiped his tear-streaked face and followed the lieutenant as they made their way toward the elevator, increasing their pace with each step. The creatures circled them, avoiding Harris' bolts and focusing their attention on the professor, attempting to attack from behind.

As Harris fought off the beasts before him, he continued to fire into the dispersing crowd. But several of the creatures bolted toward the center of the room, forcing him to quickly change direction and fire toward them. A giant tentacle suddenly dropped between Harris and his targets, thudding heavily on the floor, causing the soldier to pause and take aim at the new target.

His energy bolts pounded into the tendril, exploding through its gray flesh, and spilling thick, milky liquid onto the floor. The other creatures cried out, as if communally feeling the pain, as the giant tendril lifted skyward and away from the soldier.

Amidst all the chaos, a distant chorus of voices cried out in warning.

"Beware the soulless one."

Harris ignored them and continued firing at a bulb sweeping across the space above, tearing and ripping into its colossal head until milky liquid erupted and splattered on the floor below. The creatures all shrieked in agony.

As Harris turned back to call the scientist, he saw it was too late to save Professor Ford. The professor lay motionless on his front, Amy Caldwell, and several others holding him down while a boy kneeled on his back. Tendrils reached from the boy's body, wrapping around Ford's head, and pulling it up at an unnatural angle.

"Run," Ford managed to call out to Harris before his neck stretched, skin tearing at the clavicle, bones cracking with a sickening sound. An agonizing cry spilled from his throat, quickly turning into a series of gargles as blood spilled from his lips and throat.

In a blind rage, Harris unleashed a relentless onslaught of rapid fire from his gun into the small, fragile body of the boy. The air filled with the deafening sound of gunshots and the high-pitched screams of pain.

"Beware the soulless one," hissed a chilling chorus of voices as the boy disintegrated into pieces around the professor's body.

Without hesitation, Harris aimed his weapon at the other assailants who were holding Ford down. The crisp sound of bolts being fired from his gun filled the air, slicing through flesh and bone with deadly precision. With a fierce determination, he turned and sprinted toward the elevator door, his heart racing and adrenaline pumping through his veins.

Just as he neared the elevator door, a massive tendril dropped from above, barring his path like an impenetrable wall, a good head and shoulders taller than he. Without missing a beat, Harris bounded with all his might and soared over the obstacle, his rapid-fire shots tearing into the limb in a fiery display.

He landed gracefully on the ground, tucking and rolling before continuing to sprint toward the elevator doors. The giant limb recoiled and retreated into the air; its escape punctuated by the echoing sounds of gunfire as the soldier ripped the tendril's side open with rapid-fire.

Harris reached the elevator doors, his heart pounding with adrenaline. He pressed the panel to call for them to open. He raised his pulse rifle in a tight grip, ready to defend against any threat that may come his way. In the corner of his eye, he caught sight of a slimy tendril wrapped tightly around a nearby rod.

"Beware the soulless one," taunted the creatures with their eerie, distorted voices.

Harris aimed his weapon at the monstrous limb. "Fuckin' oath," he growled as he squeezed the trigger.

With a deafening burst of energy, the tendril violently tore apart. Its milky substance sprayed across the walls and floor like a macabre painting. The creatures in the chamber let out bloodcurdling cries as the tendril's grip weakened on the metallic rod it had been desperately clinging to.

Amidst the chaos, a sharp click echoed through the chamber as the rod shifted and slowly lowered out of position.

With a crack of thunder, a thick bolt of electricity, reminiscent of lightning, shot out from the lowered rod and struck the orb at its base near the floor.

A brilliant wave of white light swept through the room, illuminating every inch of the Shrine, swallowing shadows as it danced across the walls. As if by some powerful magic, the orb vanished and the constant droning hum that had filled the air was silenced, leaving only an eerie quietness in its wake.

The monstrous tendrils writhed in the air, stretching and twisting as if reaching out for something just beyond their grasp. Suddenly, they froze, suspended in space as if cut by an unseen force. A burst of thick, milky fluid spewed from their newly severed ends before the limbs thudded heavily to the ground, one by one, like giant tree trunks falling in slow motion. The pungent scent of decay filled the air as the severed tendrils convulsed and twitched on the ground, spraying thick fluid in all directions. Their once menacing appearance was now reduced to a grotesque display.

Like a blinding burst of lightning, the orb flashed back to life momentarily before disappearing once more. Harris was mesmerized by this phenomenon, watching it repeat several times as the massive elevator doors slowly creaked open behind him.

The orb vanished again, leaving behind a deafening, thunderous pop that filled the chamber. In its wake, more severed tendrils writhed and released their grasps on the rods around the room, dropping to the floor with resounding thuds. Thick, gelatinous liquid oozed from their wounds, creating a sickeningly sweet aroma that filled the chamber.

The crowd of infected creatures unleashed bloodcurdling shrieks, as the giant bulbous appendages stretched open their mouths, as if in a desperate attempt to call out for help. But instead, they writhed and squirmed with determined intent, hunting...for him.

The voices of the infected echoed through the Shrine, a cacophony of terrifying whispers.

"Soulless one," they chorused. "Soulless one."

Harris took a step back into the large service elevator, his gaze locked on the writhing mass before him. He reached for the elevator panel and pressed the button for the surface.

"Soulless one," the voices continued to call out, growing more urgent as the doors slowly closed, sealing off the nightmarish scene.

CHAPTER TWENTY-FIVE

"Captain?" The crackling of the radio cut through the tense silence, making Hope jump and turn her attention from bandaging Sandra Martin's foot to the lieutenant's voice. She heard the worry and urgency in his tone. "Start the engines. I'm on my way," Harris' words quavered through the radio, sounding distant yet urgent.

Moreau's response came quickly, her voice steady and focused as she sat in the cockpit with her headset covering her ears. "Already ahead of you, Lieutenant. We're ready to take off. Just awaiting your arrival."

Tinsley's voice chimed in next, full of tension and anticipation. "Lieutenant? Were you successful?"

Harris' answer was not what they had hoped for. "Negative. The singularity is closed, but the thing in the Energy Generation Chamber still lives."

"And Professor Ford? Is he with you?" the deputy secretary asked.

There was a pause before Harris responded. "Professor Ford didn't make it."

A solemn silence filled the shuttle, broken only by the soft static emitting from the radio speaker attached to Gonzalez's belt.

Moreau placed a delicate hand over the speaker cup, pressing the can against her head to amplify the transmission. She listened intently, her brow furrowing in concentration as another voice passed on crucial information through a separate channel.

"Understood," she said into the microphone attached to her headset. Twisting in her chair, she faced Gonzalez, the urgency clear in her sharp movements. "Lieutenant Harris, are you still there?"

"Still here," he answered.

"You'd better make it quick," the captain instructed with a sense of urgency. "The Quebec headquarters have just informed me that the bomber has sighted Borden Island's coast. We need to leave immediately.

"I'm moving as fast as I can," Harris reassured them.

Across the cavern from the shuttle, near the large pod structure, the elevator doors opened slowly with a low rumble. Lieutenant Harris dashed through the widening gap and sprinted toward the shuttle with determination, his boots pounding against the ground like thunder. Every second counted now.

"Open the hatch," he commanded, his voice strained. "Start rolling for the door. I'm here."

Hope felt her heart race as she quickly finished wrapping the bandage around Martin's injured foot. The impending danger made her want to drop everything and run to the hatch, but Gonzalez beat her to it.

With a soft hiss, the hatch slid open as Moreau cautiously guided the craft toward the cavern's exit.

"Five minutes out," the captain announced, her voice crackling through the speakers. "Maybe less with the message relay between IEC and Quebec."

Harris sprinted alongside the shuttle, ready to leap through the open hatch as soon as he reached it. As Moreau expertly maneuvered the craft through the giant doorway, Harris leaped inside in one swift movement. He rolled across the floor and crashed into a row of seats clumsily as Gonzalez sealed the door behind him.

"I'd tell everyone to strap in," Captain Moreau said over the commotion, "but we don't have time, so hang on."

The shuttle rocketed through the opening of the cavern, immediately encountering strong winds that rocked the port side of the craft. Moreau adjusted the throttle and pitch control, propelling them into the sky at breakneck speed.

"Holy shit!" Schwartz exclaimed, white knuckles clenching onto his armrests, feeling the entire weight of his body pressing into his seat.

"Jodida puta," Gonzalez cursed as she stumbled and fell onto Harris's lap.

Hope felt her body being pressed into the floor of the cabin by intense G-forces. Her ears popped and filled with pressure as Moreau continued to climb higher and higher, angling their trajectory forwards.

Sitting on the floor beside Martin's seat, grasping onto her leg for stability, Hope peered through the cockpit door at Moreau's determined expression. Beyond her, past swirling clouds and endless blue sky, was the promise of freedom from danger.

A sense of relief washed over Hope as the walls no longer felt to be were caving in on her. But just as quickly, a wave of fear crashed into her as she slipped and struggled to stay upright on the floor.

Martin reached down with one strong arm and pulled the trembling assistant into the seat beside her.

"Brace yourself," she instructed, gripping the armrests tightly with both hands. Hope mirrored her movements, clinging to the armrests until her knuckles turned white.

A loud alarm sounded from within the cockpit, jolting everyone's nerves.

"What's that?" Harris called out, holding onto Gonzalez tightly.

"Proximity alert," Moreau answered, her voice tense. "Radar shows not one, but three aircraft inbound. And they're less than a minute out."

"Are we going to collide with them?" Schwartz asked nervously, his body stiffening like a statue.

"I sure hope not," the captain replied coolly, adjusting the aircraft's course, and leveling it out.

Harris stood up and firmly lifted Gonzalez to her feet before stepping into the cockpit and peering out the windshield.

"Where are they?" he asked Moreau urgently.

She pointed to their left, just above the horizon. Three massive triangular objects were hurtling toward them at incredible speed.

"Those are XB-90s," Harris confirmed with a grim tone. "They can carry up to fourteen tactical missiles each."

"Fourteen!" Tinsley exclaimed in shock, overhearing their conversation. "I thought you said the payload was two, Captain?"

"I did," Moreau answered. "Obviously, someone isn't being truthful with their information."

"And I have a feeling they don't plan on simply destroying that facility," Harris added.

"What do you mean?" Tinsley asked, curiosity etched on his face.

Schwartz shifted his gaze to the small portal window beside him and caught a glimpse of the approaching bombers.

"They're going to open the Earth," he said, his voice heavy with dread. "Let molten rock consume everything under that mountain."

The deputy secretary nodded slowly, processing the gravity of the situation. "What about the aftermath? The fallout will kill any living creature for miles, and who knows how far the radiation will spread?"

"It's an uninhabited island in the Arctic Ocean," Schwartz said. "No one cares what happens up here. In its vast two and a half thousand square kilometers, who will really show concern for a tiny dot on the side of a mountain?"

"I will," Tinsley declared.

Schwartz leaned forward eagerly in his seat, his eyes wide with curiosity. "So, what will you do? And I mean no offense, but you put your report in, as we all will. You inform the authorities of an overuse of tactical missiles on an island partially protected under global environmental laws. But they will argue that the area the company nuked is contained within the five hundred or so square kilometers owned by them. Arguably, the fallout will be contained to that region and restrictions will be enforced to prevent people from accessing the zone."

"They can be prosecuted for breaching international laws enforced by the United Nations Charter and the International Criminal Courts," the deputy secretary countered. "And I fully intend to prosecute once I seek advice on the matter."

Schwartz chuckled bitterly. "Good luck to you," he replied. "Seriously. I hope you get them. After everything we've witnessed and for what they're about to do, I hope you get them good. But whatever punishment they receive will be pocket change for them. They'll pay up and possibly put some scapegoat at the forefront while continuing their operations without a hitch. My bet is, that scapegoat will be the late Professor Ford. Who better than to point the finger at someone who can't protest the allegations against them?"

He shook his head in defeat. "I doubt you'll stop them or even give them something to think about," he continued, his tone resigned. "They're a corporation. They practically own the world."

Without warning, a brilliant white light burst into the shuttle through its windows, making everyone shield their eyes and squint against its intense brightness. Moreau grunted in frustration at the blinding glare. "Merde. I can't see a thing!"

Hope turned her face toward the floor, shielding her eyes with her hands as multiple bombs dropped onto the facility. The blinding light seemed to stretch on forever, filling her with a sense of dread and uncertainty.

But gradually, the overwhelming feeling dissipated and when she cautiously opened her eyes, she found that the cabin and cockpit were now bathed in an eerie orange glow filtering through the tinted portal windows along the sides of the shuttle. The world outside took on a surreal appearance, like a sunrise on a perfect day.

Gonzalez rushed past Hope to the seats behind her, pressing her face against the portal window.

"Fóllame duro," she whispered in awe.

Turning in her seat, Hope peered out the window beside her, angling her face to view the island far behind them.

The orange glow slowly dissipated, revealing a large, ominous cloud rising from the side of the mountain, a column of dust and smoke connecting it to the surface below.

"How many do you think they dropped?" Gonzalez asked.

Hope watched the colossal cloud rise in awe, unsure if the question was directed at her.

"I don't know," Harris replied. "Maybe three or four."

Another alarm sounded from within the cockpit.

"Shockwave," Captain Moreau announced. "Hang on."

Hope sat rigidly in her chair, bracing herself for what was to come. She thought about buckling her seatbelt, but before she could, slight tremors ran through the cabin followed by a vibration. Moreau muttered something under her breath as she adjusted her headset and retrieved a pair of dark sunglasses from the console.

"They're making another run," she said as she slid on the sunglasses.

"That's overkill," Tinsley remarked.

"Best to be sure, I guess," Schwartz added, shaking his head in disbelief.

Hope closed her eyes tightly and covered them with her hands again as Harris moved to sit beside Gonzalez. Moments later, another blinding flash filled the cabin.

"Putain inutile. These fucking sunglasses do nothing," Moreau cursed as the light slowly faded.

As the golden rays of the blast fireball dissipated once more, Hope cautiously turned to look out the window again. The vibrant hues of pink, orange, and purple stretched across the sky like a brilliantly painted canvas. Sandra Martin leaned close beside her, their breaths catching in unison as they peered out at the scene unfolding before them with wide-eyed awe and disbelief.

A new mushroom cloud rose from the same location, its thick smoke and debris billowing upwards like a monstrous beast awakening from its slumber. The previous cloud dispersed, pushed outward in a wide circle as the new one expanded. To Hope, it looked both terrifying and beautiful at the same time.

Hope turned to the soldiers sitting behind her, directing her question toward them.

"Do you think that thing is dead?" she asked, her voice low and hesitant.

Harris answered with certainty. "Everything from the surface all the way down to the Energy Generation Chamber and beyond would've been vaporized in the first run. Rock and iron liquified. Nothing could have survived."

Just then, Moreau's voice cut through the tense atmosphere. "Incoming shockwave," she warned, expertly steering the shuttle to increase altitude and adjust their bearing for Ottawa. "We should be back at base in a little over two hours."

"Enough time for some sleep," Harris declared, rising from his seat, and making his way to the back row. "I'll be back here if anyone needs me."

Hope watched him curiously as he settled into his new seat.

"What's his problem?" she whispered to Gonzalez. "Did I do something wrong? He hasn't even said hello or anything."

Gonzalez chuckled. "That's just how he is. All business when it comes to situations like this. Give him some time to sleep it off. He'll be back to his boring self in no time. Take it from someone who knows."

Sandra Martin interrupted their conversation with a polite clearing of her throat.

"I know this may be personal," she began, speaking low, addressing Hope, "but your Lieutenant Harris and I were both part of an experiment that aimed to eliminate emotions from our psyche. It was deemed a failure, as you're probably aware by now, because we do possess emotions. We just don't have the capacity to express them in the same manner as most people do.

"I do okay because I learned to fake it," Martin continued. "I had to pretend in order to fit in. Lieutenant Harris, on the other hand, might not have had the same opportunities I did to learn this skill. I grew up immersed in society. I attended school with other children and held weekend jobs as a teenager. I get the impression Lieutenant Harris may not have had that kind of experience as a child.

"But I think he's starting to understand," she extended. "I think he's trying to let go of the constraints imposed by our genetic restrictions. We may be genetically modified, but we are still human beings with emotions. With time, he might become as expressive as I am."

"Expressive?" Gonzalez giggled, breaking the serious tone of the conversation. "That guy generally has a metal rod up his ass at the best of times."

Hope nodded before turning her attention back to the view outside as Moreau announced another pass by the bombers.

"How many more until they expire the payload?" Tinsley asked anxiously.

"Until that mountain is reduced to molten liquid," Schwartz interjected bitterly. "No one will be able to go back there for a million years at this rate."

Sandra Martin leaned in closer to Hope.

"I just thought, after last night... you know," Hope whispered.

The private leaned toward Hope. "He likes you. I know," she murmured back.

Hope furrowed her brow in confusion. "How do you know?"

"Because he did things with you that he never did with me," Gonzalez replied with a snicker.

"What things?" Hope asked, feeling a blush creeping up her cheeks.

"He was...expressive." The soldier stifled a snort, unable to contain her laughter any longer.

As blinding light flooded the cabin once again, Hope wondered what other secrets Lieutenant Harris might have hidden beneath his stoic exterior. She turned to see him slumped in his seat, head lolling against the backrest, already in a deep sleep.

CHAPTER TWENTY-SIX

"Breaking developments continue to emerge from the heart of the Borden Island incident as the world watches with bated breath. Limited access to the safety zone surrounding the island remains in effect as the situation unfolds. From our satellite feeds, we're witnessing the cloud slowly dissipating over the western half of the landmass, while the fallout, according to Innovative Energy Corporation's chief spokesperson, Dana Whilton, is expected to be contained within the island's borders, minimizing the risk of widespread radiation contamination."

The screen's display flicked from the "on the scene" young female news reporter standing outside the main doors of the IEC headquarters building in New York to another young woman standing at a podium with the company logo on the wall behind her.

"As you know, Innovative Energy Corporation strives to improve our impact on the Earth with insightful and reliable initiatives that benefit the lives of our consumers and enhance and promote the environment in the hope to create a clean and productive world," she said, her voice laced with rehearsed confidence. "Unfortunately, a technical error at our Borden Island Facility required drastic action to ensure the containment of an unexpected contaminant.

"The successful operation required the detonation of three tactical ballistic warheads delivered with pinpoint accuracy by an XB-90 stealth bomber," the spokesperson continued. "According to the last report, any contamination will be confined to the landmass of Borden Island. There's no danger to the shipping channels and fishing territories of the Queen Elizabeth Islands network and they will be reopened immediately with the exception of a fifty-mile radius safety zone off the coast of Borden Island. We are continuing to monitor the situation and will keep you apprised as details become available. Thank you."

Several people off camera shouted questions over each other as Dana Whilton stepped away from the podium, flanked by an entourage of men and women in suits. The reporter in New York reappeared on the screen.

"The United Nations Environmental Assembly Program and Industrial Development Organization released statements condemning the actions taken by IEC with the promise of full investigations and ensuing legal actions based on their findings," the reporter said as she stared down the camera, through the monitor and into the small boardroom where the delegation and security detail sat around a long table, drinking tea and coffee. With a sudden jerk, Schwartz rose from his chair, the scraping noise of its legs against the linoleum floor echoing through the room. He strode toward the mounted monitor on the wall behind him, his eyes blazing with anger and frustration. "Allegations of fabricating facts concerning operational procedures at the Borden Island Facility by IEC have come to light in the last hour, creating an explosion of conspiracy theories on social media—"

"I've had enough for today," he announced, turning the TV off, pivoting to face the group gathered at the conference table. "I hope that's all right with everyone."

"Fine by me," Gonzalez chimed in from her seat next to Hope.

The assistant nodded in agreement with the engineer's decision.

"It was more than three," Hope muttered under her breath, lifting her steaming cup of coffee to her lips.

"Way more," Captain Moreau agreed from her position at the end of the table.

Schwartz shook his head slowly, reliving their nightmare in his thoughts.

"I don't understand," he started, peering around the table. "Why?... What was the reason for the boy?"

Hope furrowed her brow, not grasping the engineer's question.

"Do you mean...?" Tinsley started. "Sorry. I really don't know what you mean by that."

"I mean," Schwartz replied, looking at the table as if reading from an invisible script. "Why did he exist? Why did the thing impose itself into the boy like it did? I don't get it."

"Perhaps the boy was its mouthpiece?" Hope suggested. "Or a window into our realm?"

"Maybe," Harris said before drawing a deep breath. "Maybe it doesn't matter."

"Doesn't matter?" Schwartz queried. "So many people died and you think it doesn't matter?"

Harris locked eyes with the other man. "I didn't mean it like that. I meant..." he paused to consider his words. "How does a gazelle analyze the actions and decisions of a lion? It doesn't. It just knows the lion intends to kill it, so it runs."

"We were the gazelles," Gonzalez added.

"Yes," Harris nodded. "And, I don't think we'll ever understand the actions of that thing. I'm sure it had its reasons to use the boy the way it did, but it doesn't think like us or behave like us. I don't believe we'll ever understand it."

"Well," Schwartz sighed. "At least it's dead, now."

"Is it?" Harris frowned. "For all we know, it's done this on a billion other worlds and thrives on all of them."

A thick, heavy silence filled the room.

Tinsley, sitting to Hope's right, carefully set her glasses down on the table before closing her eyes and pinching the bridge of her nose.

"How much longer are they going to keep us here?" she asked, her voice tinged with exhaustion.

"Until they think we've told them everything we know," Harris replied, seated across from the Deputy Secretary. "Then we'll be taken back to New York and asked the same questions all over again."

Tinsley studied his face as if trying to gauge his experiences.

"It seems you've been through this sort of thing before," she remarked.

"Once or twice," he admitted with a sigh. "Interrogative mission debriefings can be cumbersome. I'm expecting this one to be ruthless."

The deputy secretary's sharp gaze shifted to Sandra Martin, sitting quietly beside Lieutenant Harris. Her face was calm and composed, betraying no hint of the turmoil inside her.

"I suppose they will question you the most," the deputy commented, her tone cool and calculating. "Being that you work for IEC. They'll want to know everything you know. Access codes, operational procedures, the works."

Martin's lips twisted into a bitter smile. "I suppose," she agreed, her voice cold with resentment. "Doesn't matter, really. I have no loyalty to IEC. They left us all there to die. Many people I regard as friends are gone now."

Tinsley's eyes glinted with empathy as she looked over at the security officer.

"Does that mean you're looking for work?" she asked.

"I guess so," replied Martin, raising an eyebrow in surprise. "Do you know anyone looking for a security officer with limited social skills?"

"Not that limited," Tinsley objected, a small smirk playing on her lips. "I'm an excellent judge of character, and I like you. I might be able to pull some strings if you'd like to work for me."

A grin spread across Martin's face as she considered the offer.

"I'll have to give it some thought," she said playfully.

The deputy secretary smiled approvingly, her face alight with satisfaction. She turned to Hope, her gaze sharp and focused. "And how about you? Do you wish to continue working for me after all that has transpired?"

Hope hesitated before nodding slowly. "Yes," she replied. Her mind drifted to her cherished pooky bear, sitting patiently on her neatly made bed. "But first, I want to go home and collapse onto my bed, surround myself with all of my plushie toys, and remain there for at least a week."

"Only a week?" Tinsley raised an eyebrow in surprise, turning her attention to the private standing next to her assistant. "And what about you?"

Gonzalez appeared taken aback by the question, not expecting such a personal inquiry from the deputy secretary.

"I suppose I'll return to New York and report in with the lieutenant," she answered thoughtfully. "Then wait for my next assignment or placement."

Hope's heart sank at the thought of not seeing Harris and Gonzalez again. It hadn't occurred to her until now that this could potentially be their only encounter. A lump formed in her throat as she realized that their brief intimate moments might be all they'd have to remember one another by once they returned to their regular lives.

"No time for a break?" Tinsley pressed on.

"It's not typically allowed for us," Gonzalez explained, sharing a glance with Harris across the table.

Tinsley followed their gazes and addressed Harris directly. "Is that true, Lieutenant? You just move from one mission to the next without pause?"

Harris responded, his composure never faltering. "Usually. But I was considering visiting a guy we met recently to request some time off for Private Gonzalez and myself. After everything we've been through, we both deserve a break. What was his name? Dan something?"

"Rogers." Gonzalez smirked. "We just completed two back-to-back missions before receiving orders for this detail. The colonel asked for two weeks."

"Demanded two weeks," the lieutenant corrected her. "And if he hasn't passed that on, as the colonel told him to, I'll readjust his underwear elastic over his ears."

Tinsley nodded, her eyes showing empathy for the two soldiers. "I'll process the request for you. Only, I'll make it four weeks."

Gonzalez's jaw dropped open.

"Really?"

"Really," the deputy secretary replied.

Gonzalez jumped out of her seat and dashed to Tinsley's side, where she wrapped her arms around the deputy secretary, planting a kiss on her cheek.

"No me lo puedo creer. Eres el major," the private blurted with excitement.

"I'm sorry," Tinley said. "I don't speak Spanish."

"She said, she can't believe it. You're the best." Hope grinned.

"Oh." Tinsley patted the soldier on the shoulder. "Thank you."

"Thank you, Deputy Secretary," Gonzalez said humbly, returning to her seat.

Tinsley moved her gaze to Harris. "What do you think you'll do with your time off?"

Harris leaned back, a sly smile spreading across his face as he exchanged a glance with Hope. "I'm not entirely sure," he admitted cheekily. "But I heard about a charming little Chinese restaurant in Tudor City."

Hope giggled. "It's not Chinese," she clarified.

Harris's gaze lingered on Hope's lips, twinkling with amusement.

"I know."

THE END

THE END

ABOUT THE AUTHOR

Robert E Kreig was born in Newcastle, Australia and grew up in its outer suburbs.

He has always had a love for books, particularly well-told stories involving action, adventure and fear.

Some of Robert's favourite authors as a young reader included J. R. R. Tolkien, Stephen King, Orson Scott Card, Ray Bradbury and Frank Herbert. As he grew into adulthood, the list continued to lengthen, adding more influential writers such as George R. R. Martin, Matthew Reilly, Nathan M. Farrugia, Dan Brown, James Patterson, Michael Connelly and Lee Child just to name a few.

Inspired by movies like Star Wars, King Kong, Jaws, Jason and the Argonauts and other great adventure pieces, Robert listened to the voices in his head and entertained the strange visions dancing through his mind to assist him with writing his fantasy series The Woodmyst Chronicles.

Robert has penned ten books for the series which follow the lives of many characters, particularly focusing on a family who must face many trials before the epic conclusion. Clashing swords, strange creatures, flying dragons and sorcery inhabit the world surrounding Woodmyst.

Robert has also written two other standalone books, Long Valley and The Calm Voice.

Robert currently lives in Canberra, Australia where he hopes to one day become a full-time writer.

youtube.com/channel/UCFWQVEmxfmf50wTeiY_POtg

linkedin.com/in/robert-e-kreig-14880a105/

ALSO BY THIS AUTHOR

PIT GUARD: THE TANNER'S BOY

A YOUNG BOY MUST LEARN THE WAYS OF A WARRIOR IF HE IS EVER TO BECOME A PIT GUARD

Far to the north of Ananduil, in the province of Kedielewen, a peaceful fishing village celebrates the harvest year when raiders attack.

Orphaned and left to fend for himself after the massacre of his entire village, the tanner's boy chances upon an encounter with a seasoned soldier, Commander Steigauf. A Pit Guard of Dendadia.

Taken under Steigauf's wing, the boy begins his training at the Shiverwind barracks and quickly gathers the skills to defend himself and fight for others.

When a rider from across the land arrives seeking help with an investigation of the heinous murder of an unknown traveller, the boy accompanies Steigauf and a small band of unskilled soldiers, to Mountainfall, a place with a terrifying history and reputation.

Along the way, the boy battles his inner demons, discovers love, and prepares to stare into the face of death.

But nothing could prepare him for what awaits at Mountainfall.

THE WOODMYST CHRONICLES

The Woodmyst Chronicles is the story of a small community that faces the hardest of trials in a world filled with darkness, violence and magic.

Books In This Series...

- THE WALLS OF WOODMYST

- THE SONS OF WOODMYST

- THE HEIR OF WOODMYST

- THE WARLORDS OF WOODMYST

- THE HUNTRESS OF WOODMYST

- THE SHADOW OF WOODMYST

- THE BRIDES OF WOODMYST

- THE GODS OF WOODMYST

- THE WEAPONS OF WOODMYST

- A FAREWELL TO WOODMYST

LONG VALLEY

In the small community of Long Valley, nestled comfortably beneath snow-capped mountains, people quietly go about their business. Everybody knows everybody and there are no worries to give mind to.

But something has awakened.

A tragic accident near the valley's army base sparks a number of terrifying events, placing the local civilians in mortal danger.

A contagion is subsequently released into Long Valley, infecting pets, livestock, wildlife and people.

It's up to the local law enforcement and a small band of citizens to try to keep the town safe.

In the end, it becomes a struggle for survival as the people of Long Valley are overcome by the urge to feed.

THE CALM VOICE

No one in the remote town of Edwards Hill could have known that she was capable of such carnage.

Least of all her parents, the first to die.

Driven by the gentle words of the Calm Voice, she inflicts a barrage of carnage and death, leaving a trail of blood in her wake.

Her goal is to bring death to all who have hurt her.

All she needs to do is listen to the Calm Voice.

All she needs to do is just focus...

Just focus...

Focus...

The Calm Voice by Robert E. Kreig is a dark psychological novel surrounding the actions of one girl on a fateful morning in April 2017. Kristin Matthews is fed up with her life, her oppressive parents, and her bullying schoolmates. A soothing voice thrumming in her head compels her to seek revenge on those who have wronged her. At the top of her list is a trio of girls who have taunted her to breaking point. After careful planning, she embarks on a deadly rampage through Edwards Hill State High School, bent on destroying all her pain one last time. What follows is a haunting description of the day's events, culminating in an ending no one will expect.